QUINNEHTUKQUT

Quinnehtukqut

JOSHUA HARMON

« STARCHERONE BOOKS »
« BUFFALO, NEW YORK »

Starcherone Books
P.O. Box 303
Buffalo, NY 14201
www.starcherone.com

Library of Congress Cataloging-in-Publication Data
Harmon, Joshua, 1971–
Quinnehtukqut / Joshua Harmon.— 1st ed.
p. cm.
ISBN-13: 978-0-9788811-2-2 (alk. paper)
ISBN-10: 0-9788811-2-5 (alk. paper)
1. Indian Stream Republic—Fiction. 2. Pittsburg (N.H.)—Fiction.
3. Domestic fiction. I. Title.

PS3608.A7485Q85 2007
813'.6—dc22
2006102536

Printed and bound in Canada.

FIRST EDITION

ACKNOWLEDGMENTS

I gratefully acknowledge the National Endowment for the Arts and the Rhode Island State Council on the Arts for fellowships that offered support during the writing of this book.

"The Legend of Jimmy Frye" originally appeared, in somewhat different form, in *The Iowa Review*; an excerpt from part two of "Quinnehtukqut" originally appeared, as "Idlewild," in *Denver Quarterly*.

for the real MARTHA,
and for SARAH

CONTENTS

THE LEGEND OF JIMMY FRYE

Fence blown down in a winter storm
darkened by outstripped possession
Field stretching out of the world
this book is as old as the people
There are traces of blood in a fairy tale

—Susan Howe, "Thorow"

Late in the year, depressed with that disappointment which ever treads upon the heels of extravagant expectation, they returned from their melancholy journey across the wilderness. They seemed to expect a treasury underneath every foot of the rude soil. They imagined every rock of yellowish hue to be impregnated with gold. They slept on the mountains, dreaming of the rich ore lurking in their rocky foundations, and overlaying the roofs and floors of their deep subterranean halls. With fancy's eye they saw through the fissures of the rocks, and beheld yawning caverns starred with gems and rough with gold.

Here the country is wide and a man can see a farm from a mile off over hayfields and fences. In this country I lay as a dead man through the short summer nights blown over with stars and waited for each moment to arrive. Then the stars fell from the sky to land shining at my feet, lighting the green grass with fires that burned till morning. I ran that wide country searching for water, lost, tasting the air for salt.

The moral of a *fable* is expressed formally; the lesson of the *fiction*, if any, is inwrought. A *fiction* is studied; a *myth* grows up without intent. A *legend* may be true, but cannot be historically verified; a *myth* has been received as true at some time.

In Boston he had had his portrait taken by a photographer—years back, he said, though the face looking out at me from the image looked older than that before me, pressing the creased print into my palm. The hair oiled and combed flat across the brow, the collar and tie, the fine coat, the jaw smooth and strong. When I looked up from it to him the other face seemed to appear in the air between us but what I noticed was his voice saying Go on take it but keep it for yourself.

Near six feet; longlegged fellow; bit fallen away, as if he'd been living off roots and berries and small game in the woods; illkept beard; dark hair tending toward long; generally scurvy-looking when he first came through; blue eyes. His clothes all gone to tatters, coat and stained trousers and his boots torn and flapping. Carrying only a single leather pack as if it was all he owned. And a ratty fur cap crooked on his head. After a few days we saw him again down Baldwin's store buying some tobacco and it looked like the widow Godfrey had cleaned him up some, trimmed his hair and mended his dungarees and shown him to the washroom. Gentlemen, he said.

We never knew how he arrived here, already bearded and unkempt as though he'd been lost in the woods for years. Maybe he had. He appeared one afternoon and no one could say for sure whether he'd come in the road from Skunk Hollow and Clarksville or over from Beecher Falls or whether he'd hitched a ride up the river from Colebrook. It was the end of summer, 1918.

First few seasons here he rarely spoke but to widow Godfrey, in whose house he boarded with the principal. During the week he logged alongside all of us, yet didn't open his mouth except at dinner, when he'd empty his pail into his lap and tuck into whatever the widow had placed inside it. Any questions, he only nodded or spoke a word or two, and so we learned he didn't want to be asked. Of an evening anyone would see him and the principal sitting out on her front porch, both of them staring off at the wooded hill across the river. But neither of them came out to the camps for the poker games or the dances, and though we saw the principal in church on Sundays, singing along in a pew near the front, the hymnal held in one hand, we never saw the other. We could never figure why the widow Godfrey was lodging him, for we hadn't believed she would allow such a man, nor certainly a man with no religion, into her house.

Claude Covill said he thought it was the old word of the caves that had passed south decades back on the lips of one of the gentleman hunters who came up for a week or two holiday in the camps that had brought him, same as it had brought others. Most of them never lasted more than a summer, and one or two ended up vanishing in the woods, their bones whitening like fallen antlers, unless they'd made off with the Indian's gold, since we never saw them again. Yet with him it was his patience that made us believe Russ was wrong. We'd seen that hunger before, and it didn't allow a man to sit quiet, gazing at the country instead of heading out into it. Others of us thought he was bootlegging whiskey from Magog or Sherbrooke, searching out a trail across the border and dickering over the price per case up in P.Q. He was here near four years, logging and no more, before he vanished one March morning. Didn't think we'd ever see him again until he showed up six weeks later with that mute Frenchman.

Kwenitekw or Quinatucquet—something like that the native tribes-
men called their Great River, speaking so low in their throats that the
English, making hard work of imitation, had many versions. At last
they decided to spell it Connecticut River.

In the spring of 1939 the state of New Hampshire began work
on the Murphy Dam project, a flood control measure following
the great hurricane of 1938. Workers came from throughout the
northeast and worked into October of that year. The river valley
below First Connecticut Lake, some of the most fertile land in
Coos county, was to be flooded, and with it much of the village
of Pittsburg, ensuring regulated hydro-electricity and prevention
against future damage from floods.

A young engineer from Yale, working in town that summer,
heard a story—evidently quite popular among the villagers—
about a mysterious gold hunter who had lived for a time in those
parts nearly two decades ago. Some in town said the man had vanished years back, under mysterious circumstances, after his mining
failed to yield results; others believed he still lived in the woods
nearby, working his claim. Still others alleged to have known the
man personally. The engineer repeated the tale to some of his fellows, and by the end of summer every laborer at the dam site must
have heard the story. As of September 1, 1939, the manager of the
site estimated he had lost twenty-three men, either alone or in
pairs, who had stolen tools and vanished overnight; some of these
men, he explained, were those he had hired to replace the initial
deserters.

One fine morning, Jimmy stepped out of his cabin, his rifle slung across his broad shoulder and his tall boots shining in the sun. He watched the stream ripple gaily over its rocky bed. The air was filled with promise and his heart felt light. A gentle breeze stirred the spruce branches. "Vince," he called into the dim interior of the cabin, "I do believe today is the day we will find it at last."

That he could summon the north wind by speaking certain words over a fire of fir-cones. That if led blindfolded into any woods between here and the sea he could point the direction of the nearest town and tell you its distance and what country lay between and the location of every hiding hole large enough for a man. That he had killed one man for each year he had lived; that if ever a year passed when he did not take another's life he would surely die. That he had fathered many children by different women so that his seed would never be erased from the earth; that they walk untold miles not knowing the yearning in their own hearts.

A small house shaded on all sides by pines, no grass, the ground covered with dry orange needles. Never knew where his own father went off to—announced one night he was heading to the barn to repair an axe handle, and didn't return. His mother took up with another man from town, farmer who had a family. His sisters, all older, raised him until he was old enough to leave as his father had, in the night while everyone slept—sneaking out just after that farmer left his mother's bedroom, and following him down the road. He never saw his sisters or mother since. Downstate, all this, or else over into the Green Mountains—some town I never heard of. Don't recollect the name. Course this is all just what he told me. Thing was, he loved to hear himself talk.

He had told me he'd been abandoned by his family as a child and each night we prayed for him, for what he'd had to do to get by, things he refused to tell me from the goodness of his heart. I did not try to imagine. He was not a bad man. After supper I would shoo him from the kitchen or he would have done all my washing and scrubbing. I will not have a boarder do my work, I told him, and only then would he sit with Mr Harding on the porch where I allowed them their tobacco. Some nights the three of us would sit in the parlor and Mr Harding would read to us, his well-trained voice such a wonder, of the poems of Longfellow or Bryant, or several verses from Peter, and at these times was such a peace in my house as I'd never felt. He would study the ceiling while Mr Harding, holding the book in his palm and standing by the hearth, read and licked his finger to turn its pages, or he would look at the floor or some corner of the room where he could focus on nothing but the even rhythm of Mr Harding's voice, so moved was he.

The first time I was told it was in a cabin outside Beecher Falls where I'd come with old Hap him pointing to the cabin and then leaving in the dark his bags rattling against his legs. Both the man who told me and another man present who heard it I shot and dragged the bodies one at a time deep into the woods back of the cabin. Dug a hole the night through. The lamp had burned out by the time I came back to lie in the man's bed until the sunlight fell over the pillow. They had asked twentysix dollars which I laid on the table between us one hand atop it while the older fellow scratched out lines on a stained scrap this here's the river and these're the lakes. And this is the road from the village.

It wasn't the trees but the shapes between the trees in the dark the different colors of the dark and how I walked through it not a man could've followed or even kept pace could he have seen the path. Say a night of clouds and no moon when a man can't see his hand held before him. Even Vince I had to slow for the trail I'd shown to him down in the dirt and leaves a bent-back twig or a fern growing where it shouldn't where it wouldn't last even but would turn orange and then brown in the soil too dry for it. A branch the stars hung beyond or the one spot in a rainstorm you'd never get wet. No Vince didn't understand in his head these things I tried to put there. Vince I say. These trails the Indians walked or even later the slaves they say they smuggled up to the border this last stage of the journey before they would throw themselves on the free ground and cry for joy. The bog I have unearthed the bones from where several never saw anything later but the sunlight winking through leaves a pattern I like to think of when I close my eyes at night. The swinging motion of everything so many miles from home.

It's true, there was a time when this town belonged not to the United States nor Canada but only itself. The charter named it the Republic of Indian Stream, perhaps out of allegiance to the old stories or the Abenaki who first lived here, who some say can still be found in small groups deep enough in the woods. This was near a hundred years ago, long before any other state in this nation had taken it upon themselves to secede. Some days we still talk about doing it again—damming up the river and claiming its waters as our own, closing down the roads in and out. There is nothing we need that comes from anywhere else.

All my life I have been moving toward something I can't see the shape of. At night I can feel it out beyond wherever I am waiting for me or even speaking my name Jimmy in a whisper no one else can hear. I have known this since I was a boy. But it has followed me from place to place so that even if I am trying to escape it I am only leading it on and if I am running toward it it hides on me. I wake in the night and listen to the loons on the lake and feel it out there.

From the appointed hour I waited with some few belongings I could not bear to leave behind tied up in a sack. A petticoat with some lace embroidery, a pin my father had given me which I never wore so as not to lose it, my father's folded maps, a sampler I'd been at work on which I thought I'd hang over our mantel, the creased photograph he'd given me, and his very words which I vowed never to burn no matter what he had said. Through the night I didn't sleep, waiting always for some sign, a knock at the window or an owl call just outside. The next morning I could barely stand and my mother commented on my sluggishness in the kitchen where she was trying to cook breakfast for nineteen men. During the day, despite my state, I would look from each window I passed. I stood by the doorway every twenty minutes until one of the men asked me if I was expecting a telegram and if it might arrive sooner if I watched for it. That night I nodded over the dishes, my hair drooping in the steam and my hands under the hot water, searching. I couldn't help but fall asleep, though I imagined him waking me in the night, his hands gentle on my arms or shoulder and his face rising out of the darkness to call me away.

Three Indians and three white men were traveling together. They came to a river and found a canoe, but the boat would only carry two at a time. Now if more Indians were left on a bank, while a crossing was made, than white men, the latter ran the risk of being treacherously killed. If more white men than Indians were left on the bank while the canoe was crossing, the savages were likely to be foully dealt with. How did the whole party get across, and always have white men and Indians on either bank evenly matched?

The first day out we took several deer. One fellow I'd met over breakfast had shot a grouse though the shot had torn the wing clear off in a burst of feathers and he threw it into the brush rather than have a taxidermist attempt it. The young man named Jimmy, who'd been there when I arrived, stayed at the lodge, claiming he was sick from the homemade liquor he'd bought the night before and of which we'd all seen him partake liberally after supper. Yet when we returned we found him chatting up the cook's daughter, she in her dirty apron staring at the ground while she listened. He had handed her a mangy mink hide to woo her. Of course the fellows gave him a ribbing seeing this. Supper lasted well past ten in the lodge that night with the serving girls coming and going bringing out deermeat pies and mince pies and roast duck and all manner of excellent country fare. The young fellow watched the cook's daughter all the night long making no secret of it. Admittedly she was a gorgeous creature but most of us had not come north for that sort of thing. Later he lost seven and a half dollars at cards and broke a bottle against the doorpost, threatening us with the splintered neck. I turned in soon after.

——————————

That crooked woodpile standing against the barn I could smell what lay beneath it already but took each log to burn through the winter armloads of logs that stack getting smaller until I saw a foot a hand some knee bent was it bones under there now and nothing more or the flesh still on it the grass withered away. And now growing a bit warmer and on the roads all the trees just waking and the pails stuck into them to drain it out walking past I could see their tracks in the snow hear the drops filling everything flowing now. There was a rhythm inside my skull.

THE SEARCH FOR JIMMY FRYE: VERN AMEY.

Jed Parker and Windy Williams proposed the search party. The canoe had been found the morning after, clearly tampered with, and it was only a few minutes later that someone said what we'd all been thinking. Where's Frye.

There were a dozen of us at least, four on horseback, and we began the hunt right then, the riders galloping down the road to the village and the rest of us moving off in a ragged line across Perry Stream, heading for Indian Stream where we imagined he was wedged in some crevice or hidden in a bramble patch. The Frenchman watched us from the road, shading his eyes with his hand as we entered the trees. I looked back a few yards later and he was walking away in no particular hurry, his hands in his pockets.

I had barely slept since the night before last. My throat felt dry and ticklish and my hands shook a bit on the barrel of my shotgun. The woods were green and dark and all I could think of were the swollen eyes of the two men they'd laid out on the shore, that smell of the lake.

Cal Marsh fired the first shot. We all jumped, swinging our own guns as the echo died among the trees. A leaf fluttered down. No one spoke for a moment and all the birds had ceased singing. Cal walked in the direction he'd fired, jostling ferns with his legs. We watched him bend down.

Nothing, he called back.

For days I would refuse to let myself eat whether or not the food was available my body only emptying itself as around me the other men ate or I smelled the meals their women cooked. My stomach protested and in cramps I curled to the ground. Hands twisted the leaves in my ears with my eyes closed everything was near at hand. For days scratching at the skin over me. Beyond the hunger came vision and quickness. My body circling in it ate itself. I taught it denial.

It was Henry Cummings, fishing the shallow riffles way out Indian Stream, who found what everyone agreed was his old camp some years after anyone had last had word from him. A couple of dented old tin pans, scraps of lumber and some carpenter's tools, some contraption like a cradle but with a piece of sheet iron all filled with holes instead of slats. A coil of rope, a pile of rotten burlap, and one shovel, the handle broken off eight inches above the blade, which was rusted and broken itself.

————————

In my sleep my feet were taken. By axes cut off and on my knees I crawled into a thicket to fashion crutches wrapping the bloody parts in rags. No no I was shouting but they hearing me came back their axes still clutched and I hid my hands in my armpits. Their boots crackling twigs. A shining knife for my tongue no hands to beat them back no feet to run.

NINETY-NINE YEARS OF WILDERNESS.
Days roll by…
Days roll by.
Days roll by,
like logs down the river.

April 3 In the absence of Something to Drink Jimmy and I took a smoke and our journey is commenced   arrived in. Saint John a Six o clock put up at friend Websters.

April 4. A Young School Marm got aboard the Train about 10 o clock
    the Seats were all occupied and gave her a part of mine. Mind Jimmy asleep with his hat over his Face. She prooved quite an interesting School Mam. We dined to gether Several times dureing the night first out of my Basket and then out of hers. I was Sorry when we reached her Station. the only name I have for her is the Sweet Cracker Girl

April 5. Not getting any Sleep last night am inclined to be drowsey to day   We come to Bangor in a snowstorm this morning and Jimmy not to Pleased. Forenoon wast Spent in trying to make arrangements for Horses   Jimmy bought a Box of choclats at the five and Dime   We plan to Strike a cross country to the West

April 6 To day saw a bear   my horse started nearly Threw me but the bear run off   Jimmy laughed but the horses no good. Dont know what he paid for it. Got mad but He says just to wait till we come to Where were going but he wont Tell me yet where it is   Tired and cold and already having serious aprehentions about this trip   Dont know why he came and fetched me   says he has a Task for me and a reward   ate some Bread and dried Beef for supper. Tried our guns   Snow and wind are trying to See which can do the most Devilment

April 7 Rode 16. miles in deep snow and come to Skowhegan at dark. fearful cold. am not in a very good Humor this evening. Snow still flying thick. Jimmy wont have us be Seen in town and we camped in a Thicket   lots of Wood and a fair camping place but Wind is Howling so the tent threatens to blow over   feel I will frieze but Jimmy seems happy tonight singing of riches and a Pretty Girl   melted Snow for cooking Purposes and ate bacon

and bread Smotherd in fat   made us a pot of Tea and Turned
in

April 8. an other Windy day and what is very Strange a foggy
one   at lest its warmer but the horses having Trouble in the
heavy Snow. Started to rain by noon and no cover anywhere got
soaked through right away   went N. along the Kennebek to find
a Place for a Crossing and found an Old cuss on the bank   said
he thinks he is going to die   Jimmy said he Might travel with us
but the Fellow is clearly foolish   only fit to Bottom a chair and
look out the Window.

April 9. Our old man is not Dead yet   we gave him Some Grub
think he will make the trip   has led us to a spot in the Kennebek   sure enough we crossed just above where a brook came in.
Followed upstream and saw an old Thundershower Mill half fell
over   mostly just a pile of loose stones   frigged around the
Woods a while clearing Brush and looking for a path

April 10 Last night will be remembered for a long time. Our mutual
Friend the Bummer led us upstream into the hills   couldnt ride
and had to lead the Horses   rains turned back to snow and come
midnight our Tent was blown down Hats Blankets and evrything
that was loose was Scatterd. Some of my Tools lost in drifts   our
Blankets was filled with the driving Snow. Jimmys choclats lost too
and he cussing and digging in the snow to find them   We sleped
with our Boots on or they would have been gone   We laid Still
for ten or fifteen minits   We found that we were going to loose
our Blankets So we cralled out and tried to keep on   Our old
Friend lay up wailing and wouldnt move   Jimmy took some ugly
Fit and Stove in his head   We left him and getherd up Camp
went back downhill again   dont know what Jimmy has plans
for   known him six Years Ago but not like this

April 11. Followed a Brook upstream   Jimmy said wed find a
village   Met some loggers Nooning and they gave us a dite of
red flannel Hash. Pointed out where we wanted to go. Jimmy said

he knew this Country but were Turned Around some and Back to the South to far   Jimmy said will have to come by way of Berlin   a nother strange thing Jimmy asked if I could talk any French said he Thought Id learnt it in Halifax. Told him No and he was Quiet a While   Came to Some small place after dark only one House in Town and we had the privilage of Sleeping in the Dining Room by furnishing our own Blankets

April 12. All Ready a week out of Bangor Jimmy said six days to get there   Still wont Tell me where but were almost to Berlin at lest a Hope of dry Lodging   Past two days Sunny but still cold   in Old Specs Shadow now   Jimmy is itching to be done this trip

April 13. an Exciting day in Berlin. About noon a man was found by the river Dead   cause of Death poor whisky. Jimmy and I do our first Washing and we do a first class job after which we take a Look round   bought more Supplies and Jimmy got a few Pie Plates   ate a fine boiled dinner and it is a Splended Day   we left Town riding upriver   rode on past dark .21. Miles and campd by Philips Brook

April 14 Rode through the Notch this morning and by afternoon camped in a Pine Stand atop a Hill near Clarksvill   Only some Beans and cold meat for supper   Jimmy says To morrow morning well be There and if I cant learn any French to just Keep Quiet and let him talk   I dont know what its about   have Never seen this Country before   rolling hills now were Past the mountains all dark Trees and dont like the Looks of it

PROSPECT.

The tourist who has in summer time stood upon the top of Mount Washington can not forget the view which stretches away to the northern horizon. Immediately below him winds the Androscoggin; near it coils the Grand Trunk Railroad; and beyond rise the successive peaks of mountains, some bald and glittering in the sun, and others clothed in deep foliage, until they become blue and shadowy in the distance. The Percy range lifts its snow-white tops toward the northwest; and beyond them the green Monadnock guards the west bank of the Connecticut. In the northeast the mountains of Northern Maine are seen, with the naked top of Escohos on their left; while the ragged spurs of Camel's Rump rise directly at the north, higher even than those shattered crags which form the jaws of Dixville Notch. Lifting up against the northern horizon, blue and misty, stretching eastward and westward, are the peaks of the Canadian Highlands—that wind-swept range which forms the boundary between the United States and Canada. Sections of the Connecticut valley on the west, and the valleys of the Androscoggin and Magalloway on the east, appear between the mountains; while, sparkling like mirrors set in the deep green of the forests, the Umbagog chain of lakes repose far up in their wood-encircled basin.

Over nearly the whole of this broad and wild region is thrown the mantle of the forest. A few farms and villages are visible near by, and then comes the dense and unbroken wilderness. Who that has gazed upon this wild panorama has not desired to penetrate the secrets of those gloomy solitudes, or conjectured what legends people those gorges and ravines, or what deeds of adventure those dusky valleys might reveal?

WENDINGS.
A road that follows the descent of a valley, a stream flowing in the ditch and then crossed at the bottom by a small stone bridge. He walks down the wheel ruts toward a cluster of houses and barns, squared fields broken by stone walls. Halfway downhill a small cemetery off the roadside, the gravestones grass-grown and spotted with lichen except one new marker B. 1897 D. 1918. Cenotaph for a son laid under a simple cross over the sea. From this plot he can sit and watch as the lamps come on one by one in the farmhouses. A man walks his cows into the barn. Behind him the last strip of light fades from the hill.

Come full dark he has followed the road to the bottom of the valley. Walks bent-over beside one house and drinks from the barrel on its north side, smoothes wet hands over his face and wipes it with his sleeve. Beyond the window above him, voices. Through the thin curtains he watches the shadows lift cup and fork to mouth, listens to the scrape of silverware on crockery. He can smell the biscuits and gravy.

Later the moon lifts into the sky. Wrapped in his coat he has slept three hours under an apple tree.

The low coastal blueberry country in summer rain. He stretches on his belly under the bushes, breathing the smell of salt air and the stink of smoke and sweat from his sleeve where he rests his chin. Water trickles down his forehead, beads in his lashes. He has wrapped his supplies in a burlap sack then placed this inside the leather pack. But his blanket becomes heavy and smells of wool.

Jimmy them long lashes of yours near break a girls heart if that smile dont.

After Caleb Lyman's raid against the Cowasuck Indians on the upper Connecticut River (June 1704), their settlement at Cowass was abandoned. Cowass became Cahoos and Cohos and later Coös (county est. December 24, 1803), finally Coos.

No abiding place. A circle amid the trees where winds and words cannot penetrate a mossy rock and a faint view of stars obscured by smoke. My fire burning the scraps I have no use for in cold weeks I would throw my life there if I could. Through it we all must pass it licking at our edges. A man I saw on a corner in the city chanting as everyone passed him I stopped to watch his hands fingering the air. *This world is not my home. This world is not my home. This world is not my home I'm just a-passing through.* His dull coin eyes finding me even here. *And I can't feel at home in this world anymore.*

As if blindly seeking the magnetic pole his feet over the years led him north.

VERN AMEY.

I laid low out in the woods once to try to see what Frye and the Frenchman were up to, but lost the trail about two miles from the village. He is good at woodcraft from his years knocking about here and there, I imagine. I cast off into the trees, making a circle from the spot their tracks ended, but couldn't discover their path, not even a broken branch or footprint in some mud. I hunkered down behind an old deadfall and tried to wait them out. Sometime well past dark I woke not knowing I'd been asleep. I lifted my head over the log but there was no one near. Don't know what it was that woke me. I stayed put till dawn and never saw anything. Walked back to town with one eye over my shoulder the whole way but they didn't approach me nor had they returned during the night and did not come for several days.

It may be interesting to know that the Indians had several well-marked trails from Canada across northern New Hampshire to Maine, the most used one started from Clifton, P.Q., across by South Bay, Connecticut Lake, thence across the northern part of Clarksville, New Hampshire, and down the Magalloway into Maine.

That he worked for a time at a textile mill in Lawrence we can prove by the books locked in the safe, the key available only to the bookkeeper and the manager. The pay records, the word of the Italian woman from whom he rented his room. And after his shift one afternoon he walks along the Merrimack with a young woman from town, the wind blowing loose papers and dirt along the street. Their arms linked, her scarf and his upturned collar flapping. He studies the brick façades, the tall windows with dozens of panes, and tells her of the smell of balsams, the wild cries of loons, the northern lights wavering green behind the trees in summer. She tucks a loose strand of hair into her scarf and with her fingertip flicks soot from his lapel. The river gray and full this time of year flows behind them. Later, alone, he watches trains rattle slow through the trainyard, men stepping over the shiny tracks.

When we heard him speak the first time we knew why he'd kept quiet so long. Why he hadn't come to church to sing with the assembly. Why no one had heard tell of the plans working themselves out in his mind. We could never have imagined such a voice could come from him—the few words he'd spat out during his time working in the camps had not even hinted at this voice, and we knew right away that it was how he had charmed his way into the widow Godfrey's keeping. Those of us with daughters and wives kept them close at hand.

MR HARDING.

He kept the room across the hall from me. A very courteous fellow, he took great care to keep quiet while I was reading or studying in the parlor. Yet at night I'd occasionally hear all manner of noises from his room and once found myself standing in my robe and slippers outside his door while inside the room he moaned and mumbled in his sleep. Something thumped the wall. Mr Frye, I said, knocking on the door and trying to keep my voice low as not to wake Mrs Godfrey. Mr Frye. There was a pause in the sounds coming from behind the door and a rustle of blankets perhaps and then silence. I stood there waiting, my hand poised before the doorknob. But I have always valued my own privacy and would never intrude upon another man's without good cause. Mr Frye himself has always been a discreet man and this too I took into account. The noises did not continue and I returned to my bed leaving my door open a crack to hear should the noises resume. I did not sleep for some time after that. Something about the sound of his unconscious voice had unnerved me as if I had witnessed his naked soul. At breakfast he seemed himself and I did not see him again until after supper when we took a smoke on Mrs Godfrey's porch as was our custom. I lit the bowl of my pipe and rested my hands upon the porch rail, gazing out at the lawns before us, and Main Street and town hall at the bottom of the hill. Out of sight in the trees behind the hall and down a small bank the river ran south, and beyond it rose Ben Young Hill. I studied Mr Frye from the corner of my eye. He seemed innocent enough of what had transpired the previous night and I was loath to discuss it. We took our smoke in silence but for the murmur of the river. To this day I am certain that he was merely asleep and fighting some invisible enemy who had assailed him there.

Yet John Redskin appreciated beauty when he saw it mirrored in the River—tall trees and mighty oaks, the trout pool blushing under the sun's last kiss, the stars, the tender sickle moon; and his heart swelled within him so that he needs must fashion a flute of a reed and make a song about it all full of wild high pipings. He sang of the three jeweled lakes where the River was born far up among the larch-hung mountains.... He sang of the wide intervale below it, the Coos Country, through which the river writhed laughing in summer's sun, or reeled drunk with a foaming brew poured into it after thaw or heavy rain, by those mad torrents, Ammonoosic, Passumpsic, Ompompanoosic, Cascadnac, Ottaqueeche, and all the soberer tributaries which form, along with Quinatucquet itself, that long lovely valley he called the Smile of God.

The sky was sudden. A strip of blue peeping out where the clouds had begun to tatter some hand reaching down to pull them back to cast light on this patch of hills and woods. Or the narrow view of low rainclouds through branches so dense a jay could not fly through. That tired sun lighting the boles of spruce the dead limbs still clutched to before it passed below. A man could never see his shadow before him.

MARTHA HENNESSY.

I'd seen Jimmy since the first time he came to town. Must've been only ten or so but I recall him a longlegged fellow with scanty beard, not too old himself. I met him up the lodge one day while I was running an errand for my mother, and he called out and said did they breed all the young girls up here this pretty, if so he thought he might stay awhile. I looked back at him for a moment and then ran on away. There were men around the lodge all the time and mother had told me never to speak to them. I didn't hear him speak to me but once again for four years, and that time he was overheard and walked off right quick. But that voice played itself out in my mind every so often, a faint sound like the wind in bare branches. Then one day, not long before sugaring season, he found me alone again and told me he was off but would be back for me shortly and to sit tight in the meantime. True to his word he was gone the next morning. Vern Amey came up to the lodge with a load of firewood and said Jimmy'd left the widow Godfrey's house on foot that morning, and good riddance.

I started planning but I didn't know what for. I walked in the dooryard after supper and if my mother knew I'd some foolish ideas in my head she never spoke of it.

Each of us is a hundred men known and secret even to each other as a crowd in a tavern vying for attention the old man and the fresh boy and yes they moved inside me at times. Sitting on a rock in thick woods. All answering to the same name though it meant differently. If I could cut a man open like cleaning a fish. The things we say. Jimmy I shouted till the trees understood.

HISTORIES.

Soon we came to a larger tributary, practically the same size as the River itself, and knew it for the rivulet which had given name to the Indian Stream Territory, whose history is among the strangest of all River tales. It is difficult to believe that this jagged corner of New Hampshire determinedly maintained complete independence up to about a century ago, but such is the truth.

The history of the next controversy, as to the northern frontier of the State, will be given in a few words, and without particular comment, as the dispute is still pending before our own judicial tribunals.

Certain purchasers and their grantees, it is understood, claim the title to the soil under a deed from one Philip, an Indian occupying all or part of the premises. It is dated, June 28, 1796, and a copy of it is given in a report by a select committee to the Legislature of New-Hampshire, November session, A.D. 1824. It is stated, that the Provincial act against purchases from the Indians had then been repealed four years.

Whatever laws may since have been passed by Congress as to Indians, these purchasers would doubtless question the power of Congress to legislate at all about the title of land within the limits of an old State, and never ceded to the Union. This deed includes all or most of the land north of the forty-fifth degree of latitude, and since the execution of it, sundry surveys, conveyances and settlements have been made under it.

By another report of another committee, the same year, it appears, that on an examination of that country, they found the population over 100, and though some of their farms had been occupied as early as A.D. 1795, yet the present settlers had mostly removed there since A.D. 1814.

In November, A.D. 1820, the Attorney General was directed, by the legislature, to institute proceedings against the inhabitants, with a view to ascertain by what authority they occupied this tract. Proceedings were accordingly instituted, in May, A.D. 1821, the decision of which must depend on many other facts, beside those of an historical *character before stated, and which, till those proceedings are closed, it may not be proper to state or discuss.*

But it is understood, that both the title and jurisdiction of the State to any land north of the forty-first degree of latitude, has been, or will be, brought into consideration, and both will doubtless be settled on those sound principles of evidence, and public law, the purity of which are of more importance than a victory can be to either party.

Portsmouth, N.H. April 20, 1827.

———

Indian Stream, Indian Stream Settlement, Indian Stream Territory, Township of Indian Village, Township of Liberty in Indian Stream, Indian Grant, Bedel's Grant, Bedel's and Others' Grant, Bedel's and Associates' Grant are all names which were applied to a tract of land situated in what is now the extreme northern portion of Coös county, the northernmost county of New Hampshire.

The assumption usual in regard to border settlements, however, should not be too readily made in the case of Indian Stream. The conclusion that the region was a haven for the lawless and indebted, who trusted in the ambiguity of its location for protection against legal authority, is unwarranted by its history. Indian Stream had its disorders, but nothing is more certain, in light of the record of their activities, than that the great majority of the settlers were men of good character, serious purpose, common sense, and no mean degree of ability. The amount of lawlessness from which the community suffered was probably the minimum, and the serious attitude assumed toward it was due to the natural Anglo-Saxon desire to enjoy perfect system.

———

The treaty of 1783 defined the northwest boundary of New Hampshire as "the most northwestern head of the Connecticut river." The country was wild and unsurveyed. The British considered that their title under this treaty extended down to the forty-fifth parallel of latitude, and the real head of the Connecticut, while New Hampshire did not concern itself with the subject. In 1789, however, Col Jeremiah Eames was on a commission appointed by the legislature to survey and establish the boundaries between Maine, New Hampshire, and Lower Canada, and his journal shows that they made the head of Hall's stream, the northwest bound of this state, and established it by suitable monuments. Hall's stream is the northwestern branch of the Connecticut, and this survey brought all the land between Hall's stream and Connecticut river, including the fertile valley of Indian stream, within this state. The advantages of this region becoming known, in 1789 two settlers made their homes on Indian stream. Others followed, led hither by the richness of the soil; others, to seek in this remote district an asylum from pressing creditors or punishment for crime.

In 1819 the British and American commissioners attempted to jointly establish the boundary line between Canada and this state, but they could not agree. The American commissioners held to Eames' survey and Hall's stream as the bound made by the treaty, while the British commissioners contended for lines according to their construction. From the survey in 1789, the settlers here had known nothing else than that they were in New Hampshire territory, and, so far as they were amenable to any law, acknowledged that of this state.

In 1824 Indian Stream Territory was inhabited by about fifty-eight settlers, who, with their families, made a population of 285 persons, having about 847 acres under improvement.

The settlement, in 1830, numbered ninety voters, and there was a large enough number of disaffected men to lead them to talk of resistance to the long acknowledged authority.

July 9, 1832, the voters of the disputed tract met, by notification, formed the government of "The United Inhabitants of Indian Stream Territory," adopted a constitution, which created an assembly and a council.

March 12, 1835, Deputy Sheriff William M. Smith, from Colebrook, attempted to arrest C.J. Haines and Reuben Sawyer, and was violently beaten and driven from the Territory by several men. March 13, Milton Harvey and an assistant were assaulted while trying to attach some property, and also driven from the Territory. Wild reports came *down to Lancaster of this resistance; it was asserted that the Territory was organizing a military force, had made an alliance with Indians for war, and were building a block-house for an intrenchment, under the name of "jail."*

A posse led by Sheriff Harvey and Miles Hurlburt of Colebrook, crossed the border into Canada, rescued Blanchard, and took him to Canaan, Vermont. Here they joined a large mob in front of Parmelee and Joy's Store. Sheriff Smith offered a reward of $5.00 for the capture of Tyler. Ephraim Aldrich of Indian Stream called for volunteers to capture Rea, Tyler, Flanders, and Clough, and promised them all the liquor they could hold. Three or four others offered additional bounties.

A second and larger posse was organized. Captain James Mooney of the New Hampshire militia, then on call at Stewartstown, joined it. The posse crossed the border into Canada and headed straight for Rea's house. There Rea and a deputy named Bernard Young met the crowd. In the confusion that followed, Rea was wounded in the head by a blow from Aldrich's sword and Young in the groin by a shot from Hurlburt's pistol.

Indian Stream War was caused by a boundary dispute when the town of Pittsburg, for a short time, was an independent nation in 1829.

One occurrence of the war was often related by old settlers. The town had no prison so when a Britisher or Tory was captured he was confined under a large potash kettle, overturned on a large flat rock, a smaller rock placed underneath the edge allowed air to enter the prison. He was there confined until tried and justice meted out.

The large flat rock has been pointed out to me as the spot where stood the "jail" of the Indian Stream War.

Jimmy Frye is an old wives' tale, a story someone invented long ago during a time he was snowed in his cabin. A story to distract himself from the drifts mounting in front of his windows and the blue light he knew he would wake to in morning, the water melting down his stovepipe to hiss on the logs when he got a fire lit. My grandfather told me how he had heard about Jimmy and the gold years back, how even his grandfather told him stories of a character he called Jimmy Moonshine, who would come to town with the summer thunderstorms, steal the corn and the livestock, foment discord among the men, despoil the women, and then vanish under cover of darkness. That this story somehow got tangled up with the other story of the Indian's gold—which according to some may go back to the time before any white men lived on this continent—is only natural. In this remote corner of the world there is nothing but wilderness and darkness and drink. Any man can be forgiven an evening's dreaming as long as it is not passed on as fact. There were many hoboes in those years, and while there may well have been a man named Frye who passed through the village at some point, this Jimmy Frye they speak of has never walked the earth except in men's minds or the stories they tell.

I knew you were out there. I looked for you in the face of every man who came to the lodge, every pair of eyes that met mine while I carried my mother's steaming trays of trout and potatoes around the table. And recognized each time that I had longer to wait. At night I stood by the shore of the lake, listening to the silence that hid everything inside itself. I thought of any far-off place, the sound of train whistles. Your face as you cupped a match to your cigarette. Imagined what life we would have far from these woods. Where are you, I said, knowing that you heard my voice. When I looked down the empty road to town I was seeing you already.

I swear he used to shit his pants. We boys would go out there to throw rocks against the roof or ask him to show us the best spots for trout. Some claimed he'd left decades back but the whole town knew he was still in the woods whether or not they'd say as much. Most people wanted to forget him, as though he'd never lived. His shack was sixteen by twenty, pine boards and tarpaper, his bed in one corner and the rest workbenches covered with junk. Old traps rusted shut, pelts of muskrat and raccoon and fox, some in piles, some stretched out and drying with flies crawling on them. All kinds of rusty and worthless tools and frayed ropes and tin cans filled with Lord knows what all. Way out in the frigging woods by Indian Stream. He'd piped the stream in through his wall, and it poured through his sink and back out again, running all the time. It was dark inside, only one or two windows, and those often curtained with rags. Come closer, he'd tell us, and we'd step forward while he sat on the edge of his bed unmoving. His beard white and wild, hiding all of his face but his blue eyes. His wool trousers soiled and patched and his hands on his knees. Closer, he'd say. I remember gripping tight to my fish pole and trying not to breathe. From under his pillow he'd pull a small pouch and out of that shake into his palm five or six dull lumps. He'd put one between his back teeth and bite, showing us the marks. The stream tinkling in his basin behind him. You'd like to know where the rest of it's at, he said, wouldn't you. He showed us the shotgun he'd wired to the underside of his rough table, the trigger in easy reach of where he sat. In case the warden comes, he said, winking, or anyone else I don't like and that means any one of you. Then he'd take us along the stream and point out the places to drop our lines. He came to town only once a month, leaning on a polished ash cane, to buy what he needed to eat. Everyone said he'd been out in that shack for years and years, since before my father had been a boy, hunting for it. Yes, we've seen it, they'd answer, when we told of his pouch. Still I wonder if it may have been a ploy. He never seemed to want for food and no one knew where he got his money. Once when he hadn't been to town for some weeks, they went out to check up on him and found him dead, and though they tore the place apart, no one found anything else, nothing to back up his stories, not even the pouch we'd all seen so many times.

Me in a tub with an Irish whore in this great city of Boston Massachusetts where outside the cars rumble over the cobblestones and ships sail into the harbor after journeys of several years and hundreds of strangers walk the streets and alleyways with hands concealed in their pockets. She pours water over my head and the hair slicks into my eyes the water slurring past my ears and off my chin she laughs at me this paperwhite girl I have secured with the last coins and bills in my pocket. A dozen paper lamps burn around us and steam rises from the water. She soaps the space between my shoulders and again I ask her name and again she asks me to speak into her ear. I raise a hand dripping strings of water and foam and brush back the black hair from her face.

Once at a sawmill outside Lebanon I watched as a man named Toby Moore lost his arm in the belt of the steam engine powering the saw. The blood sprayed everywhere and Bill Page who'd been working beside him keeping up the fire was covered in it some his own from where a chunk of Toby's bone had gashed his cheek. That sight I hope never to see again the strands of muscle or tendon holding the pulp of Toby's arm to his shoulder and the instant white of his face as he passed out there and every man jumped down into the pit where the engine was. Bill Page on his knees screaming. I never found out if Toby lived or died in that moment of the saw ceasing its spinning and the whine quieting I ran from the mill the shouts quieting behind me too.

Down the niggerhole for two days buried I ate nothing but carrots Vince had thought to stow there when we first opened it up. Chewing them in the dark and thought I would gag before the end. I clenched my bowels tight and let out piss a little at a time and when I climbed out the packed earth all damp from it.

JAILED.

On the ceiling a circle of water dripped by me and each time I watched that mouth in it open and close and the sound of the drop on the cement at my feet. I sat against the wall. Knees against my chest and arms tight around them to keep off the chill.

At dawn three men had surprised me climbing out a window with a gold necklace and a set of sterling candlesticks in my vest pocket. Some hilltown far to the southwest of here I had been just out of Fort Edward in the Dutch country then and passed a rollicking night with some boys met in the lake valley. They'd left heading west where I'd just come from gave me a jug of whiskey and some bread to take on the road with me. Next night I lay up in the hills and finished both watching the stars fall below the edge of the world where other strange countries lie. The long hour before light I saw the house sitting lonely on the road and shimmied up a tree to the porch roof. Man and wife asleep in the bed didn't stir while I grabbed a few things off the chest. Their mouths wet breathing holes I looked at the yellow teeth and flat tongues. Stepping barefoot across the floor and pulled my boots back on at the windowsill.

The men were riding along the road with a wagonload of wood when I squirmed my head and shoulders through the window. I ran along the roof and made a leap into a leafpile came down hard on my ankle and all three were on me.

Six months there and when they let me out squinting at the sun half the village followed me at a hundred yards until I came to the signpost on the road where they stood to see I did not turn back.

Dark turned above us caught us on the road and witnessed a pressure of my hands around his throat and then a barehanded rock. I was redhanded while he lay choking in the dirt turning in his coat and leaves stuck to it and his hair. Then the rock again and he was quiet. I panted there some time the house behind me where yet no one knew I was not though it had been a half hour I had followed his shape down the vanishing road. Where mother slept not knowing and another part of me watched stars purl through the oak branches.

Into the woods leaf-covered I left him in a ditch scraped over with moss and branches then was into the deeper woods still in darkness. I washed in a standing pool and by dawn straddled the crotch of a tree five miles away.

———————

Struggling along, we worked our difficult way onwards until nearly noon, when suddenly we came through a perplexing thicket of blackberry briars, out upon the steep bank of a filthy, muddy creek, that came slowly down from one side of the river valley, through a wide, flat, alder swamp. Neither of us had eaten more than a mouthful or two since the day before at noon. Our various rambles in the forest, if laid off in a straight line, could not have measured much less than thirty miles; and that not of smooth walking over a cleared road, but of crawling, stooping, shoving, scratching, squeezing, jumping, and climbing: for such a vile tangle of a forest, full of stumps, stones, briars, hills, bogs, and all imaginable impediments, I am sure never was penetrated before.

The border between New Hampshire and Vermont is the winding line of the Connecticut River.

Part of the border between New Hampshire and Québec is formed by Hall's Stream.

Several bodies of water, including Umbagog and Aziscohos Lakes, and the various branches of the Magalloway and Dead Diamond Rivers, lie on or near the border between Maine and New Hampshire.

A common story told in the region recounts the experiences of a woman from Exeter, in the southern part of the state, who was abducted by Abenakis during the mid-Eighteenth century and brought north by her captors. After a journey of many days, the woman, whose name is not recorded, was able to escape—according to differing versions of the story, possibly by fleeing while the Abenakis slept, or by killing them in their sleep with their own tomahawks. The woman took her bearings by the sun and walked south for several days before she came upon a small settlement. She learned from a farmer that she was in Vermont, on the western side of the Connecticut; but in her travels with the Abenakis she knew she had not crossed the river. Only then did she realize how far north she had been conveyed, beyond the headwaters of that river and into dangerous and unknown lands. It was claimed that following her return to Exeter, the woman was subject to visions and fits.

A countryside surrounded by moving waters is said to experience frequent psychic phenomena.

He is, perhaps, seven. Yet already in his eyes one could read his fate. A skittishness in league with a certain wildness. He roams the woods days, snaring rabbits and tracking squirrels and raccoons he kills with a slingshot. He discovers a shallow cave where he stashes a stolen box of matches and a supply of small rocks. He does not know what for but all his life he has pocketed loose things and concealed them in places only he has knowledge of.

Entry from a misplaced day. He sits in melting snow by a stream, yellow grass lifting through the dirty slush. The stream is still mostly frozen and he watches green bubbles slide below the ice. Above him in bare trees a few birds, chickadees. With a fingernail he peels the wet bark from a branch. His horse's breath hangs still in the air.

For miles around him not another man stirs. Only wary deer browsing the stripped thickets, the moose standing in muddy bogs, coyote roaming the spruce woods in small packs. Even the bear remain asleep.

A hand-drawn map sketched by a dead man. He has been a week in the woods, sheltering under a fallen spruce and lighting few fires. But now he will return to the village he bypassed before dawn last week—the small white church and clustered houses, the town hall and general store, the valley farms—and find lodgings.

Four years is near enough to drive a man mad with frosted windows and clocks ticking all night and the cold never leaving his bones for months. But I stayed waiting for the one I needed to wait on still young and unready and I waited long winters where I did nothing but work beside the other men in the hidden timber clearing woodlots and sending the lumber downriver where I'd come from and where each time I wanted to go. Knowing all along I could've struck it and found more than enough to settle somewhere. Biting my tongue to keep still as the blankets covered me in the dark. In hiding away from me I imagined her the hair curling down her back and all the things her eyes would see. I waited. The world and everything in it in reach of my fist. Four years out of my life.

One morning Brown and I, after a night spent in a hayloft, sat down to a breakfast which set at unblushing defiance every rule sanctioned by approved usage. The scene of the repast was a log-house, at the source of the Connecticut. Hard by, breaking from its parent lake, tossing, foaming, and fuming, the Yankee river made its start in life in a spirit of lawless riot which held forth indifferent promise of the prosperous respectability of later course....

What peculiar attraction we could discover in three log-houses and a saw-mill, which then formed, and perhaps form to this day, the settlement of Lake Connecticut, it might not be easy to explain. But the settlement of Lake Connecticut was to us but the jumping-off place whence we proposed to dive into a remoter world of mystery.

Northward, beyond the lake, ridge above ridge in hazy distance, rose the high mountains which form the Canadian boundary, savage, pathless, unfrequented—because there is nothing to be got by going there: in short, a howling wilderness.

A midwinter barn dance and that Hennessy girl as sour as old milk. The floor pounding under so many feet and she stood by the wall with her arms crossed the whole night, an empty cup in her fingers. Refused the few boys who dared ask her to dance. Oh she's always been a snooty one and it's only been worse since her poor father passed. And then this business with the hobo last summer. Told her own mother she was off to the city to search him out and then didn't speak a word for a week when her mother told her she'd do no such foolish thing. If my Maryanne ever. But one look at her face and you can see she's just counting the days. As if any sensible girl would even think of it. Mr Currier's son comes in the sleigh to pick her up after school and she won't say a word to him either, just climbs in and rides the six miles up to the lake in silence, not even seeing the snow-covered trees or the ice edging the river in the valley.

DIVINATION.
A girl wishing to know her destiny must go blindfolded into a cabbage patch, turn around three times and point to the cabbages. If she designates a hard head, her future husband will be all she could wish for. If, unfortunately, she points to a soft head, she is doomed to live with a worthless mate.

No man in this town is as brave. No man as handsome. No man as cunning as he and soon when we leave this godforsaken country forever we will have a large house in the city with maids and many doors and closets large enough to stand inside.

He had not been back but a day when he came for me. I had heard already how he had come into town with some friend of his, both of them looking as though they'd been beset by wild Indians in the woods. But when he called at the lodge the next day he was shaven and his clothes neatly pressed. He stopped me in the hall and whispered to meet him at seven o'clock by the shore and then he was clapping on the back some of the men who'd remained during his absence, asking them how their luck had been.

At seven o'clock I told my mother Mr Currier had an errand for me. I ran through the woods away from the shore should anyone see me and then crept back through the trees to the edge of the lake. He stood in the shadow of a tree and came forth only when he saw it was I.

I am certain of you, he said, are you certain of me? It was a dark night overcast with clouds and I couldn't see his eyes. The lake lapped the rocks by our feet. I will take you far and you will not see this country again, he told me. I thought then for a moment of the farm, father in the rocky hilltop, the kitchen and the sound of men's pinched laughter from the dining room, their eyes as I walked from the room. I could hear his breath, feel it stirring the hair on my forehead.

I would help father check the traps he kept in the woods during winter, the pelts he could sell to bring in extra money. One time when I was younger I had pulled the brush off a fox hide stretching in the shed by petting and petting it. It meant more money than I care to think about, but father didn't scold me. He wrapped it around my neck and hoisted me inside for mother to see.

Father and I walked the loop each morning the snow wasn't too deep for me, and he carried both a gun and a heavy stick for the animals. Sometimes we found a fox or a fisher cat but more often rabbits and coons and such. This morning he had stopped for a skunk that had somehow tangled the chain round a bush, its blood tingeing the snow pink. I ran ahead up the trail, the sky bare of clouds and the snow already blinding me. In the next trap was a bobcat still quite alive and hissing at me as I approached it. Its hind leg was caught in the jaws. I knew what it was only from the stories I'd heard about them, never having seen one before. I picked up a stick and, as I'd seen my father do, gave it a wallop on its head. It hissed and spat and jumped sideways, dragging the trap through the snow. I gave it another crack with the stick and it yowled and slashed the air with one claw. My father came running up the trail, and when he saw what it was said oh Jesus and dropped his sack and drew his pistol and shot it. After he was sure it was killed he showed me how the trap held it only by two toes. Thereafter he walked the loop alone and I helped mother in the kitchen as it has been ever since, all this time, she handing me a bowl of eggs to beat or flour to sift down into a bowl, snow over the valley.

Years later, by the lodge, he gave me the skin of a mink, and, as I held it in my hands rubbing my fingers over the fur, told me to have my mother make me a set of mittens from it.

———————

As I became deaf blind and mute.
As I left my own body.
As the body a map the voice a flame.
As this name never spoken.
As a journey answers a question.

THE CIDER-MAKER.

George Belknap owned a few acres of orchard on the side of a hill in southern Vermont. His cider-mill stood beside a stream that in summer and fall was a shallow brook cascading over rocks and in spring, green with runoff, often flooded its banks. His family had possessed the land for five generations going back a hundred and eighty years. In one of the beams inside the mill were carved the initials of his father and grandfather and great-grandfather who had raised it. He had been born his own father's child the year the man turned sixty. And never marrying had worked the mill alone, pressing cider and burying the pomace in the woods or leaving it for the deer. His orchard Baldwins and Northern Spies and Mc-Intosh. The bones of his family were buried on the hillside, and sometimes after a day's work he climbed to the flat stones placed in the grass and imagined their voices spoke to him.

The hobo had appeared by his mill one morning in September, asleep on a pile of oat straw. Belknap poked the hobo with a stick and stood back while the man pulled his hat from his face and with it shaded the sun to look at Belknap looking at him.

Belknap instructed the hobo in the operation of the grinder and the press and let the younger man use his greater strength to crank the bar while he layered the pomace and straw and boards. He gave the hobo the spare bed in his dark-shingled house, the bed where for thirty-nine years no one had slept though its linens were washed as regularly as those on his own, and in the morning they took their coffee together. At night the hobo sang while he soaked in Belknap's tub, his voice tentative and boyish.

> Jimmy crack corn and I don't care
> Jimmy crack corn and I don't care
> Jimmy crack corn and I don't care
> My master's gone away

A pressing took them all day. By evening they poured the cider from the tub into five gallon kegs, the sediment sinking slowly to the bottom. Later they brought a keg into Belknap's cellar and after supper the hobo descended the steep wooden stairs and drew a pitcher, and as they drank the hobo told him of the places he had been, west to the thundering falls at Niagara where he and a crowd of men women and children had watched a man die in a splintered barrel, east to Cape Breton where he had seen the sun rise red from below the sea. By winter, when the hobo left unannounced in the night, Belknap could no longer recall his tales of the road, and the granite hills and the sea-broken shores the hobo had conjured became confused in his mind, and he wondered if the stories had not been something he had dreamed, or some tale his father had told him from the gloom of his rocking chair one evening some fifty years back. But now in his mind instead of his father's voice he heard the voice of the hobo, drunk on their cider, only the sleepy words and the ticking stove and the wind beyond his windows. All that winter the snow fell thick and in the mornings still stuck to the tree branches, auguring a good apple year.

In those days, after the fear of King Philip's War and the raids had long since ended, and when Indian and white man had in places begun to work together as they had at first, the Abenaki Migounambe (called Sheepscoat John by the settlers) showed his friend Nathaniel Perry, one of the first white settlers by the Connecticut Lakes, the cave with walls streaked with gold far into the wilderness. This cave had long been known among his people as a sacred place where they had once gone to commune with the great spirits. It was a half-day's journey into the woods from the village in the valley, down faint and forgotten traces no eye but that Indian's knew: for Migounambe was even then one of the last of his people. On the return journey, Perry's mind was consumed with thoughts: his plough set aside for a pick, the rocky earth yielding at last. For even though the valley was fertile where the young Connecticut meandered, the growing season was short and the farmers had to put much care into their work. Each step of the path back, Perry thought only of how he could obtain the gold in secret, and forgot the many kindnesses Migounambe and his people had shown his own family and the other early settlers. And so in the woods, when they had almost neared the village, Perry slew his friend, shooting him from behind as the Indian guided him home. Migounambe fell and knew he had but a moment of breath. Ahead of them through the trees he could see the first fields. And so he said, 'Out of greed you have killed me, but your greed will be your undoing. No white man will again see this cave, and your valley will one day be flooded with angry waters destroying your homes.' These final words were never heard by any in the settlement until Perry, wasted and gaunt, overcome with sorrow and filled with repentance on his deathbed, bade that they be recorded.

Some nights I tried to remember the lines of his face and from them piece together the man he had been or maybe still was somewhere I didn't know of. Always those turned-away eyes escaped me and the mouth drawn into a frown. For years I never let anyone touch that axe handle splintered six inches above the blade where he'd been splitting unseasoned red oak. Why he had chosen that rocky plot of land to settle and raise a family.

The roads I walked I asked after him to people who didn't bother to think hard on it. No they said and soon I stopped asking. After some time had gone by and I had grown into myself I knew he was nowhere in this country but somewhere far out west or bellied in a ship across the wide and raging seas wherever his own star had steered him. Each time I thought to give chase I could feel the hills calling me back to them their rocks my bones and their dirt on my feet. The sea had never agreed with me its stink of things rotting and the muck washed onto its beaches and shores. The churning motions of the ships I'd been on had angered me that man had yet to find a way to remedy it. But for all I knew he had just waited for us all to leave one by one and now was returned to his home the crooked corners he had raised among the pines where now he listened to the wind in their boughs by himself. I could never bring myself to go back there to see fearing what I might.

The axe I buried still broken before I left.

———

Jimmy Frye was at least half Indian himself, which is why he knew of the gold to begin with. His great-great-grandmother was an Abenaki who knew the exact spot. She left for some village down east where she married a white man and raised a family. The legend she passed on to each of her children, and they to each of theirs, until it came to Jimmy. His mother had married a Pessamaquoddy, which accounts for the extra Indian in Jimmy, and that blood is what drove his feet along the empty roads to this town.

Six or seven men came on him, arming themselves from the wood-pile of the man whose farm it was. That farmer had found him sleeping in the barn when he went out in the morning to tend the cows and had driven him off, only to find him again on a pile of moldy hay when he carried out his lamp the next morning. This time he didn't thump his ribs with his boot as he'd done the morning previous but stepped out quietly to fetch the hired hands and several men from the farm a half mile down the road. And still somehow in the short minutes it took them to gather he had awakened from some animal sense and stood in the shadows just outside the barn door. He had no pistol nor even a knife, nothing in his hands but a clutch of that hay he'd been using as his bed. Sure, you think, he aimed to throw it into their eyes, or to use it to ward those split logs off his shoulders. And that may well have been his aim. But he didn't let them get close enough to hit him. While they circled in he began in that voice you've all heard for yourselves. He may have told them that he was a preacher from distant parts who'd fallen on a hard spell and had simply put his trust in Providence to furnish him with a shelter for the night. If only you'd let me explain myself yesterday, he may have said. Or perhaps it was some incantation that stayed their blows, as some of you would have it. No matter. You can imagine as well as I. For the truth is that none of those men laid a hand on him, but instead let him pass through them while the sticks they held dropped to their sides. What he spoke none of them has ever said and likely never will for shame at his tale's flimsiness.

This is a story I heard down Lancaster way from a man I know there, who I'd gone to see about a horse. You should have heard the voice on this fella, the man told me. That was what kept them from him, more than his words. He could've talked his way out of a nest of vipers. And once he'd said it I knew it could be none other than our very own hobo.

PORTLAND.

Up the stairs two at once my hands sliding over the plaster walls
and through the door my coat heavy with water the whisky still
flooding the space behind my eyes. They told me Louis and his girl
were staying here. Inside the room was in darkness and my breath
made hearing hard I banged up my shin on a table. Everything in
the room a sleeping animal to snare me and a trickle of light coming
through the gap in the heavy curtains. Felt a chair arm the wood
smooth as a girl's belly. Into the next room.

The bed stood there clothes draped over the posts and before
anything else I could smell them that smell of bodies asleep in a
shut-up room a winter smell the coals in the grate barely glowing
at all. I reached under the covers with my hand found her leg first
she could not have been eighteen yet and with thumb and finger
I circled the tiny bones of that ankle and held her fluttering pulse
against my palm. Then I fished around under there and came up
with his foot gave a mighty heave and he fell to the floor trailing
half the blankets and making a quick burst of air from his mouth.
She bolted up and I turned to see her before she drew the covers
back over herself. Winked.

I fell atop him pulled the blankets from his face and we were
both of us laughing while the girl still silent looked at us drawing
on her clothes beneath the quilt she held. Even that patched fabric a map of something. My beard dampening the sheet dripping
rain.

It's me I said I need something. He dropped his head back
against the wood floor my eyes growing accustomed enough to
the dark to see the hair on his head stood every which way. I need
Vince Bouchard. Have you seen him.

Not in six years. Not since I last saw you. How did you find
me? Again I smelled him her their bed and she was up now and
hunting for her shoes under the blankets. Stay he said.

Well where is he. Where is he goddamn him.

He can't be anywhere near or I would have heard.

I'm leaving.

Louis I need a place to lie my head. The rain pouring off the
eaves I curled into the warmth her body had left holding it in my

hands while he went to the kitchen fried an egg and drank some coffee cold since supper. You're just drunk he said.

In one place what I wondered was how the other places still were the people still there still walking and working still eating each meal. But me not there but here unless a part of me has stayed. How a man's head cannot begin to take in the places he has been or the people each word spoken a line somewhere in the land. And if everything behind us to return in circles the only way my feet then have worn this old ground bare.

VINCENT BOUCHARD.

He told me to gather my tools. Only the finest ones, he said. We placed them in a bag. We can find other things we need when we get there, he said. Where? You'll find out. I wrapped my hammer in a cloth, tied twine around it, and put it in the bag. The matches in a metal tin. Hurry. Hurry, hurry. Is it a secret? Lock your door you won't be back for some time. Let's go.

June 2nd, 1922

A most curious and disturbing thing has happened yesterday and last night. Just after noon, during a thunderstorm, a canoe of sportsmen overturned on First Lake. We heard of it in town some hours later. Earl Young's boy came by with the news. Apparently many others attempted to rescue them, yet by the time word had reached us only a fishing rod and an empty lunch pail had been retrieved. Many of those listening rode up to the lake at once. I accompanied the boy to his house and heard the rest as we walked.

At supper Mr Frye did not return from the woodlot, and, while Mrs Godfrey kept the dishes waiting for a time, he still did not return so we assumed he had stayed at the lake to assist the others. After we had eaten I paced the parlor rug, the clock's loud ticking ringing in my ears. Shortly thereafter Mrs Godfrey came into the parlor and as I was too agitated to read we discussed the day's events. Only a few minutes had passed when we heard horses on the street and I went to the porch. Mr Covill, Mr Young, Mr Rolfe and several other men were traveling past. I hailed them and went down to hear the news. Mr Young said that they had recovered the two bodies, both those of men from Massachusetts. It appears that nearly the entire village took part in the operations on the lake. Now as it was turning dark I asked them if they had seen Mr Frye at the lake and none of them had. It was a curious whim that had made me ask the question and I regretted at once this trespass on another man's autonomy. Nor did I want to seem overly concerned for Mr Frye's welfare, nor too curious about another. Certainly there are times when he travels to Littleton to see his ailing mother and is gone from Mrs Godfrey's house for a time, but before these journeys he always tells us that he will be away. Other than these times I am pressed to recall an evening when he was not at home to share our supper.

Mrs Godfrey and I waited up for a time past dark, lighting the parlor lamps, she fussing over some embroidery and I pretending to study the pages of a Latin grammar. Finally I announced I was turning in and heard her do the same while I lay in bed upstairs.

Her own room of course is downstairs and I set down these facts only because of what happened during the night.

Past two by my pocketwatch I heard steps coming up the porch. I thought it a bit odd at once because nearly everyone who visits uses the back door and Mr Frye had never been known to come in this way. Of course I assumed it was he, back from the lake at last after perhaps lending a hand in whatever final arrangements were necessary. The front door opened and whoever it was stepped inside and closed the door behind him. The footsteps paused in the parlor near the door to Mrs Godfrey's bedroom, which I attributed to Mr Frye determining that he had not woken her. Next the footsteps seemed to walk toward the kitchen, which I thought rather odd until I realized that Mr Frye must not have had anything to eat since dinner and was likely famished from his hours at the lake and the long walk home. I turned over to my side and waited to hear him come upstairs. I half-fancied meeting him in the hall to hear the details about the rescue and the two drowned men and by what means their bodies had been retrieved. It seemed I waited a long time and when I next held my pocketwatch to the moonlight coming in the window I saw that an hour had passed and I must have fallen back asleep in that interval.

In the morning Mrs Godfrey and I prepared to take our breakfast at the usual time but Mr Frye did not rise to join us. She too had heard him enter during the night. Before we started I went back upstairs to knock on his door. There was no response from within. I knocked several times and finally opened the door an inch and called his name through the crack. As there was again no response I opened the door wider. The bed was still made without a wrinkle on the quilt.

Mrs Godfrey is in a terrible state. Neither of us can imagine where Mr Frye is, nor who came into the house last night. I have tried to assure her that our nightly visitor was only someone troubled in his sleep or perhaps a drunk fellow who believed he was entering his own house and, when he realized his mistake, tiptoed out the kitchen door to avoid any further embarrassment. But these rationalizations cannot persuade me, nor her I suspect. At noon I will go to Baldwin's store, where I'm convinced a crowd will have gathered to mull yesterday's events, and hope that if I do not find Mr Frye there I will at least come by word of him and will find last night's trespasser.

Moose Hillock towers over the Connecticut below the Fifteen-Mile Falls, by which latter all further navigation of the river is precluded. Above and below the Fifteen-Mile Falls, on the Connecticut, are tracts of country, called respectively the Upper and the Lower *Coos* or *Cohoss*; which term implies, according to some, a fall in a river; according to others, a bend in a river; and, according to a third party, a parcel of meadowland; but the true interpretation is pineland, the word being derived from the Indian *cohâ* or *coä*; a pine-tree. Some Indians, of this part of the Connecticut, still remain at Saint-Français, where they call themselves *Cohâssiac*.—Such is the origin of the name *cohass*, *cohoss*, or *coös*; but, the pine-trees having been removed, their place is occupied by meadow; while, at the same time, the lands lie on bends of the river, and are contiguous to the Fifteen-Mile Falls:—hence, the diverse explanations.

Oh, it was terrible when Al Hennessy passed. Nearly the whole town came to the service, as if none of us could believe him gone unless we stood in the cemetery. Some said it was the mustard gas, some said it was the flu that took so many others that year, some said that what he'd seen and survived had ruined his spirit.

I remember that spring. Cool days, apple blossom petals swirling in a wind to catch in your hair and the folds of your clothes, the scent of lilacs, bleeding hearts thick in the dooryards of the valley farms—all that blowth a fair promise. Finches, fiery yellow, flew over the greening fields. We thought summer would be that gorgeous. Then the rains ended and the unbroken sky burned away such hopes. No one much noticed how sick Al took those months, since everyone else was drawing wells dry, bailing water from dwindling streams, watching the lakes leak slowly back into the earth. For weeks he had been—so we heard—shut away in his bed, attended by Dr Rowell, who permitted no visitors. When his wife sold the farm, we knew he wouldn't last.

Al had been one of the few to enlist when the recruiting party came through Coos County, despite being nearer to forty than twenty, despite never having any proper training. I can shoot straight, he'd tell us, I'll be all right. Those two years he was gone his wife had a starved and harried look to her, her hair beginning to gray, her face a flurry of feeling, her eyes unable to fix on any one spot long enough for her to see it. Currier's son would drive her between the village and the lodge, and I'd wave as they passed our place, though she appeared not even to notice me. No matter. I understood. I had no peach pits to collect for charcoal for the gas masks, but I spent evenings knitting socks for soldiers; I did not bake with wheat flour; I gave seven cents for Belgian children on Envelope Day; in the newspaper, I studied each letter home from the trenches as if it were written by my own. But even once Al returned, his wife seemed unable to see him; at church, she clung to him fiercely, and studied his face while he spoke to us in his soft way.

Al's daughter, Martha, cared for the herd and managed the farm with only their old hired hand, and him so worsted by drink we wondered how they did it. Martha would climb in Currier's wagon herself some mornings, to help at the lodge during those busy weeks in the fall, when the mist hung thick in the hollows, when our own woods rang with the echoes of gunfire.

If she suffered like her mother, she didn't show it—even after that summer, when they returned to the Curriers', this time to stay for good in a room above the kitchen. Some say she grew as bitter as her mother, stranded so far from town with those uncouth men, but I don't believe it. She was a rare beauty, and like all things beautiful left us too long ago. Boston, I believe. Sometimes even now I remember her in my prayers, her face still clear in my mind as I kneel before bed: a few words I hope find her well, wherever she may be.

———————

He lived in a windowless shack two day's ramble into the woods, in a narrow valley where the sun arrived late over the hills to the east and fell too early toward those to the west, where the trees had grown dense and crooked in the winds. A nameless stream poured through there, green with runoff as it fell toward the Magalloway, and he roamed the hills from which it coursed, hunting and trapping. When the snow had mostly melted, and his supplies run out, he'd tramp to one of the remote homesteads to beg for food—sometimes by himself, sometimes with a vagabond Indian or two, all of them loud and sloppy and stinking with rum. At one cabin, near Errol, he was said to have surprised a young wife alone; her husband had gone down to Berlin overnight on some errand. He demanded that she set a good table for him; then he ate with his hands the supper she cooked; then he murdered her. Some said he butchered the woman's body to bait his traps; others, that he preserved it and bore it away to his valley for some foul and unknown purpose. An armed mob headed by the widower set off into the woods upon the discovery, but lost his track; further pursuits, including many by lawmen, proved as futile. For that crime or perhaps another, he was said to have been hanged in Maine, though some reported that he had fled to Canada, and that they'd seen him years later in Moncton, or had heard that he was shot and killed in a tavern fight in Shawinigan. But more than one woodsman declared that for years he still checked his old trap lines deep in those same woods.

IN THE CAMP.

Was a young guy name of Amos Duncan who knew how to play the fiddle. He had one carved and fitted out of some gorgeous-grained hardwood he kept polished to a fine sheen. Evenings at the camp when everyone was gathered he would lift it out of its velvet case and clamp it under his jaw, one foot tapping out a rhythm on the ground. The fingers on one hand darted up and down the neck, and with his other hand he stroked the horsehair bow across the strings. Some kind of wild music to hear it at night with the stars scattered over us and only a lamp or two keeping back the dark. Those songs would stay an agitated man from speaking as he followed the notes of the melody out into the night, though in some they may have only made more wildness as Amos stamped the ground and scratched the bow back and forth, his eyes closed and the sweat standing out on his brow.

TALL MEN & TALL TIMBER.

The last long-log drive had gone south a few years before, and though in those woods you could still find stands of old growth spruce, some of it two and a half feet through on the stump, now we ran a pulpwood drive downriver, working not only in the winter but during all the year. When the timber had been felled we set to it with one-man bucksaws or crosscut saws two men to a trunk and cut it into four-foot lengths for the teams to twitch out. The chips covered the lot a few inches deep in places, so soft a man could twist his ankle in it. We wore kerchiefs tied over our mouths and hats to keep out the dust and shield our eyes. Any sawdust got down your neck you'd go mad itching. It was a rainy spring and bad for blackflies. Jimmy was the one who showed us how to cut up the mushrooms growing on the sides of the trees and burn them. Didn't say much, just put them on a stump and set a match to them. That smoke was thick and kept off the flies.

He knew old Ned Mascamah the Indian, who was maybe only a halfblood but who had been living in those woods so long he knew more about them than many pure Indians ever did. Ned came to town only twice a year, three times, buying groceries and tools and whatever else he needed and hauling it out into the woods in his wagon. It wasn't a small wagon, either, and we never figured how he got it down some of those bridle paths or through the wet spots. Ned had been working the lost Indian gold mine for some years, after hunting for it all his life. He and Frye were friends, sure, more than he was friends with any other man, and Frye always claimed that Ned had told him that before he died he'd pass on the secret location of the mine to him if he promised to keep it only to himself. Old Ned was old long before Frye got to town, and so he figured he wouldn't have long to wait. Sure enough it was only about some four years after Frye arrived that an Indian no one had ever laid eyes on before came running down Tabor Notch one morning saying that Ned had need of Jimmy Frye. We all went downstreet to Baldwin's store and found Frye out front and soon he and a few others were off through the woods toward Ned's cabin, led by this strange Indian. Don't know if they got turned around or stopped for dinner but by the time they reached the cabin old Ned had died. The thought of that old Indian, waiting and waiting. Silent leaves falling in the woods all around his cabin and sunlight through the branches. Frye shook those hands, still warm, but no words came from Ned's mouth and his eyes just looked up at the ceiling. They said he kneeled there sobbing. Right after that was when he disappeared. Some said he vanished into the woods, looking for Ned's claim, trying to track his prints and discover it for himself. Others said he went back away wherever his people come from and still others that he became mad on the spot and rushed off raving among the trees never to be seen by human eyes again.

TOPOGRAPHY.
The high ridge of land forming the elevation or divide between Indian and Hall's streams is a slate formation, through which large and frequent dikes of quartz have been ejected. The most southerly point of its surface-indications is one mile north of the Connecticut river. It crops out quite often towards the boundary northwardly (a distance of eighteen miles), varying in width from two to four miles, and covers an area of probably not less than 35,000 acres.... It is in this formation that gold has been found on the head waters of Indian stream, at several points over an area of 4,000 acres, and more frequently in Annance gulch, a vein leading into the middle branch on the east side thereof, three miles south of the Highlands, where evidence of quite extensive mining operations (probably by parties from Canada), such as deep excavations in the banks and former beds of the stream, marks of quite extensive camping grounds, and sluice-boxes in the last stages of decay, are found.

———————

I remember him as an old man but then I was so young everyone was old to me. White beard, crushed hat, wool pants held up by suspenders. He washed maybe once a week.

———————

It was my stomach collapsing on itself as the old fools talked of what they had seen going back every day of a man's life a lonely road not even a crossroads just a place between other places no reason to stop. Still the voices spoke and the earth hummed under my feet it was my stomach telling me here.

Vince I met down Penobscot Bay where he worked on the boats
and built anything from a lobster trap to the finish work on some
rich folks' house his hands callused but gentle and one finger gone
at the top joint from a saw. I just coming from some months up
north in a shack by Ktaadn eating potatoes and shooting moose. A
quiet man mostly we went to the tavern and he sat with his mouth
to his glass for hours. And never got an edge on. Vince standing
over me in some street stars behind his head and a halo round
the moon I could feel already the blood dried on my mouth and
the ache back of my head. Vince lifted me with his arm and we
walked back to his mother's house him never speaking one word.
He laid me out in his bed and come morning woke me. Was still
half jingled. His mother in the kitchen frying a mess of sausage
and eggs. Didn't think you was ever going to rise she says and I
Morning Mrs Bouchard.

Not long after his mother took ill and Vince brought her on
the train up to her people in Halifax. I drove them over to the station in Ellsworth Falls with a borrowed team and trying to keep
those horses steady. His mother coughed behind me like a clatter of stones and Vince bundled blankets around her. Already she
seemed gone and shriveled up like a cornhusk. How quickly it
comes. Vincent she said and one hand reached out of the blankets
for his. I watched the train pull out then went back to the horses
hitched outside the station just standing there stupid I have never
thought much of any horse. Brought the team back and the next
morning packed my own bags and left too heading out anywhere
a man could go.

---

*On December 10, 1840, the town of Pittsburg was incorporated, con-
taining the territory of Indian Stream, the Carlisle Grant, the Colebrook Academy Grant, and sixty thousand acres of state lands.... Since
its incorporation Pittsburg has enjoyed unbroken peace and prosperity,
and is a favorite resort during the summer weeks and the hunting
season.*

Once a man's gone woods queer he'll never change. I heard he killed the Indian who drew him the map to the cave. Windy Williams told me he paid the Indian twenty-six dollars and shot him right in the back once he'd turned around. Fetched back his money and whatever else and buried him out in the woods. A trapper and his boy checking their line in the woods out past First Lake heard the shot just after their dinner break. Said they thought it was just someone out taking an off-season deer until they saw him on the road back to town that night, his trousers muddy to the knees, his jacket torn and his hands raw and bleeding. Oh sure he joked with them, told some story about something, why he was in a state, I don't know what. Later they realized that Indian never turned up again. Real old Indian everyone called Sam. Windy told me he buried him with his bare hands seeing as he had no spade.

It is constricted I feel and have felt always the clothes never fitting to my body in the proper way a way I imagine they fit to anyone else. As if they were never made for me though the first time I laid up some money I had a suit fashioned an old man wheezing to his knees to measure the distance from my crotch to the floor unwinding a yellow tape. But even inside that brown gabardine I could feel the drape all wrong a seam too tight here or loose at my shoulder even sometimes a pressure on the chest or even on my head say woken in bed by it. At times a boy I felt a sharp pain trying to breathe as if a string circled my lung and beat my chest and threw myself to the earth to dislodge whatever it was. A dizziness my breath coming shorter until what I saw was the distant mouth of a cave and all else only pure dark.

A BRIEF CHRONOLOGY OF J.L. FRYE.

1897. Born October 12, near Cuttingsville, Vermont. Only son to a dairy farmer.

1908. Father dies. While his mother and sisters manage the farm he is sent to work at a sawmill in Rutland to supplement the family's income.

1917. United States declares war on Germany, April 6. Enlists in the 26th "Yankee" Division of the New England National Guard. Arrives in France September 20, at St. Nazaire.

1918. Falls in combat at Château-Thierry, July 24. Is buried in a cemetery in La Ferté-sous-Jouarre.

1933. Mother dies. His correspondence from France is preserved at the Rutland Historical Society.

TERMINUS.

Late in the afternoon they came upon the ruins of an old birch-tree, which was long the corner between the States of Maine and New Hampshire. It was covered with hieroglyphics, the initials of names once famous in the two States who had visited the spot long years before. Twenty rods beyond stood an iron monument, now the real boundary between the United States and Canada, as well as the corner of the two States. The line established by the Ashburton treaty runs from peak to peak of those Highlands which separate the waters which flow into the St. Lawrence from those which flow into the Atlantic.

This was the end of the trip. Nay sat himself down in Canada, hugging the iron monument, with one foot in Maine and one in New Hampshire, but declared that he felt no better in three dominions than he did in one.

Old Molly the Indian lived out in a shack by the Dead Diamond River, way off in the puckerbrush where no one could trouble her and she heard the voices of her people on the winds. That corner of the country, from Clarksville down through the notch toward Bungy, is the windiest corner of this state, the windiest spot on God's good earth perhaps though why He saw fit to bless us with such winds is His own mystery. Old Molly was an old woman even when I was young and now some said she was past a hundred, that the blood flowing through her veins had never mingled with the white man's and that was what accounted for her longevity. Or that it was by some kind of ghostly magic that she kept herself going long after she should have been called back. Molly might not even have been her real name. It was what we called her as long as I remember and after enough time she may have taken to calling herself Molly too.

I say was. For all I know she may be there still. Smoking her pipe and walking those empty woods, touching wrinkled hands to the trees. She used to come to town every so often, whenever we least expected her or had near forgotten her. However many years had passed she had not changed, an old scarf wrapping her wild hair, her black eyes bright. She would ask after folks dead twenty years and buy some sundries at Mr Baldwin's store, spools of thread and odd ends of fabric and barrel hoops and empty bottles, things no one else would have any earthly use for. Some said she paid in wampum beads, others said she used French coins minted two hundred years ago. I don't think she has ever tried to keep herself a secret but has chosen to live apart from the race of man and even the few of her own people who remain up on St. Francis. Now it has been some six or seven years since we have seen her in town.

Some of the old hoboes or lumbermen could have pointed out the way to her shack, or perhaps some who hunt that river and may know its exact spot. Scraps of lumber held together by rusted nails, twine, and mud, the cracks plugged with old leaves and rags and more mud. I have never seen her shack but from those who have I have been told everything about it: the smoke funneling from the crooked stovepipe, the door so low anyone would have to bend clear over to step inside. Not that anyone would, unless he was foolish or drunk or both, or if he was after something no one else in this country remembered anymore. For that there have been many of us who wished we could question her, who wonder when she'll come back from the woods.

Dearest Martha. I have given this to Vince for you as I am occupied presently but need to send word. Any moment you must be ready at the word go I will come sudden in the trees and we will be gone from here forever away. If you are in need of anything just ask Vince and he will see to it. He can be trusted but no one else this country is filled with watchful eyes and listening ears. Do not tell a word of this to anyone especially not to your ma or anyone at the lodge. Do not listen to what they may say. I am in fine health and condition is fine too. When you have done with reading this put a match to it and stay by the flame until you are certain not one scrap of it remains. Your Jimmy.

If you want a man to clear a pasture, send Art Hollister, for he's strong and handy with an axe. If you want to get a message to Canada, send Tom Phelps, for his sons live there and he would like to visit them. But if you want to get word to hell, send Jimmy Frye, for he will have to go sometime and it is time he was there now.

THE OLD SQUAW.

She told me to take a reckoning of my life. The smoke from her stove blew all around us so thick she was hidden in it but her dark eyes burning as if to cut through me. Above us from the rafters hung drying weeds. It is not in the land she told me and with a feather and a black rock drew circles in the air and after her hands had dropped back to her lap I could see them still shining there like rings of gold in all that smoke. The ghosts walk with you and ask you to look she said. You have already seen your own fate. Coughing I reached for the circles. Soot whirled around us. She began to speak the words long like the rain falling on a roof all night and I shoved back the door and still choking crawled out on my hands my eyes watering with smoke into the clear wind blowing everything away amid the trunks of pines and my empty hands sticky with pitch. The door swung shut.

Nit msiw kisi mawewsehtit, nit mace tpitahatomoniya tan op al te 'tollukhotiniya. Stehpal msiw siwaciyukuhtit eli wapoli pomawsihtit. Yukt kci sakomak 'tiyaniya kotokihi, "Yut elapimok asit weckuhuhsihiq, knomihtunen eli pokahkonaptuwoq. Knomihtunennul kehsok ewapolikkil. Yuhtol pekahkonikil tomhikonossisol olu, naka tapihik, pahqihil, cuwi puskonasuwol askomiw."

November afternoon in the woods, any woods, old hardwoods and conifers, the ground rusty with dead leaves or needles, or white in patches where snow fell last night, the week before, woods outside some unremarked town or between two such towns, near a small river, its name perhaps changed many times though he could not speak any of them. Say rain falls and his hat brim droops with it, the water running off it to his shoulders and his breath obscuring his beard as the low clouds drape the hills. A stone wall the marker of someone's old land, each stone placed by hands he can never grasp, he thinks as he sits beside it, the stones against his back. He rubs his own hands together. Above him a crow's nest, a clump of leaves and twigs.

April 27. Jimmy is not a Handsom man but he has a way with ladys   has Found himself a young girl calld Martha from the lodge on Second Lake   Says when were done here soon hell run a way with her

April 28 Staying in Town at the Hotel while Jimmy is back at his lodgings with the Widow. To day she went out for Lunchen and he took me through the house to test the Walls   sure enough after some hunting we found the space Between the floor and the old sassholl   very good Construction and got it opened up in no time   greased up the hinges and the latch. Cunning airholls to a Bit musty but Jimmy says it will do fine

May 9 Building Jimmy a rocker and sluice box cross Indian Stream   a bout Four Miles into the woods he says no one is to see us out here   Spend the days shaking the Rocker and pouring water through while he Shovels the gravel   tiresome work but so far weve filled a leather sack and Jimmy says Evrything is lovely   prospects Bully   after Supper He panned out a bit he says for Marthas Ring

May 23. Not Sure of the date but think that one is right   have been in the Woods at lest a fortnight. Last night at Happy Corner

Jimmy got cocked as a Cannon and walked it to some fellow as had it Coming   Fellow was teasing Jimmy about waiting round the lodge   after hed pound him up calld to me and said lets go so We left out into the night   Jimmy led us round Back Lake in case our mans friends tried to follow   rather Id staid and drank

May 26 Jimmy has shown me the Trail through the swamps up to the Border   Something confusing but he tells me its the only way when the time comes   and says its soon   twenty miles strait north through P.Q. and from there a train back to Halifax without entering U.S. teritories once   Enough he says I wont have to Build another cubbard again and can quit the Shipyards

May 28. Jimmy getting antsy   he says there is more to dig out but he has need to Get a way soon   in Town he showed around a nuggett and some old timers asked if wed found the indians caves after all. Jimmy laughed and said we still Couldnt find much   I said nothing   Think of leaving soon not telling Any One. he is getting careless

---

BALDWIN'S STORE.
Vern I ever tell you I used to be on the stage?
    No...
    Oh sure I rode the stage from Albany to Connecticut once...

He came one afternoon to the barber's in Colebrook with two week's growth of beard and his hair matted with pine pitch and dirt and that mute Frenchman by his side. The barber was a Frenchman himself, called Frank by everyone but the other Frenchmen who came to get their hair cut and who called him something I could never make out. Frank kept his scissors on a neat white cloth and used a clean cup and brush to lather each customer's face. His hands were small and delicate like a woman's. He didn't talk much but his shop was usually busy with a few men and young boys sitting there arguing about something and watching as the wet clumps of hair fell around his feet.

By this time the stories of Frye's brawling and such had made it to Colebrook and Frank looked none too pleased to see him and his companion march into his shop smelling of weeks in the woods. It was me and Charlie Hubbard's boy and one other fellow I didn't know, plus Joe McCabe in the chair. When Frye came in this other fellow took a look at him and then looked at his shoes a minute and then got up and left without a word. I had no acquaintance with Frye beyond seeing him at Young's once or twice and what I'd heard at Baldwin's store up in Pittsburg, which wasn't then as much as it is now.

Me and Ben here are in no hurry, I told Frye. Why don't you go on ahead. He sat down without paying me any mind and his friend stood by the window for a while looking out at the street and chewing his fingernails. When Frank finished Joe's cut Joe stood up and dusted off the hairs on his hands and while Frank took his money Frye had already sat down in the chair and was busy wrapping the cloth over him.

Okay, okay, Frank said, and tried to straighten the cloth. He started to comb some water through Frye's hair but the comb caught in a tangle everywhere he put it and soon he gave up and got a hot towel for Frye's beard instead. This whole time Frye seemed to be dozing in the chair and had yet to say a word to anyone.

Presently Frank brought out the cup and brush and lathered up Frye's face. He stropped the razor some and then set to work making even paths through the lather with the bare skin peeping through. He'd done Frye's mustache and sideburns and was scraping off the last white flecks from his throat when he drew a bright line of blood below Frye's chin. That mute one was watching all this and started to laugh and I got a bit worried given what I'd heard of Frye's unnatural temper. He was still sitting slouched over while Frank dabbed the blood away with the corner of one of his clean towels. I gave Ben a coin and told him to run downstreet and see if he could find me a pouch of pipe tobacco. He headed out looking back through the window at us all as he passed in front, and as soon as Frank took the towel away the blood rose to the surface again and Frye's companion laughed a second time. Frank made a few more strokes with the razor to clean up the rest of Frye's beard and the blood was beading up when he finished. Aside from everything else I ought to add that Frye's face looked little older than Ben's without its beard.

Frye lifted his head and turned to his friend. What is it, he said. The Frenchman nodded at his chin. Frye lifted one hand from under the cloth and touched his throat. He looked at his fingertips smeared dark red for a moment and then rubbed his thumb across them thoughtfully. A smile broke out on his face. Vincent, he said. Come on. And with the cloth still draped around him he put his hat back on and walked out of the shop, bleeding. I have yet to guess what is so funny about as common a sight as a shaving nick on a man's face. He vanished soon after that afternoon but for some years it was told how Frank the barber was the only man in Coos County to ever draw the blood of Jimmy Frye.

THE GIRL.

It was ropes around me keeping me from rising, and all the while
the wind fluttered the curtains but did not reach me. Outside, the
men's voices low as they shouldered canoes. Only a corner of the
sky showed itself to me where I lay still unable to close my eyes. She
returned and looked in at me, said something then left. Returned
again still later and the sky turned orange. It was as if my head
against the damp pillow as if my ears the river swollen as if spring
and rushing green carrying sticks and things with it away.

————————

He. A vision. The oak. Heeled to a branch thicker than his waist
a dark pool of blood soaking the ground below the slit neck. The
rack raking the dirt. That peculiar mud rubbed in his hands, the
rich smell, the creases in his palm. At the corner of the eye, its, a
lash. Bare branches and bare branches behind them in rising pattern against the low sky. Steps in the leaves, a whistling. A hand
on his shoulder. A voice.

ISLANDS IN THE CONNECTICUT—DIGGING FOR GOLD.

*In the Connecticut River, just below the mouth of the Passumpsic, there
are no less than fifteen islands. The most prominent one is Gold Island,
covered with spruce and cedar. Many years ago some persons, who had
been led to believe that the Indians had buried gold there, dug the island
over in search of it, but their efforts were not rewarded with a yield of
the precious metal excelling a California placer. Between this place and
Lunenburg, Vt., are the famous fifteen miles falls in the Connecticut.*

Those last months he was down to Littleton so often to care for his poor mother, who had fallen ill there; he'd found her after all these many years, he told me, and had forgiven her. Some nights he would join Mr Harding and me for supper, and then I would bake his favorite Boston cream pie for dessert. I often wished I had had such a dutiful son, a son who would pardon my failings, a son who cared for me so well that he often forgot his own wants, but then I always considered him less a boarder than a child of my own. My Jimmy. How anyone could have abandoned such a child I will never know.

I only regretted not being able to say goodbye. He sent me word later that his mother was failing at last and he must depart for good. Oh, my heart about broke then. I packaged the few belongings he had left in his room, and nearly cried when I brought them to the post office. But I know I'll see him again, knocking at my kitchen door some afternoon when his road brings him back north.

---

*Among the hills of Northern New Hampshire and the mountains that abound on the Southern border of Lower Canada, the "*QUONEKTACUT RIVER*"—the Long River—has its source. Forming, for a long distance, the boundary between Vermont and New Hampshire, it sweeps across the Western portion of Massachusetts, and, passing through the State to which it has given its name, discharges its pure waters into the sea.... This river, these meadows, these inward looking slopes, and these tributary streams, have determined the character of the industry which has appropriated them to the purposes of human life. There is hardly a farm or a workshop, a dwelling or a church, a road or a mill, but is connected in some way with Connecticut River. Its waters feed the pride of local feeling, and mingle with every local association.*

SUPERSTITION.

He would never name a thing until he grasped it in his hand, never speak the word of what he wanted until he was certain it was his. So that word for what he hunted never passed his lips during the time he was determining whether the old cave existed and obtaining maps and scouting the territory, nor even when he had probably found already the first small flake or nugget and then another and finally had set off to find Vincent Bouchard and bring him back.

No one had ever believed a word of those old campfire tales about the gold. All of us had spent enough time out in those woods and casting for brook trout in Indian Stream that if it had been true there would have been an afternoon when someone, reeling in his fish, would have wondered enough at a shiny stone to draw it dripping from the bed of the stream. And in no time the entire town would have decamped to the woods to pan and build whatever contraptions are needed to draw up the ore. Of course nothing of the sort ever happened and I'll tell you why: there is no gold in these woods, nothing under these hills but granite and the bones of the dead. Where would an Indian have got the gold to begin with? Even when he couldn't resist boasting to the fools gathered at the bench at the store or passing round the soft nuggets most of us guessed it was simply stolen or else fool's gold. If it was honest, he'd been up and down this country enough times to have somehow stumbled on some cache that was Lord knew how old. I'm sure there were some simple enough to have ventured out to the woods, most likely in secret pacts of two or three, after he'd shown his discoveries, though if anything had ever come of such foolishness every man woman and child in this village would have heard of it within the hour.

VERN AMEY.

I mistrusted what he was doing from the start of things. No kick-about like he was has ever shown himself honest nor respectable and he turned out no different than the rest. Everyone said he had a way with words but he's just so crooked he couldn't piss a straight hole in the snow. He claimed to work well with a team so one day we had him in charge of twitching logs with a single sled and two horses. The horses balked and he started talking to them, patting their ears to get them to move. Gave them each a cigarette to eat, most simpleminded thing I ever saw. I came up and got on the sled with the whip. Cleaned out the woodlot in a week and he went back to swamping and helping us limb out. But mostly he had a bad case of blanket fever in the mornings, as I recall.

Old Hap Jones the tinker came through town round that time, first visit in five years. I'd always got by well with Hap and planted every season a small row of corn at the edge of my land for him in case he visited. In winter he'd cut some wood and I'd give him dinner. Never knew how long he'd stay in town. Sometimes a few months, sometimes only a short while. You'd wake up and he'd be gone with never a word. When his star moved, he moved. Then before long he'd be back. This five years was the longest he'd been away since I first saw him as a boy. My father had started the cus-tom of planting the extra corn for him back then.

We took dinner and set to talking, him telling of things he'd seen on the roads or other farms he'd stayed at. Speaking of what had happened in town I mentioned Frye and his hunt for the gold. At that Hap said he knew this Frye and had met him on the road outside White River Junction some years back. They'd traveled together some and swapping stories one night Hap had told him the legend of the Indian's cave. So you're the cause of his coming up here I says. I guess I am Hap says.

Next morning I went out to the barn where Hap was sleeping in the hayloft but he was gone and all his things. I didn't think much of it, because that was his way. But they found him a few mornings afterwards, and he'd died out in a pasture somewhere down the valley. No mark upon him and Dr Rowell up from Cole-brook said it was natural causes.

Hap Jones wasn't his real name. That's what he went by. His brother had been a prospector up in Alaska. He came here later to ask people about Hap, and he gave me a big gold nugget for the kindness I'd shown him. I gave it back. We've had enough of that around here, I told him.

———

All the faces the eyes meeting mine for an instant some still clear in my mind years after apart from the face even rising like my own from the lake's surface as ripples still and clear enough I couldn't tell whose they were or how they had searched me out with plain seeing. Yet at one moment or another everyone has seen everyone else despite our best devices. What is exists beyond the designs of men and so is obvious to pure vision.

———

Jimmy lifted his pick in the air above his broad shoulders. There was a shower of stones and gravel as he swung it into the earth at his feet. In short order he had dug a large hole. Beside him Vince toiled over his own hole, then paused to mop his brow. The sun was high and soon both men were stripped to the waist. Jimmy struck the earth again and then dropped his pick to sift through the dirt with his fingers. He thought he had seen a strange glint—unless it was only the sun playing tricks on his eyes. His fingers closed around the shiny stone and he lifted it into the light. Could it be? Then: "Gold!" he shouted, "gold!"

Later we pieced together how he'd been interested in the crawl-spaces and hidden closets carpenters had fashioned for escaped slaves. Several homes right in the village had secret cupboards and such. He'd had a lot of questions for Jake Stark, whose grandfather had harbored slaves beneath his staircase. This had been the last stop before the border, the last hills before those wide fields around Chartierville and onto Sherbrooke or Québec where many of the fugitives ended up. Course he'd hunted out the old trails through the bogs the river gets its start in, the spots where in summer the blackflies chase the moose out of, but no one put much thought to why, or else no one knew but a part of what he was up to, and that part seemed innocent enough. Him coming to town of a Saturday afternoon and pulling a bottle of gold-flecked water from his pocket for a pretty girl, or trying to pay for a gun with a nugget he'd found in some isolated place where Indian Stream flows shallow over rocks.

No one'd known that that other fellow he kept as company when he returned, the dark little Frenchman who Frye said came from Halifax, had once worked as a cabinetmaker.

———————————

They said he could walk through the woods on a new moon night without snapping a single twig or once stumbling over a root. He may have had some Indian blood in him himself, or it may be that he possessed some kind of magic which allowed him to pass unseen. Every man in the village knew better than to follow him into the woods alone. Some even believed the birds were his spies, singing certain songs to alert him of danger.

June 2 Jimmy is in   evrything worked as Expected as I assume he fixed the Canoo   The whole Town stood by the shore while they tried to bring the Poor Bastards in. Finally did after midnight a Sorry sight   and now I am to Saddle up the horses we purchasd and leve them at the Camp. Saw the Girl at the Lake and hidd in the trees she drawing water   whistled and when shed seen me Gave her the sign to Pretend she hadnt   then Showd her the Note and as she watchd Dug it under the Needles and gave her the O.K.   now am off to camp   Jimmy has it All with him he Thinks but there is what Ive set aside and still a night of Work to do   To morrow before he rises I will have Left

June 3. A Long Night in the Woods but a little to show for it   Scared off horses so they will have to Find an other way. He thought hed had me Fooled I know what he wouldve Done when he came Back to Camp   have not slept in some Thirty Hours and feeling Tired. Only a Week and the trail seems Diffrent back-trackd through dense Woods and Swamps all morning looking for the Path Jimmy showed me   up the Stream and follow the east Branch but cant find the lightning struck Hemlock he markd out   No trace even of our Own Tracks made just a week ago dont want to rest yet as Tonight he comes   I want to be a cross the Border and hidd in that country he dont Know

Previous to the survey of Dr. Jackson, the scenery at the extreme north of the state was little known. Its striking features were observed by him, and are known, to a few persons who have since visited them, to be among the grandest exhibitions of nature in North America. Indian Stream is a small settlement near the falls at the outlet of Connecticut lake. It is the most northerly inhabited place in New Hampshire, and comprises, in the whole, a colony of three hundred and fifteen persons, scattered on the undulating shores of the lake. They are far removed from any other settlement, and for many years refused obedience to the laws of the state. Desiring none of the benefits of civil government, they claimed exemption from its burdens; and under a simple government of their own, they resisted the officers of the law, until they were visited by a military force and reduced to subjection.

At once it was clear to me as nothing in my life has appeared terrible in its certainty there in the clearing by the stream I stood as it rushed over the same rocks as if nothing had happened as it may still rush for all I know. Through the night I had carried the sack from the village creeping from the dank and stinking hole my legs at first cramped and trembling enough I fell but kept on for the horses which my own labor had purchased and which in several hours would bear me across the border so that at dawn when the first fools stirred here I would be on my knees kissing the very soil as had others before me and deliver the girl from this country of trees into the wide empty lands beyond the north. Ran dark miles. Yet before me the new diggings and the tether posts standing bare in the moonlight and only the shape of him in the shadows that remained. And deep in the woods I could feel that which I have hunted all my life calling to me except now it was myself who was calling my own voice coming back to me from the last hours of night reaching back to yesterday each night turns two days. I bent to the stream the pools still muddied from his work and splashed water on my neck though I was already chilled with sweat from stumbling through the woods and the night air. He had left me no provisions even but a heel of bread spotted with mold. This I ate as the mooncast shadows stirred in the faint wind and then headed off along that trail the sack across my shoulder and my legs and arms and chest burning.

After the first few seasons the village seemed to take him in as its own, the way it has with others who have arrived some chance morning without histories or names. It may have been his silence at first drawing respect, or the honest facts of his hard work and his quiet living. He was unseen. I do not know when he first told of his plans. It may have been only on returning. Yet the leaving and the return in themselves were enough to alter respect to suspicion. If he had settled here, why leave, and if he had left, why return—so they thought. Or the plan may have slipped before he left and therefore at his return the village realized he had the will to see it through. Yet what no one knew was the part I played to draw him back, the fact that it was not only the gold. He told me he had seen my face each night when he closed his eyes.

His second passage, whenever it occurred, was not his choice, that much I am assured of each time I stand by the lake's far shore and wait for his voice to come to me with my own echoing from the hills.

THE TRUE STORY OF JIMMY FRYE.
When the fire dies to white cinders and the snow drifts all during the dark hours, or when the heat forces us to the porch and the loons laugh at us from the still lake; when the supper has been eaten and the last drop drunk; when I want to see eyes grow round with wonder, or hard with suspicion; then I tell my listeners the true story of Jimmy Frye.

Now I must confess that I am not sure that his name was Jimmy Frye. I do not believe that he ever told me what his name was, but everyone else called him Jimmy, and Frye is a good name, as good as any, so we will call him that now. But the rest of the story is as true as true can be. It all happened, just as I am telling it, in the North Country, many years ago.

The train tracks follow this small river and as the engine passes the steam drifts back and sinks in the humid air, settling over the motionless water where already mist curls. The sun is still below the earth's curve and as the train moves through the dusky trees a man steps from one of the cars as if stepping off a curb. His pack cradled in both arms. He rolls down the bank and into the brush so quickly that no one notices him, unless perhaps the train's whistle as it approaches the sleeping village has caused some passenger to stir in his sleep and see the figure through a smeared windowpane. But the passenger yawns and, believing he is still dreaming, closes his eyes again. The conductor walks between the rows of silent people in second-class. Prochaine station Rosaire, he murmurs. He stoops to stir a woman awake.

Ici la campagne est vaste et on peut voir une ferme à plus d'un mille de distance par-dessus les champs et les clôtures. Comme un mort, j'y ai passé les courtes nuits d'été balayées par les étoiles, attendant que vienne chaque instant. Du ciel, les étoiles tombaient à mes pieds, étincelantes, allumant des feux qui brûlaient jusqu'au matin dans l'herbe verte. Je parcourai cette vaste campagne à la recherche d'eau, perdu, humant l'air pour en goûter le sel.

TOWARD THE INTERIOR

A man sets out on a journey to a place he has never been before. Another man comes back. A man comes to a place that has no name, that has no landmarks to tell him where he is. Another man decides to come back. A man writes letters from nowhere, from the void that has opened up in his own mind. The letters are never received. The letters are never sent.

—Paul Auster, *White Spaces*

In dreams are none of these beige walls. There, the nurses—Alison and Renee, Carol and Natalie—do not exist, except for their white uniforms, which blur into the snowfields all around us.

At times I feel I am a young man again, but I do not know if that young man is me. Other times, it is all my snow melting, all that water rushing in, that frightens me. Of these things I have heard rumors.

She came to me from out of the snow herself, wrapped in a scarf and a belted coat. The snow had just melted and she was still wet behind the ears. Snowbird, I called her. From the northern hills. Martha, she answered. I walked with her along the Charles, my arm about her and the wind in my face. She would name each bird we saw, even the iridescent starling new to her. It came from England on a ship, she said. It has taken over our cities. Before coming here I had only read about it. I went south on a ship, I told her, the gulls following our wake from the harbor into open sea, their wings barely moving as they tilted on air, crying and crying of everything behind us.

Just stay still, Renee says. In her hand is a white globe, a ball of scented snow. She pats the snow over my chin and cheeks, on my throat, then stands and walks to the bathroom. Water runs. She comes back to me holding a basin of water.

The snow covers my town for months, she told me. We can see the aurora some summer nights. Yes, it is no different than what I will see, I told her.

Your name is Samuel, Renee says. Today is Tuesday, October second, 1979. You are in Havenwood Manor. In a few minutes you will have breakfast. Please hold out your arms so I can help you put on your sweater. It's a beautiful day outside, but you'll want it for the breeze. See it ruffling the pretty leaves out there?

From my window, I can make the view melt from the parking lot slashed with yellow lines, the slope of bright grass and saplings and trimmed bushes, to the ice at the end of the world, one of two points a man can stand perfectly still while around him everything else spins.

Renee takes me in the chair, down the hill to where the water flows past us, and onto the wooden bridge where the water flows beneath us. The wheels of the chair drum across the boards of the bridge. Each thump as Renee scoots me over the boards interrupts my thoughts.

The morning is the hardest time. It is hard enough anywhere for a man to begin the day's work in darkness; where I am it is doubly difficult. This morning I had to admit to myself that I was lonely. Try as I may, I find I can't take my loneliness casually; it is too big. But I must not dwell on it. Otherwise I am undone.

Just look at these leaves today, Renee says.

We kept three cows at Little America. One stood up all the time and refused to lie down; another, accustomed to lying down every night, lay down with the coming of the winter night and refused to stand up; and the third, poor thing, couldn't make up her mind just what to do except roll her eyes at Cox, the carpenter, who haunted the cowbarn.

That Cox was a bastard, chewing his food so loud at mess, sneaking into our trunks while we cut ice to melt for water and worked to repair the tractor engines. A bastard, and no wonder he stayed away from us.

It is the words themselves I cannot see to say. Leaves, I can think, but the letters drift away before I can speak them. The wind lifted them, curled and dry, in small eddies before us as we walked, our arms linked, those last days. How can I arrange it? A word is no simple task. It is the game the doctors used to play that I remember—one eye closed, toes at a line drawn across a linoleum floor, and the black type swimming against a white background.

In a hotel facing Dartmouth Street, under a gaslight on Beacon Hill—in a cemetery in the North End, a hill, a view, a rainstorm, and gray water stretching away. I cannot remember where I told Martha I was to go to New York to ship on the Eleanor Bolling. And was there something I held in my hand? Papers, an umbrella, a watch?

Your name is Samuel, Renee says. Today is Tuesday, October second, 1979. You are in Havenwood Manor. In a few minutes you will have breakfast. And then I can no longer help you.

Those last weeks. We left in October. A message from Byrd in each morning's mail. A candle burning. White wax flecked the base and hardened overnight. In two more candles, she said. She wet her fingers with her tongue. The wick curled, black; smoked. She would read to me at night, brushing my hair with her hand and then turning the page. Her legs tucked beneath her on the couch. When I returned my hair was as long as a woman's. We grew it to cover our necks in the cold, shaved once a week only to keep the frost from catching in our beards as we breathed.

The cedar waxwing lives in the northern spruce and fir woods, a gregarious and noisy bird which alights in large numbers on berry bushes. Their wings appear to have been daubed with melted wax, red and yellow. Their eyes are masked.

Which we soon learned to call the Evermore Rolling. Our faces soot-blackened, our hands clutching our sides as she rolled. But now, they tell me, I have stopped speaking. I could not tell you if this is so.

But what was it Martha told me?—her face, wrapped in scarf and windblown ribbons of hair; her eyes, gazing across the water, have replaced the words.

That winter night we never saw the sun. I learned the Morse Code, the dashes and dots, long and short. That has stayed with me. I tap the arm of the chair with my fingers, and behind me, Renee hums under her breath.

Sometimes I do not need to read the stories. They are so familiar to me I can tell them to you without looking at the words to remind me. She told me these things. There was a time, she said. Far away in the north a man came to a small town for the first time in his life, a journey of many miles. Yet he knew exactly what had made him come, exactly what had brought him there. The valley and the river were just as he had imagined them, just as they had been told to him so many times before. The farms and dusty roads. He had seen them many nights in dreams.

What day is this? I ask Renee. Today is Tuesday, she says.

To imagine my back curved like this, the muscles which hang loose in the folds of my skin, the shaking of my hands I cannot control even by clasping them together.

Silence I crave, those lost nights when my breath was the only sound, and cold so deep that in the slightest breeze, I could hear my breath freeze as it floated away, a sound like Chinese firecrackers. No one here knows that silence. There is no peace where men are, where words transact our business. Yet even now I know the feel of Martha's touch, those last days in Boston. A hand pressing my own, a warmth I recalled at 56° below, when the kerosene froze inside our lanterns. When these memories and the words to name them fade from my mind, I still will own the white spaces, wide and empty.

Those white spaces were what brought me into the south, seeking that point from which any direction is north. This was years ago in Boston, the end of summer and fall of 1928. I saw the handbills soliciting men for the Byrd Expedition. I imagined that snow a blank page I could mark myself upon, the tracks of my feet the only language in that everlasting winter. It was not until those first hours on the Barrier that I discovered the snow was frozen too hard to take the traces of a man's foot.

The night of the last candle. The days had passed more quickly than had guessed. Her hand shook touching the flame to the wick. Melted wax spilled and ran. I closed my eyes and listened to the sounds beyond the windows. Footsteps through fallen leaves. A late trolley car along the street, electricity clicking the wires.

No, I said, your story is wrong. It begins: Far away in the south a man came to an empty country for the first time in his life, a journey of many miles. Yet he knew exactly what had made him come, exactly what had brought him there. The ice stretching to the horizon, with little history of the lives of men, was just as he had imagined it.

May I have your hand, I said.

Martha turned away. Beyond her through the window the sun was beginning to rise. A red light bled between the roofs of buildings. A suitcase by the door.

The cold has entered my bones so much I cannot move, or speak. Why, the doctors ask me, with lights and rustling coats and gloved hands softly clutching my own.

I am presently thirty-one years of age and enjoy fine health.

She rode with me in the taxi to South Station. Still neither of us had slept. She rested her head against my shoulder. The glass was smeared with the fingerprints of countless strangers and beyond it I saw nothing but the blurred outlines of objects, buildings and lamp posts and signs. The driver's eyes glanced backwards in the mirror.

I doubt whether a dozen men on this expedition have any idea of the difficulties that face us. It is only natural that they should not. Very few know anything about this new world we shall enter into.

My hands gone yellow with frostbites. My hands were eloquent. The flesh had been burned and shriveled by the frost; the nails had turned black and were rotting away; and blood was oozing from sodden blisters. It is said you can tell the character and quality of a man's work from his hands.

That spring Byrd made the headlines every week. We all read the papers, dreaming our own futures somewhere in those printed columns, the black ink rubbing off on our skin.

It is a small room I live in, four beige walls and a thin carpet, the bed, the chair. None of these are my words. The nurses pass in and out all the time, the heavy door following them slowly and closing with a snip. They stick tubes in my arms and pills in my mouth. A man comes to talk to me, though I do not know who he is. Is he another doctor? The nurses, smiling, admit him through the door; he stands in its frame a moment, then folds his jacket over one arm and sits in the chair by the window, haloed by the light. He says his name is Donald, David, Daniel, unless this is my name. Do you remember? he asks, and what I remember is D, one long and two short, the lever's gentle resistance to the finger, the words coming out in another language.

The silence of this place is as real and solid as sound. More real, in fact, than the occasional creaks of the Barrier and the heavier concussions of snow quakes. It fills the air with its mood of unchangeableness; it sits across from me at the table, and gets into the bunk with me at night. And no thought will wander so far as not eventually to be brought up hard by it.

There is motion in the leaves, and a flicker flies from one tree to another, wings flashing yellow. Did you see the bird? Renee asks, pointing.

Martha made me promise to travel north with her when I returned, into the hills and woods from which she had come. Just across the Forty-fifth Parallel, she told me. And from there, I asked. Further on, she said.

I went there looking for peace and enlightenment, thinking that they might in some way enrich my life and make me a more useful man.

WGY Schenectady and KDKA Pittsburgh broadcast to us, the radio waves curling around the sides of the earth. Saturday afternoons we stopped work to listen. Byrd stood apart, hands in his pockets. The governor of New York, opera singers—so many people spoke to us from the studios, offering their encouragement. Our families, our friends. What they said I have forgotten. Martha came on the radio once only—a cough, a hesitation, and the sound of my name; her voice lost in the numberless miles.

Any fool remembers how to tie his own shoes and button his own shirt.

At night, when everything was quiet, I could sometimes feel the floor of my shack heave gently from the swell pulsing against the ice basement, hundreds of feet below my bed. These times I wondered why Martha did not speak again through the radio.

I took a train north. I kept my promise.

I have never known such utter quiet. Sometimes it lulled and hypnotized, like a waterfall or any other steady, familiar sound. At other times it struck into the consciousness like a sudden noise. Up on the Barrier it was taut and immense; and, in spite of myself,

I would be straining to listen—for nothing, really, nothing but the sheer excitement of silence.

Your name is Samuel, Renee says. Today is Tuesday, October second, 1928. Home is back there now. Yesterday was the last day.

Byrd wrote books after the expedition. In this room I can never find them, though I know they are here. I looked up Byrd at 9 Brimmer Street in Boston years later, and he gave me his books, pressing them into my hand as I left. Please, I think you'll like these, he said. One is blue; the other, red. But what Byrd said is not true. What happened is this:

This is the honest truth. On more than one occasion the glass of water which I put down beside me was skimmed over with ice before I had time to drink it.

I looked up Byrd at 9 Brimmer Street in Boston, and a man I had never seen answered the door. Yes? he said.

I looked up Martha when I returned to Boston. I took a train north.

I think it is the pills they give me that make me sleep. Pushed too far, a man will lie down in cold enough to freeze him in half an hour, sinking into the drift. Outside the window, cars move in and out of the parking lot. Sunlight winking off glass and chrome. Distress signals. An airplane circling, a runway inscribed on ice and snow. There is a voice, a hand on my shoulder. The rustle of my hair on the pillow. Martha? Or is it Gould, waking us into the dark for breakfast?

In the winter dark I dreamed a radio that would carry my voice back to Martha. A way for her to hear how the cold had crept into my throat, an excuse for me to try to form the words.

Everyone is always leaving me. She said everyone is always leaving me.

We watched each other's faces for the dead-white patches of frost-bite. A blossom on your nose, Petersen, somebody would say. Petersen, until then unaware of the danger, would mold the flesh with his fingertips, his fingers stinging the instant they left the warmth of his gloves; then the blood would come surging back with stabs of pain. Jesus, he would say. Then back to work.

My name is Daniel, the man says.

Past Concord the hills closed in, their slopes covered in dark pines. The man on the seat next to me slowly rustled the pages of the *Globe* he had been reading since North Station. I leaned my fore-head against the glass and closed my eyes. A faint swaying motion as the tracks climbed a grade. My best hat lay on my knee and in the suitcase above me was a fine gabardine suit I planned to change into when I reached Littleton. Soon we came down from the hills to the river.

In the streets of Boston the cold fingered out every shelter I devised.

I worked as a cook at a lunch counter in Central Square when I returned, broken and penniless. Byrd came into the restaurant quite often to take his meals. Through the swinging door of the kitchen I could see him, plates spread before him, his companions clapping him on his shoulders. A haze of smoke, the endless scrape of cutlery against heavy china. Steam. The waitresses, Alison and Renee, told me he never left but a nickel tip. But such a gentleman, they said.

The letters I wrote to Martha returned to me one by one, stamped in red ink. In the apartment she had rented, another woman now lived. How many times I had passed that door and climbed the stairs beyond. At night, looking up at the lighted windows, I saw this other woman's shadow move behind the curtains. I did not know if this made me another man.

She told me of the bobbing flight of the goldfinch and its love for thistle; of the way a swallow will dive toward a man who walks too close to the nest; of how other birds will feign injury by dragging one wing along the ground and, keeping just out of reach, lead you away from their young.

The actual building of the shack was done by Ivor Tinglof, a cabinetmaker, in a Boston loft. The shack was as tidily built as a watch. Fine white pine stiffened the frame and flooring, but the rest was mostly shell. The walls were only four inches thick. A three-ply veneer, one-eighth inch thick and composed of a layer of wood between two strips of cardboard, sheathed the outer and inner walls. Loosely wadded in the hollow between was insulation of kapok, which resembles raw cotton.

Of how any smaller bird will attack a larger bird: a robin or jay after a crow which has tried to steal an egg; a crow after a hawk has captured a fledgling.

Daniel, he says. Don't you remember?

Years later, after the War, I found myself in many places.

It was said to be a cold spring. I sat on the Esplanade in my shirtsleeves, my face inclined toward the sun. Crocuses. Even the name sounded odd to my ears after two years. I had seen the clusters of yellow and purple flowers on the walk here. Yet on the river floated small chunks of green ice. Behind me, the huddled brick of Beacon Hill rose against the pale sky.

I believe I first saw the man who comes to me now sometime in those days in Boston. Perhaps it is Byrd come to see me, silent as ever as he sits in the chair he draws close to my bed. Sometimes he takes my hand in his lap as he sits near me, and at these times he seems to want to tell me something. Only occasionally does he speak; the rest of the time he too studies the four beige walls.

Your name is Samuel, Renee says. Today is Saturday, January twenty-sixth, 1929. The Bolling has just reached the Barrier. Byrd will give you further orders shortly.

I called it the city of the dead and for years I wandered there after my return. Mt. Auburn. As if I would see my own place there among the maples and elms. It was the only spot where the sounds of traffic faded and above me in the branches birds flicked from one tree to the next.

But you never left the city, the man says. We imagined you miles away, anywhere we could name—and to think that all that time you were there.

All of us digging, the supplies in crates and boxes on the Barrier, the tractors casting long shadows in the low sun. Our breaths made a continuous fog. Later we worked by the light of pressure lanterns and the heat of primus stoves. Scraping away the ice and snow to what lay below us—a strange rocky soil or deep green water. Even then I dreamed I was digging my own grave, carving out a space in that world to place a part of myself. Or excavating something long lost. We buried ourselves all that year.

At Littleton I sat on a stool and leaned over a bowl of soup, wiping my mouth with my napkin after each spoonful. In the fir trees, the pulp mills, the gray river: I could place her here, conjure her to my elbow where she rested her head. Outside it was as if the wind carried her voice. Even the river spoke of her.

The man spreads the photographs on the table. Each small square opens like a window, framed with a white sill. Do you know her? he asks me, pointing. He lifts the window closer to my face. What's her name?

In his books Byrd did not mention my name.

A week had contained entire years and during a single day men had been born and died. I returned home after my long sleep in the ice to find a life gone. Men I had known as boys stood in lines on the street to receive bread. Though even then, standing in line too, I felt a word could undo it, return us to that past which filled the stories we told each other while we waited.

Those nights were spacious and fine. Numberless stars crowded the sky. I had never seen so many. You had only to reach up and fill your hands with the bright pebbles. I remember a monstrous red moon climbing into the heavens some nights. The stars were everywhere. A sailor's sky, I thought, commanded by the Southern Cross and the wheeling constellations of Hydrus, Orion, and Tri- angulum drifting ever so slowly. It was a lovely motion to watch. And all this was mine: the stars, the constellations, even the earth as it turned on its axis.

I learned the other woman's schedule and waited for her to leave the house in the morning. Ten o'clock. She walked toward Harvard Square and I walked behind her. I imagined she would somehow lead me to Martha. I thought that they must be acquainted; in those days the city was still small enough. But each time I only fol- lowed her to the copper roof of the subway kiosk and watched her disappear underground. The shape of her back vanished among the people descending the stairs. In my pockets my hands clutched damp coins.

In July heat, for years, I have thought always of weeks of no sun.

The drift covered all of our signs—buried the Citroëns, the empty crates, the flags we used to mark our trails—erasing us from that continent even while we still occupied it.

There was another room, some time ago, in which I lived. Down the hall, past one red door, was the bathroom; down the carpeted stairs and through the archway was the kitchen. About this room I can remember the smallest things—the crack in the plaster above my bed, the tarnished light fixture, the one creaky floorboard, the morning light through the window, red-gold, at the end of slow winter nights.

Later I stood in shadows across the street and watched the woman unlock the door. In that moment I cleared my throat and swallowed should she call out to me. Yet she passed inside, her shoulder against the door. Soon the light came on upstairs. This happened for months. We never spoke, though I believe she came to expect me as much as I her. Once, looking over her shoulder at the sound of my cough, she smiled.

After two years, my key no longer fit the lock.

At midnight on February 15th, by the light of gasoline flares, the shack was dismantled. Here, a voice said. I could not make out the stars through the pink haze. Buildings loomed and a thousand lights burned. They had found me. Snow fell. And my house pulled down around me, a blanket around my shoulders, my hands covered with wool socks. Easy, easy. The tiny flakes stuck to my lashes and the folds of the blanket. Here.

You were dressed for winter when they found you. One sweater over another, two pairs of socks, an overcoat pinned shut and stuffed with newspapers. Watchcap pulled low. A scarf hiding your face. And bottles in your pockets.

Byrd screwed on the cap as I entered. He slid the bottle into his drawer and lifted his eyes to mine. Of course everyone knew. In that place were no secrets and knowledge could pass by other means than voices speaking behind another's back. Each of the planes was rumored to carry a crate of whiskey; other crates were hidden among the stores, though despite our searches none of us could find them.

Yes, she told me many things about you, the man says to me. He rises from his chair and stands at the window, his back to me. I've thought about this moment my entire life, he says to the glass. And now there's nothing to say. In the sky beyond him an airplane stitches a white trail across the sky.

I find, too, that absence of conversation makes it harder for me to think in words. Sometimes, I talk to myself and listen to the sounds, each one hollow and unfamiliar. I can feel the difference between this life and a normal life, I can see the difference in my mind's eye, but I can't explain it in words. This may be because I have already come to live more deeply within myself; what I feel needs no further definition, since the senses are intuitive and exact.

But now, in the leisurely quiet of the New Hampshire hills, I have had time to go back, to pick up the threads of the narrative; to see things steadily and to see them whole, with all things done and all hopes and fears having run out their sand.

Here you are, he says. Inside the window he shows me, a man's shoulders are draped by a woman's arms. She, eyes closed, rests her head in the hollow of the man's neck; the man smiles and seems to wink. January 1929, he says. Cambridge. Here you both were.

I want to tell Renee that I do not know this man, that he has wandered in from the street to sit in a warm room for a moment, to steal the food they bring to me, to tell stories to anyone who will listen. But his stories make no sense. He carries pictures he has found on the pavement, in garbage cans, in abandoned houses. Look, he demands. Don't leave me alone with him, I will tell her. But my tongue loose against my teeth. The man plucks his pantlegs and sits down.

Those New Hampshire hills, beyond the mountains, north, the hidden country Martha had escaped—there I imagined her hidden again. Where else would she have gone? A salesman I met in

Bethlehem offered to take me as far as Lancaster, and we drove up Daniel Webster Highway along the river, through a countryside of lost farms and ruined fences, Holsteins and Jerseys staring at us over tangles of barbed wire.

Things I had perhaps hoped you could confirm or deny, and in your denials confirm them, he says.

I brought with me a smooth stone from the shore at Marblehead, a July day I could press into the hollow of my palm to let the sound of waves rise and drown out all others. A letter which sometime during the black days of winter I mislaid though still I could recite its contents from memory. My Dearest, it began. A loop of ribbon which had held back that hair. In Boston, after returning, I found a single dark hair caught in the weave of a wool shirt—a hair too long to be my own. I eased it from the fabric and curled it around my finger. Later with a strip of Scotch tape I stuck it to a blank sheet of paper.

You have been sleeping again. I have sat by you, watching the motion of your eyes behind your closed lids and waiting for you to wake. It rained while you slept, dreaming of summer rainstorms. The ground is still wet but already the clouds are breaking.

In the dim lecture hall I sat near the back row while on stage Byrd stood at the podium and behind him photographs of Little America and the Queen Mauds and the Bay of Whales filled a white screen. Between each image, a moment of blessed darkness, Byrd reaching for his glass of water or pausing in his remarks.

The spruce grouse is so passive that a man can walk up to it and kill it with a stick. My father called it the fool hen, she said. But they are hard to find, living only in the deep woods.

Our forks and knives crossed on our pushed-forward plates, we talked for hours some nights while the windows grew dark. Or rather she talked and I listened. Things I could never have known.

The smallest scrap of your life would fascinate me for days. You would not speak in the morning until you had drunk your coffee. In bed you could sleep only on your left side, with the window open in even the coldest weather to let in air. Your habit of sprinkling sugar on sliced tomatoes. Your fear of bridges. Your hair already turning white by your thirtieth birthday.

But it was not only the other woman's window I watched. At night I stopped anywhere lamplight fell onto the sidewalk, shining on leaves or grass silvery with rain. And each window was another occasion I carried away with me. A woman with a telephone cord curled around her arm as she spoke into the receiver; a child reading in an armchair; a couple seated at a piano; a man kneeling at a hearth to build a fire, his back and shoulders dark, but streaks of light showing when he moved his arms.

We left what we no longer needed or could not carry; what had broken down beyond repair; what we imagined some future expedition might make use of. Under the ice. We dug up biscuits from one of the first expeditions, and found them still quite edible.

To what is already written I can add little more.

Byrd has tried to rewrite his past, our past, to change facts to suit his current whims, to erase what has become inconvenient.

I was handled roughly. At first it was Byrd shaking me awake, his voice close to my ear. Get up, he said. You'll freeze out here. Give me your hand. His face was lined and just showing the start of a rough beard and I realized at once that his youth had passed. I found myself weeping. He turned away for a moment, as if to gauge the strength of the wind or allow my moment of weakness, and then I was lifted up by several arms at once. Easy, a voice called. A pair of hands cradled my head. Here.

There has been no man in to see you, Renee says.

The sooty brick and concrete of the city could not contain your dreams, you believed. And so while she waited for you to return from work one night you began your travels, escaping down whichever sidestreet first presented itself. By that time the earliest dispatches had come already from Little America, the stories of life at the base had appeared in the papers. Still silent, you sipped a second cup of coffee and ate your breakfast while reading of pack ice and sled dogs and the first flight over the Rockefeller Mountains. There it was summer, but here snow fell and frost coated the windows, and every man imagined himself living in the ice.

I can only hope that the man whose misfortune it is to fail will have the manhood to hold himself to blame.

Men and women passed me and I wanted to touch them, to put out a hand and feel the soft fabric of their coat or shirtsleeve and the warmth I imagined beneath it. The throb of a vein at a wrist, the fine hairs on the back of a neck. My own skin felt bloodless.

I do remember what their voices were like, even if I am not sure of what they said. And I do remember thinking that much of what they said was as meaningless as if it were spoken in an unfamiliar tongue. I was the stranger.

The taste of hot soup: the spoon lifted to my lips, the mouthful of heat, the salt on my tongue, the trickle to my chin which the spoon lingered to catch. How long had it been? I held it in my mouth, felt it burn my throat.

Time for your supper, Renee says, opening the door to this small room and standing in the middle of the carpet. She pushes the chair before her on silver wheels.

There were many things I never told Martha, many things I never told a soul.

But I was wrong. The woman did not lead me to Martha; she led me to Byrd. As she descended the steep stairs into the earth, Byrd rose, climbing two at a time, one hand clutching a bundle of papers and the other gripping the metal rail. Admiral Byrd, I shouted. He looked up then and I saw him as I first remember seeing him, the stiff hair swept off the elegant brow, the keen eyes seeking me out among the crowd. I pressed through as he reached the curb, grasped his shoulder as he was about to step into the street. He swung about to face me though his expression did not change. Admiral Byrd, I said. Admiral Byrd, sir, how have you been? I'm sorry, he said. Sorry, I don't think I know you.

Of Devil's Graveyard I have never spoken, have tried to forget: everywhere, those stricken fleets of ice wandering hopelessly through a smoking gloom. The engine-room telegraph bells never stopped ringing.

And what I wondered so many nights, those years, was if you ever, sometime in your wandering, found your way back to your own window like the character of a story—our window, I should say, behind which she and I may have even talked about you, wondering when you would return. Did you stand in the darkness outside, peering in at people you no longer recognized?

Massachusetts Avenue. Commonwealth Avenue. Harvard Avenue. Columbus Avenue. St. Botolph's Street. St. James Street. St. Alphonsus. St. Paul. Marlborough and Charles Streets. Hanover Street. Summer Street and Winter Street. Hemenway, Boylston, Brookline, Longwood, Wigglesworth, Heath. Here I made my home, among nameless faces, gaslamps, damp pavement. Raindrops hung on wires. The wind brought news to me as scraps of paper, cigarette ends, fine grit that stung my face as the drift once had. I knew Byrd would come to me there. And he did. One night we spoke on a bench along the Fenway. Weeks later we met in the shadows of a warehouse near the wharfs, the air scented with salt and gasoline. During a summer rainstorm we walked west on Huntington Avenue, lightning illuminating the hills before us. It has driven me from everything I thought I loved, he told me, one of these nights. Or shown me what I did love. It was rare for him to display any emotion but I recall him gripping my arm, his face mere inches from mine. Do you understand, he asked.

I woke to mourning doves in the predawn hour. Rose from my hotel room, quickly washed, and without waiting for breakfast paid the night clerk and left Lancaster for the dark hills and shadowed fields to my north, following that slow river to its source.

It was long ago when I found white hairs on my own head. Longer than I care to admit.

In the room Renee wheels me into, strange men and women sit around a table, their hands collapsed in their laps, or folded on the plates before them. Feet make no sound on the carpet. In white, the nurses come and go like ghosts. Some of the men and women do not talk. Some talk so softly to themselves that I cannot hear what words they are speaking, or if what they speak are indeed words. Among these people my tongue refuses to shape sounds.

If, looking up from our supper to your face at the window, we would have recognized you ourselves.

Are you going to be difficult tonight? Renee asks me.

The sleeping pills were on the shelf. The flashlight fingered the bottle. I took it down and dumped the pellets into my cupped palm. There were more than two dozen, white and round; they bespoke a lovely promise.

She told me how she searched for you in the streets after you disappeared, that she walked circles through the city every spare hour she had. She said she once grasped a man's shoulder from behind, not even thinking he was you but out of pure desperation. It was years before she gave up.

I have seen the stars from every corner of the globe. Navigated by them—their positions fixed only in my mind—charting a course as well as with any map.

Alone, I took walks in the evenings. In the milky fog that rolled in from the water objects lost their forms. I wandered across the ice in my windproofs, hearing behind me the cries of our dogs. Some days I would imagine that my path was the Esplanade, on the water side of Beacon Hill, where, in my mind's eye, I often walked with Martha. I would meet people I knew along the bank, and drink in the perfection of a Boston spring.

Byrd did not return my letters. Byrd, once he set foot again on American soil, vanished.

She told me that, at the time you left, she did not yet know about me. That it was only after you were gone that she suffered the first symptoms of my unmistakable presence. She told me once, long ago, that I was your final gift to her, as if you knew you would be leaving and wanted me to keep her from loneliness. And then I think about her now and realize how young she was those years, though it never struck me until I was older than she was then. Of course she never told you about me. Of course you never knew. Though some nights as I tried to sleep I wondered if somehow you had guessed, if that was why you left.

She told me we can only say what we believe.

Byrd told me a man must believe what he says is true.

For years I believed in a certain idea of you. Someone who could never match this person I now see before me.

Byrd was always going and returning. In the end it was his secret mission during the War. Yet I stayed. So many times I imagined the feel of the cold creeping up through my mukluks, the patterns of frost inside the sheds, the brief red wheel of the sun during winter.

The sudden blows when outside everything turned dark, and drift burned like grains of sand—men were lost six feet from the hatch they had just climbed through, and stumbled back only by blind luck. I kept myself from running into that fury only by staying underground. Here there has never been anywhere to lose myself.

The tracks of my feet lead in circles.

What day is it? Renee says. You don't remember? Fifty-two years ago this day you were on the Eleanor Bolling, steaming into Dunedin harbor.

Years later, I was working in the harbor at New Bedford. On a street corner one night a man accosted me, grasping my shoulder. The face I turned to smiled at me; the shadow of a dark beard colored the cheeks, and the hat was pushed back from the low forehead. Don't you remember me? the man asked. Other people passed me on both sides, their arms and shoulders brushing against my own. You look so surprised, as if you'd never seen me before. It's Cox, from Little America.

For years I have wanted nothing more than to find you, to sit by you, and to ask you questions. To listen to your answers. To have some way to try to understand, to compare what you say against everything else I've been told. To hear your own explanations, in the sound of your own voice.

The radio signals ceased days ago.

I'm sorry, the man says, covering his face with his hands.

The nurses button blue sweaters over their white smocks, and carry trays of food to the table where we all sit. Steam rises in the soft light. Next to me, a man scrapes his fork across a white plate. This sound too means something.

Her town was far into the country—beyond hills and rivers and small anonymous crossroads where men rocked on cane chairs, their feet on warped porches, watching me pass; beyond the bald granite peaks and the valleys they shadowed hours and hours each day—miles I traveled, deep into this country, toward a point on the horizon where the fields lay flat, no sound but wind and the hum of telephone wires. If I stopped, could I have heard the voices? Those sagging fences kept nothing out.

At the long mess table, elbowed in together, we chewed the meat of Weddell seals or steaks cut from whale; sucked limes to prevent scurvy.

Dusk, and the dark shapes of birds fly overhead. Byrd lifts one hand from a ragged cuff and points. Nighthawks, he says. They nest in chimneys and come out to eat the bugs when it starts to turn dark. He kicks his heels against the packed dirt before the bench. It is a dangerous time of day, he says. I've never liked it.

I wanted to find you for her, the man says. Now it doesn't matter.

No man can hope to be completely free who lingers within reach of familiar habits and urgencies.

It was the city where I had been born. The city I had roamed all through my youth, hooking an arm on a fire escape and climbing to a tarred roof to survey it, stretching away from me until it met the water in smoke and gloom. But after I returned it became only the city in which I had lost her, the place I was doomed to wander searching for her.

It is one thing to instruct the mind; it is another to make the mind obey.

Byrd crumbled a fallen leaf into a fine dust between his palms. We sat on a bench on the Riverway and past us walked women in long coats, a group of children chasing a dog, a man swinging a briefcase in a small arc. Above us the sky had faded to white. November. Byrd reached into his coat pocket for his flask and unscrewed the top. You have always stood by me, he said. You've always stayed loyal. In no hurry to make a name for yourself at my expense as were so many others. He closed his eyes and drank and from the gathering dark behind us the children's voices carried. You know the importance of a man's word. He wiped his mouth with his sleeve and handed me the flask.

As I walked the tipped squares of sidewalks through the city I would see, sometimes, a boy crouched in a weedy alley shaking a can and then applying ribbons of color to the bricked backside of a building. It was an urge I could recognize. A code for someone else to identify. But when they saw me watching, the boys ran, hurdling wire fences with a rattle and vanishing around corners. And the weeping letters they left behind formed words I could not say.

It was with a feeling akin to the forlorn that I looked back at my sledge tracks disappearing into the limitless white to the south.

If I have stopped talking, others seem to have traveled in the opposite direction, shrieking and babbling rivers of words to fill the silent corners of rooms and bare halls of the place where we live, even though no one else may notice. If I could find the words, I could tell them what I know to be true, but what it is I want to say eludes me, its shape lost in the sound like a figure in a whiteout.

Once, in the winter night, flu laid half of Little America low—the result, the doctor said, of opening a box of old clothing.

Byrd leans his face toward mine; his breath hangs in clouds. His hand bears a surprising heat against my arm. He opens his mouth as if to speak but says no words, his lips parting then closing again. In this quiet even the motion of his arm, the rustle of fabric, the faint intake of breath, each blink of my eyelids make sounds. Finally he looks away and only then says I have always dreamed this, always waited for this moment. To be here. His hand on my arm tightens. Here.

She told me each bird had a song and each song was a secret tongue—the nuthatch's nasal bleat, the cardinal's liquid whistle, the rough voice of the crow. Only the mockingbird can speak in the manner of another, she said, though he doesn't know what he says.

What are you doing here? I asked. Why have you come here?

In my bed Renee pulls the sheets to my chin, and the blankets drift and settle across my chest. The view through my window is dark. Here the stars are faint, different, not stars. My hand in Martha's, her warm breath on my neck. The ice closes in around me until I am no longer cold but burning up all over.

Give me your hand.

It is never as an old man that we see ourselves in our imaginations, never an old man we imagine ourselves one day becoming. New Year's Day, 1966, I woke feeling suddenly old, as if I'd been stricken sometime during the night: had I never noticed the wrinkled skin of my hands, the shallow tremble of my heartbeat? I remember this day as clearly as if it were yesterday. I did not look in the mirror for weeks afterward, afraid of what my reflection would confirm. From the window of my room I watched snow fall over Tremont Street. People walked below me with newspapers tucked under their arms, their coats flapping; pigeons stepped along the curbs, pecking at bits of garbage. One taxi idled past, breathing white smoke. The telephone had not rung in weeks. That day one of the few days of quiet I've had in this hemisphere.

I awakened with a violent start, as if I had been thrown down a well in my sleep. I found myself staring wildly into the darkness of the shack, not knowing where I was.

I imagined myself a character in some story, walking until holes spread across the soles of my shoes. I paused at the last rise in the road, a crest where the land dropped away into a green valley, just as she had told me so many times it would be. Off to my right the shining surface of a lake appeared among the trees, and from it a river flowed down the valley. Sweat snaked behind my ears and down my back. My shirt damp. Hours since I'd eaten. Yet in all of the stories she told me it was in such fashion that the man came out of the wilderness at the end of his journey.

I woke in the woods, soaked with dew. White light streamed through the leaves overhead. Somewhere not far off a dog was barking. Dirt stuck to the heel of my hand. I pulled a cigarette from the crushed pack in my shirt pocket and tried to straighten it.

Even thirty years ago seems impossible to conjure now.

Why had she come to Boston? So often have I asked some darkened ceiling in a hushed hour of the night. Why here? Wind banged shutters on the white house atop the hill, swept aside clouds to reveal a huge moon shining over rocky pastures. This too I saw; she had told it all to me so often those nights we lay together. I would be no farmer's wife, she had said. A branch ticked against the window.

A visitor for you, Renee says, swinging wide the door.

Even in the city—the city where I once knew every street and alley, the factories and churches, the quiet cafés, the newspaper vendors—the landmarks were erased. It did not happen one by one, slowly, the way we had watched the Barrier gradually push itself into the bay that year, ice shearing off in small shards. No, it was everywhere around me, all at once, buildings torn down and raised, parking lots scraped up, streets re-routed, tunnels dug below the harbor, the subway's warren stretching farther and farther from its center. Would my feet still follow the same path to Martha's door?

The terrain continually shifted and neither map nor memory could describe it.

Underground. The train rocked side to side as in the window across from me I watched my blurred reflection and the rushing wall behind it. Byrd, half-asleep, rested his head against my shoulder. An old Chinese man studied the floor between his feet while all around us other men fluttered the pages of newspapers or clutched briefcases to their laps. A woman held two silent children. Nurses clustered at the door for the next stop, their white shoes muddied from the melted snow we had all tracked in with us. No one spoke. Sparks flashed.

The man steps into the room as Renee's head disappears from behind the door. Snip. In his hands he holds a book, and I struggle up in the bed, the light from my window streaming all around me, to see the cover. Blue, or red?

Our voices, Byrd once told me, and this too I remember—they are something we can do without.

All of my life you have been dead to me.

Just outside the shabby store in the center of the village, slack electric wires hung humming above us. Martha Hennessy, I repeated to the man who sat on the store's steps. I did not know him, did not know his name, doubted I would ever see him again, though in that I was proven wrong for I see him often in dreams. He lifted his hat and scratched behind his sunburnt ear—this is what I remember, his answer contained already in the simplest gesture, what I had known even as I boarded in the hiss and steam of North Station. He cast his eyes to my thin leather shoes, edged with mud, and cleared his throat to speak.

But you were never listening.

No words can fit the horror of the moment. At such a time the mind sees a long story in an instant.

How I've constructed your life from photographs and someone else's words. Trying to make sense of something I cannot see, even now.

Yes, the ice was like that, I want to tell him. His gaze falls to the shape of my legs under these blankets Renee flaps each morning. Then wanders beyond the window. From where you stood you could see nothing but white, though you knew so much else existed somewhere past your own limits.

Nights when sleep cannot find me, it has often come to me that what we call stars may be something else entirely, or that even if we lose the name the lights do not wink out, still prove our relative locations, determine our lives; that what I feel exists whether or not I can tell it in a way that someone else may understand.

But the man does not stay in this northern country he has come to, she said. It is beautiful, he thinks, its balsams and firs as tall as the buildings in the city he has come from, yet whether this country defeats his attempts to possess it or whether his own restless feet lead him elsewhere, he turns his back on it and returns the way he has come, losing himself in a city where any man may go unnoticed.

It is a country that has long resisted outsiders, a country which many have died trying to claim.

Answer me.

Byrd ripped the newspaper into sheets and balled these up in his hands. He stuffed the loose padding into his trousers and then began working on his torso and arms. His sweater stretched and he rustled as he lifted his hands into the sleeves of his coat. Now you, he said. It's the only way to keep warm. His hands, black with ink, found the flask in his pocket. And this.

Entire years of my life I find myself unable to account for now.

Try as I could, screwing the eyes, I could not make out the distance of things from us, nor their shapes. Skiing, it was the same. I glided smoothly over a surface and then all of a sudden came to a cropper on a slight upward slope I failed to see. I sighted a mountain of snow, miles off, and it turned out to be a haycock twenty yards away.

My hands, ruined from a lifetime's work. I fold them on the blanket, and gaze through my window, waiting for the man to leave as, after enough time has passed, the man always leaves.

Renee shows me the book the man has left behind. Yellowed tape holds small squares to black paper and in each square a face or some faces look back at me. Eyes squinting into sunlight, a cap casting shadow, a hand holding a cigarette by a hip or tossed over someone else's shoulder. And, behind them, trees or long grass or dunes rising against a white sky or bricks in staggered rows, the flat line of the sea, a road disappearing around a corner, a laden table, a faint pattern of wallpaper against which still more pictures hang.

In winter, in whatever trees I could find here, I sought out the empty nests of birds. In the bare branches they seemed to me absurd—lonely, conspicuous clumps of twigs and leaves stuck in the crooks the boughs made. Only snow filling the carefully-shaped bowl.

What could I have told Martha, then or ever? What can a sound do to change what has been? A lifetime I have spent fleeing sound or else searching for the correct sounds, the precise words to explain away my own deeds—leaving me in the end with only the echo of what was spoken.

There is a moment, sometimes, upon waking in the vanishing dark, when all I can hear is the pulse of my blood in my neck. The intake of breath, or breath's release.

Day is coming on, heaving ponderously into the north, pushing back the darkness a little bit more every day—a gorgeous signal along the horizon to a man who has little else to look for.

QUINNEHTUKQUT

SECOND CONNECTICUT LAKE

Other New England lakes have been exploited in prose and verse to the neglect of these three highland jewels.

—Marguerite Allis, *Connecticut River*

ONE

1920

That July day the feet of men and women crushed the paper-dry yellow grass to powder, and everywhere was dust—dust coating shoes and hems and cuffs, dust rimming fingernails and settling in throats, dust chalking the corners of mouths. Her head half-turned, a woman coughed behind a fist. The horses' hooves and the wagon wheels lifted great clouds of dust which hung in the windless air. Dust whitened the least leaf or pebble. Cicadas competed from the fading foliage. The girl's hand found her mother's; her fingers laced her mother's thumb. Stones and tall men cast the only shade on the barren hilltop and sweat shone on lips and temples. Darkened the hollow between shoulderblades of the men who'd removed their coats and stood, hands on hips, looking at that sparse grass and the pale earth it rose from. The river—even low, its banks cracked mud—gave a sound through the trees. A hawk circled in the sky, though that blue was too bright to look into long. And was not even blue, but a blue that faded into a white haze, a color too faint to notice. Even along the river the corn was starved and skinny, the stalks drooping or dragging limp leaves on the ground. From the woods rose plumes of smoke where dry needles and ferns smoldered, and each day men dug trenches to ring barns and houses—that parched earth lifted shovelful by shovelful, metal ringing on buried stones. Windy Williams sat in the line of shade at Baldwin's store and remarked to anyone happening by that his shoulder ached, an ache he said foretold far-off rain despite the troubling sky. It would be an overnight rain, he said, a drizzle by dusk turning into a downpour on tin roofs to keep the town awake all through the night—to swell the streams and the river by morning. Kill a beetle and it will surely rain. When the swallows fly low over the meadows, it is a sign of rain. By the girl's count it was thirty-four days and the last rain little more than a heavy dew. Each night he had coughed into a porcelain basin, each cough lifting him from the pillow. His hair lay damp, wicked to his forehead. She had stirred honey into hot water, made him drink before the red-gold coils settled to the bottom of the glass. The windows were closed and the curtains drawn. In the mornings Charlie Chase milked the cows and she tended the horses—their warm breath on her hands, their sidelong eyes as she unlatched the stall door; that oaty reek. She filled the bags with feed, brushed coats, lifted hooves for rocks she prised loose with a blunted blade. Those moments before the sun climbed above the trees she imagined each day would be overcast, that she would not have to squint against the day's increasing light, would not have to tie back her hair and at night peel her damp dress from her skin. The trees at the far end of the pasture would fade, trunks black, in indistinct light, low clouds, needles of rain. Now she squeezed her mother's hand and did not look at the sky. Here came Mr Currier and his wife and sons over the rise, beating the dust before their feet. It was not the dry spell. No. It was not. Even if it had been pouring down buckets every day, her mother said. Even if we'd had to roost in the spruce to keep our feet dry from the rising waters. It is nothing we can place blame on, only something we must accept. She tried not to breathe the dust that stirred and then settled every time she moved, pressing a corner of her scarf over her nose and mouth. Her father had drawn a map when he'd returned. Each night he lit a lamp and sat at the kitchen table; she heard the pencil scratch on the paper, the faint snick of his pocketknife sharpening its point. Every place he named she could not say until he repeated it several times. Even then she hesitated.

The hawk had vanished—a goshawk, Martha had decided, from its thick body. A quarter mile up, what could the goshawk see—nothing but these people clustered on a hill. Men in the woods had found listless deer chewing any green shoot, legs unsteady, their mouths and flanks flecked with white foam. Young moose, legs sprawled over last fall's leaves, picked at by turkey vultures. The catamount that had not run when Boots Gorton found it stretched in his dooryard, tongue a pale pink. The stories reached her. Walking into the dark of Baldwin's store for fresh handkerchiefs or camphor, she heard the men talk. She placed coins onto the counter and hurried outside, her feet mute down the two wood steps and then, on the gravel, amplified in the heat. She saw only the stretch of road before her, her short shadow upon it. Her head bent low, she ran to the hill's yellowing blur. Windy Williams called after her words she half-heard. Rain, rivers, her father.

And her father drew names on the map, shaded forests and hills and farmers' fields. What had been. The land is so flat, he said, it goes on and on for miles. Here we camped for two days. His fingernail blunt against the paper. It traced a straight line. This was the way we walked. I wrote you and your mother a letter describing the river and the round orange moon one night. I am sure she has it still tucked in a drawer. Here we dug holes in muddy earth for a week, the water seeping in as fast as we could dig sometimes. No one was clean those days. If you could have seen me, you would not have recognized my face. Here—his finger hovered, circling slowly over the paper—here—well, no. Here I most missed these hills, this house; your face and your mother's. The sea he marked with curved lines—the sea I spent four weeks on, two weeks each way while black smoke blew backwards over our heads and the deck canted back and forth, pitching my clumsy legs against anything solid. Some of the gulls followed us from one shore to the other, chasing the rough wake we cut across the waves, resting on the rails and wires when they tired. One month of my life lived with no solid ground below me. Nothing like our lakes. You can hardly imagine it until you see it, until you watch the land slowly vanish behind you and then sink below the horizon. But we will go some-day soon to look out on it—borrow Mr Young's Nash, or take the train. He talked until his voice and the ticking clock were the only sounds—had she fallen asleep? His hands cupped her shoulders, her back curled against him. He lifted her. She felt her arm slip down, her hand's weight. Blood rushing. There was so much rain, he was saying, gray sheets over gray fields. Men sneezing in early dark. On some of the quiet nights we could hear them sneezing in their damp holes ten, forty, a hundred yards from us. And men were taken away simply for calling words across that torn earth.

But each of those nights they sat at the table, his large hands and the sketch in the circle of light the lamp cast, her hands under her legs on the wicker seat or reaching to hold back a corner of the page while he pointed to a line or a dot or a name written in his small script, both of their faces shadowed while yellow light flickered and jumped on the ceiling, a thin stream of black smoke rising straight before it curled and rolled—those nights it was the cold she remembered—the ticking of the woodstove as he let the fire die, the snow piling up unnoticed while they talked so that when she woke in the morning the wind-shaped drifts would surprise her. Her mother wordless at the doorway, and then the creak of her feet climbing the stairs.

The people were speaking quietly to one another. Boys toed and heeled the dry ground until a father glanced or a mother touched a finger to her lip. One girl flapped her skirts for the breeze. Sweat traced the curves of ears. The four young men—Rob Marsh's two eldest sons as well as Henry Cummings' weedy boy and young Freddy Young—lifted it from the wagon and, faces reddening, walked to the center of the circle the standing men and women described. He had always been a tall man. Wide-shouldered and dark, a crooked smile, keen eyes—and what a shame, the townspeople had said, he had never had a son. A son approaching his own height, a son who would grow into his shoulders, whose sinewy arms they could watch thicken as each successive summer he stripped off his shirt to split next winter's wood. In the glare of light against the dull grass and dust it seemed to them impossible that he did not exist somewhere among them, this son, that it was not his voice they listened for, that he did not stand beside his mother while she lay her head against his shoulder. No, only a daughter. Only one girl. But at least he did come back to us, her mother had said, even if just for a short while, and for that we should be thankful. The bank had sent men from Colebrook, their Ford trailing clouds along the highway and then up the hill, while her mother stood on the porch looking over the valley and Charlie Chase mended a milking stool in the barn's shadow. Her mother, wiping a hand on her apron, walked them through the house and out into the barn while Martha watched from her father's window upstairs. She's showing them into the stalls, she told him; when he closed his eyes she let the curtain fall shut. And Mr Currier had cleared a spare room above his kitchen and would send his wagon to town, his two sons sitting on the sides to load as much as it would carry, then walking alongside it the miles back to the lake. Charlie Chase was, he said, headed far downriver and across it, to a tobacco farm in Putney. The view from that side will be much different, I imagine, he had told Martha, while she helped him pack his suitcases and he clasped his palsied hands together, and already the silence at night his wheeze had once filled kept her up. The moon rose late, red behind the trees. A wind blew the curtains into the room and then sucked them back. Its sound through fir branches. It was the winds, her father said, that they had to watch out for, what it would carry toward them. Whenever it blew in our faces we knew to be careful.

The four boys uncoiled ropes. The men who stood in this knot watched, lifted hands from pockets to hang at their sides, but said nothing and made no move. The others looked at the bare patch of earth they had worn away while standing and shifting weight from one foot to the other, looked at the darkness under the trees, turned away, shut their eyes, or fastened them to that rough wood—not oiled, not polished. And all it seemed we did was dig, he had told her. If I never have to dig another hole. He lay his head back against the damp pillow; his voice faded. I'm getting sleepy, he said. Has Charlie taken care of the cows? She pulled her sweater sleeves down over her hands and watched his eyelids hover. Can I bring you more water? Women boiled lakewater, then set the lidded pots outside to cool. If the water boils out of the kettle, it is a sure sign of coming rain. Each morning she stepped to the porch, the barn and trees still dark, and carried in the pots, spooning out any flies that floated there. They hummed and buzzed all around her. Lighted on necks, wrists, hats; were brushed away. It's a sign of rain when the flies bite, Windy Williams said, scraping the dust from under his fingernail with his pocketknife. But all signs fail in a dry time. Now pastor Franklin opened his book and fingered its pages, a green ribbon dangling from them; now the men and women stopped speaking at all and held their hands closed; now the sun burned the backs of bare necks; now she wet her cracked lips, tried to swallow; now the four boys arranged the ropes, and, slowly, the rough strands rubbing their hands raw, lowered it in.

Her mother's hand tightened around her own and then pulled away: her mother covered her face. The pastor's voice, the swish of the horses' tails, the creaking rope, the cicadas the only sounds. Above, the blue bowl of sky.

And it was just downriver, people thought, in Columbia, that Hayes McFarland sat in his cane chair on his porch, looking over his fields and the men he paid to work them; that on the first day of every month a check came and would for twenty-five years; that the price of his loss was more than a man's life. His hired men hammered new shingles to the peaked roof, repaired the stone walls surrounding his land, shoveled manure, walked the plow through the fields left fallow for two years, the soil breaking before their feet, releasing its own keen breath there where the lazy river looped back on itself and a man standing in New Hampshire could fire a shot at a deer lapping the silty water, the shot traveling through Vermont before it hit the animal standing on the same bank as the man. Those fields will grow nothing, she had heard him say. If you could only have seen them. Here we cannot imagine anything like it. What has soaked into that soil will keep it barren. In a hundred years they will still be unearthing rusted metal, heaping scraps and shards in the corners of their barns. Bois Brule, Marvoisin, Belleau, Givry, Menil-le-Tour, Bouresches, Epieds, Bois d'Haumont. Did you think everyone says the same words everywhere? her mother asked. He's just learned their words. But he seemed now to speak less and less, his voice only a whisper when he coughed into his slack fist. And this she knew: at the dinner table Hayes McFarland bowed his head and said the grace—his voice a low murmur, the thanks he gave reaching the ears of no one present, who knew to unclasp his hands only by watching McFarland's lips. His wife and daughters poured coffee. The hired men, their hats on their knees, looked at the dull white circles of their plates. Hayes McFarland picked up his fork with an unsteady left hand. If he had had a son, the people on the hill thought. One morning we made pancakes in an old fireplace, he had told her. It was in a ruined farmhouse. I imagined it must once have looked something like this one. He passed his hand before his eyes. All we could buy in those villages was eggs. It was considered bad luck to keep any money, since every dead man we brought in had some francs in his pockets. We couldn't send it home so we spent it as quickly as we could. And in those villages we ate omelettes. I don't remember where we had found the flour this morning. The only coffee we had was given to us in an empty sandbag, and the sand that was still caught in the seams and the cloth found its way into our cups. Penfield was flipping the pancakes into the air. Only some of them fell back into the pan; most ended up on the sooty bricks. Still, we smothered them with Karo and spent the morning with our feet up and our backs against the one wall of the house that still stood. We will be responsible for helping with the breakfast and the dinner, and perhaps for the supper as well, her mother told her. We must always be punctual and courteous and we must remember that all of these men are on holiday. None of them will come back, Mrs Currier believes, unless they remember our cooking and our hospitality after they return home. I'm sure we'll be glad to see some of them leave and never return, but we must remember too that it's only because of them that the lodge is here at all, and only because of the lodge that we're not at the poor farm. The Curriers provided for us while your father was away, and now that he's gone we'll do all we can for them as they have done for us. I will not have Mr and Mrs Currier nor anyone else in town think that we are here from charity. The charity and hospitality of those people was beyond anyone's expectations, he said. Only a half dozen miles from the lines they lived as if nothing were happening. Sometimes we were billeted in barns and haylofts, ten or a dozen of us heaping the straw into piles and peering through the door at those endless gray fields, or through holes in the roof at shifting clouds. All the people there were old—old men and old women with wooden shoes and heavy black coats. Still, they gave us cigarettes, potatoes, coffee; some of the old women would cook stews for six or seven of us. All night we listened to the Boches' guns.

The dirt, shoveled, sifted back into the still air as gray powder. Hit the wood planks with a thump and a clatter of stones, a sound nothing like the drumming wings of a grouse surprised in deep woods, her father's foot poised in mid-stride while he swung his gun around. She waited for the echo that did not come. Next time, he said, lowering the barrel slowly, his hands red with cold, the skin chapped white at the cracks of his knuckles. He was said to know every deer trail from the river to the border though if asked would deny it. We walked those woods every day. We walked those woods, he said, bellying through barbed wire that tore our clothes and peeled pieces of skin from our hands. The shells landing did not explode. There was a ping and a whistle and then the smell—horseradish, I always thought, though the others said mustard and so it came to be known. The klaxon horns wailed from the blackened trees ahead of us and we all groped for the masks around our necks. The Boches waited until the wind blew from the east, let it drift toward our positions. That smoke. A line of men clutching cloths to their eyes, their hands on the shoulders of the man in front of them while they waited for the medics. We went straight for the ditches and shell holes before they told us that it collected there, even days later, so that a man sleeping low would wake to find the skin on his back near burnt off. Sometimes we had to cut the uniform off a man to smear the Sag paste over his swollen skin. We walked a road one night while the moon lit the crosses along its edges, shone on charred and splintered trees, on bloated horses missing legs or heads, on the water that had seeped into craters. The engineers filled them in so our supply carts could follow. The dirt slithered over the sides of the box. Began to fill; and pastor Franklin let his voice hang in the air like the dust before it trailed off. They packed dirt into the holes. The earth itself was wounded. Those old Frenchmen told us the river once ran red.

When he tired she read him stories as for years he had read them to her, sitting on the edge of her bed while his weight rolled her toward him, the book held in one open hand and the lamp casting moving shadows on the walls and ceiling. As she read, his eyes closed and at times she closed her eyes as well and, without looking, turned the pages at regular intervals and continued the stories. Fog on the hills, more water for the mills. And then. And then. Every third morning until the start of summer she had filled the basin with heated water, wetted a cloth in it, and draped it over his mouth. His eyes fluttered shut and he inhaled. For two years his cup and brush had stood in their customary place in the cabinet, and at times washing her face she would sniff the stiff bristles, run her fingers over their tips. Steady, he said, while she scraped the blade toward his chin—his face inches from hers, eyes still closed. His pair of boots had stood by the door. His shotgun hung from the wall and not even Charlie Chase had disturbed it. Twice her mother had washed all his clothes to clean out the dust, squatting all day by the tub in the dooryard. His shirts and trousers, empty, flapped and waved on the line. Can't expect him to put on dusty clothes when he gets back, her mother said. Martha told him all of the stories she knew, the stories he had once told to her, the stories of things that had happened while he was gone. One night at Young's Otis Langley had been bragging about the two-year-old colt he had purchased a week before. At breakfast the next morning Charlie Chase had told her the story, how Joe Parsons had bet Langley ten dollars he couldn't lead his colt upstairs. And Langley got that horse up the stairs, Charlie Chase had said. He took the reins and brought him right through the front door and through the crowd of everyone laughing and right up to the upstairs hall. That colt snorted and his flanks trembled but he didn't buck. We all stood there watching that tail lash the air until it disappeared around the corner. Langley's voice shouted down. Claude Covill went up to check that all four of the colt's hooves were upstairs, and Joe swore as he drew out his wallet. Here it is, he said, counting out the bills one by one and rubbing each between his fingers before he set it down in the creased pile on the table we all surrounded. For a moment no one said anything while we all waited for Langley to come down with his colt and collect the money and ride home to bury it in his root cellar. And then we heard another oath from upstairs and presently Langley came down alone. He counted each of the bills as carefully as Joe had and put them into his pocket quickly as if to make us forget he had them. Then he climbed back up the stairs two at a time and we heard him swear again. The colt whinnied and there was a loud thump. We all gathered by the bottom step and looked up at Langley trying to tug that colt back down, but those front hooves were planted and he couldn't have budged them even if he was a bigger man than he is. We watched them struggle for a minute. Can someone lend a hand? Langley said. No one moved, and he went back to pulling. Then Vern Amey drained his mug and shouted up to Langley that he was thirsty but if Langley would buy him more toddy he'd help him push. And every dime of that ten dollars went for toddy to persuade the crowd to push that colt down the stairs. By the end of the night Young had the biggest grin of anyone and some suggested that he'd somehow been behind the whole production. Her father smiled though his eyes stayed shut. So Parsons paid Langley to buy everyone a drink. I suppose so, she said. But there was another story. Once upon a time, a farmer lived with his wife and children in a country where the weather was dry for weeks. The crops failed and the animals died. Each day the cupboard grew emptier and emptier. Finally there was no food for the farmer to give his children and so one night he suggested to his wife that he would lead them into the forest. Better they starve there than here before our very eyes, he told her. At last his wife relented and in the morning he gathered his children for the journey into the woods. There was not even any bread for one child to break into crumbs as they walked. The trees bent and creaked. Dry leaves crackled under their feet. The farmer told his children to search through the dead thickets and orange ferns for any nuts or herbs they might eat, and, while his children bent over the brush, he turned to steal quietly back home. But before he had taken a dozen steps he felt something strike his neck. He looked up to see what it was, and saw skies dark with clouds. Another drop hit his forehead; soon the rain came harder than he had ever seen. And he ran quickly back to his children. Already the waters pooled around his ankles. With his axe he felled a tree to float back to the cottage where his wife waited for her family. There was one night, her father said. We lay in our ditches in the rain. The drops hung in a row around the brim of my helmet. Dull flashes lit the bottoms of the clouds. The night before one of our men, an Irishman from Boston named Shea, had been lost with a few others during a patrol. The Boches had shot at them, making them scatter out beyond the barbed wire, and only half of the men had crawled back to our lines by daybreak. The rest we assumed killed or captured. All that day we watched mud collapse into our holes, stood in puddles and waited. Around noon an observer saw what he thought was a body in a shell hole halfway between us and the Boches, and we guessed it was one of our men. The rain began to fall furiously after sunset. A few of us talked about trying to retrieve the fellow from the shell hole. But in that rain and with the Boches so close no one wanted to move. Then around midnight I heard voices down the line. Shea had come in, covered in mud so that he was barely recognizable. He had been separated from the patrol when it was shot at, had been turned around in the dark, and when the sun had risen that morning he was still in no-man's land. So he said he just crawled into that hole to play dead until it turned dark again.

The men shoveled. Pale roots reached out from the sides of the hole and below them the dirt covered the wood planks. Mrs Folsom took her mother's shoulder and turned her away to the trees ringing them. There are some of us back at the house, she said. Will you let us bring you? Her glasses winked in the sun as she looked at the wagon her husband steered toward them. All of the people climbed into wagons or walked away but for the men shoveling and Pastor Franklin, who still stood clutching the book to his dark coat. Then Mr Folsom was holding her hand and lifting her onto the seat. Her leg pressed against her mother's. There, Mr Folsom said. Flies, fat and shiny, flitted over the horses' backs. Mr Folsom swished the reins and the gravel below her began to blur. Still no breeze. Dusty leaves bowed. The back of Mr Folsom's neck was burnt a dark red-brown, and when he turned his head side to side she saw seams in his skin. The ends of his hair beneath his hat brim were damp. The horses led them downhill, into the village, the sun blazing on the white clapboards of the church where they had all stood and kneeled only an hour before—where, in the stuffy dark, she had shut her eyes and imagined that Pastor Franklin's voice was that of her father, lying in his bed with the curtains drawn. Let me bring you more water, she told him. Thank you. My throat is dry with all this talking. Then I'll talk. Shhh. In that quiet even the rustle of sheets as he turned to one side seemed loud. When she returned with the cup he had fallen asleep, one hand curled to his shoulder, his jaw loose, his breath ragged in his chest. She lifted the blanket over his legs and blew out the lamp. Shut his door without letting the hinges creak. Undressing by her window she could see the moon on the river in the valley. The night was bright enough that the barn threw its shadow across the pasture. Keep Jerseys for butterfat and Holsteins for bulk and you will never want, her father once told her. Every morning the milkman came in his wagon to take the metal canisters Charlie Chase handed up to him. In the winter months the milkman was covered in bearskins and heavy blankets and wrapped in scarves. She stood in the barn, breaking the ice in the trough. Lamplight spilled onto the snow, and the breath of Charlie Chase and the milkman and the horses shaped a drifting cloud that hid them from her. On Fridays the milkman gave to Charlie Chase an envelope he gave to her mother when she returned from the lodge in Mr Currier's wagon. Tom Currier drove the horse up the hill and helped her mother down. And he waved at her while she shook out a rug or took laundry off the line and her mother walked toward her. I'm tired, her mother always said. Do you have supper ready? Martha pulled back the sheets and slipped her legs beneath them. Her nightgown bunched. But I will be no farmer's wife.

The horses, their shoulders glistening, began the climb to the farm. Other wagons were already gathered at the hilltop, and hitched horses stood with mute faces, watching them come. Her father had pulled back the edge of the curtain to peer out whenever he heard anyone approaching, and even when he was too weak to lift himself up on one arm to look his ears were still sharp enough that he would ask her who it was before she had heard anything. But you didn't let me finish my story, she said. Which story? The farmer floated the tree back to where his cottage had stood, but the timbers had been washed away by the rising waters. His furniture had been splintered against the trees that poked above the flood. One of his old shirts flew from the end of a branch. And when he turned to his children he saw that not one of them still clung to his raft. Mr Folsom reined in the horses, turning them. The wheels made a sound like something burning. Look at this, her mother said. Look at this. She shook her head. Mr Folsom jumped down. Men and women stood and watched from the porch's shade, but once her mother's skirts began to brush the

stubbled grass before the house some of them came forward, taking
her arm or blinking in that light. The house admitted them to its
dusty hush she had conceded months back though now its chairs
and sofa were occupied, and men, ties already loosened or unknot-
ted, leaned against doorjambs or stood awkward in corners while
women carried plates to the table. Had they knocked or simply
pushed open the door as if it were their own? Her mother was
ushered to a waiting cushion and a glass of water brought. The
curtains remained shut, the windows closed. Mr Currier stepped
in from the porch, pressing a handkerchief to his tanned forehead.
The aroma of his cigar clung to his coat. Despite the dust his shoes
seemed glossy. He smiled at Martha, one corner of his mouth
creased, as she turned to climb the stairs. Below her the voices fell
one by one into a murmur. Someone's tentative laugh. The hall's
length was broken only by the dust that hung in the air, caught in
the curtained light from the window at its end. She opened the
door she had come to open so many times each day and sat on the
bed before sliding off her shoes and lying down. The last days leaning against the door to try to hear Dr Rowell's words. Nothing like.
Before. Somewhere a fly buzzed against glass, the noise of its wings
louder than the words her mother and Dr Rowell spoke while her
father, she imagined, lay between them smiling faintly at the ceiling. I am. Equipped for such. Should. Veterans. I can. Some alkaline, but. Know. Quiet. Suppose. In Littleton or maybe. Can't tell,
we. The voices paused; she did not breathe and waited for them to
resume before she pushed herself away from the door with her
fingertips and took a step down the hall, and another, until she
stood at the top of the stairs looking down at bars of sunlight slanting through a window onto the kitchen floor. And two nights ago,
her mother, stripping the sheets from this bed, had made no sound,
though once again she had listened by the door. Nothing but the
flap and rustle of cloth, feet on the floorboards. Yellowed and still
damp, the bedclothes lay bunched in the basket only moments
while her mother filled the washtub with water she would otherwise have waited a week to use. Each day the house had grown
more and more quiet until today; now the voices of those gathered
downstairs reached her in this room, their words as muddled as

those her father had spoken when he returned from the other side of the ocean. She turned her head on the pillow, looking at the dresser, the lamp, the ladderback chair where for months she had sat. Her mother had plumped the pillows as if to remove even the impression of his head. She closed her eyes. In the heat, the un-moving closed-in air, she could smell herself, her skin still warm from the sun, her sweat, her hair. Only once had she bathed since the dry spell had begun, when her mother had filled the tub half-way with wellwater. Her father had merely shaken his head, had not mentioned the cows cropping the withering grass to the roots, the milk some no longer gave. She and her mother had lifted him in first, arms and legs dangling over the sides, and then helped him out when in a quarter hour he complained of the cold. She had sat in the tub after her mother had. Dusk on an evening early in June. It will rain soon enough, her mother had said. And the well isn't dry yet. This will make us all feel better. Martha had soaked until the mosquitoes lit on her knees where they poked through water gray with soap. After that night her father allowed only the basin, and that filled with water from the river or the lake, where daily the mud at the shore grew wider. Hundreds of tiny flies hovered. Weeds stank in dark clumps. Later, she squeezed a cloth over the basin and wiped his forehead, the corners of his mouth, his neck. Listen, he said. One year there came a summer of terrible drought. No rain had fallen for weeks and the farmers believed that their crops would be ruined. Then the minister set a day for the towns-people to gather at the church and pray for rain. There was a man who lived at the edge of town, and as he was going to hitch up his horses for the ride to church he saw clouds beginning to gather. Well, he thought, it looks like rain, so I may as well stay home. And the rain came that day, enough to save the crops, though it stopped at the edge of his land, where the corn curled and shriveled, the husks pulled back from the kernels like withered lips over old teeth. Her father's own dry mouth shaped a smile. Did Charlie tell you that one? Charlie Chase told her he would write when he reached the flatlands to tell her what the country and people were like. Most of what he owned fit into two suitcases, the same two he had brought the day he had arrived at their door and her father had called her out from the kitchen to meet this awkward man, his large hand already trembling as it took hers, the skin around his watery eyes wrinkling. He told her he'd been across the country and back more than once by swinging himself onto a slow-moving train and sleeping on sacks of potatoes or between stacked lumber. Later her father told her Charlie had never been south of Carroll county. What is it like in Kansas, Charlie Chase? He set down his axe, blade by his foot and handle against his leg, and drew his handkerchief from his pocket. Twisted the end of his nose in the cloth and sniffed, then wiped one hand in the other. So many miles of nothing, flatter than you can imagine. Oh, the car I was in showed me the world only through a slat in its side and we passed through there at night. Kansas? I don't believe I went that way. He swung the axe, splitting kindling, and while she watched him he sang to the rhythm of his blows, his voice quieting when he bent to stand a new log on the block: Over the water, and over the sea, and over the ocean to my Charlie. Even when her mother had told him she could no longer pay his wages he had decided to stay, he said, until things were settled. I'm in no rush to see anywhere else. But the farmer in Putney had written that the planting season was upon him. The next day Charlie Chase herded the cows to Bill Coombs' farm, the only man her father had agreed to sell to, sixty-five dollars a head. And the following day he was gone. Still the voices carried up to her, the faint scrape of cutlery on china. Now she imagined Charlie Chase walking where grass waved by a roadside covered by the moving shadows of leaves. So somewhere a wind blew. It has a nice ring to it, she told him, folding his shirts for him so they wouldn't wrinkle in the suitcase. Putney. Don't you think? The day Charlie Chase had pumped and pumped to draw up air her mother had only watched, her dress a white shape inside the door in the day's vertical light. Then turned and vanished. Her father had said nothing for a moment when she told him. He fingered the hem of the thin blanket covering him. It will rain again someday, he said at last. Lifting the edge of the curtain, she had seen Charlie Chase squatting in the dirt, his shadow huddled at his feet and the pail filled with sunlight. Martha shifted to her side, the pillow warm under her cheek; stretched her feet out, then curled them back.

She woke to the shadow at the edge of the bed, the room's blur of darkness, a strand of hair roping her mouth. Her arm, her back damp. She leaned up on an elbow, slipped a finger below the strand and pulled it loose. Her dress had tangled around her legs, bunched at one shoulder, and as she plucked the fabric her mother spoke from the dark beside her. Have you been here this whole time? her mother asked. Didn't you know they had all come to help us through? You could at least have given them the courtesy of knowing their troubles were appreciated. They've all gone now, they all left hours ago. Don't tell me you've been sleeping. One night. Had she been sleeping? The sky lit itself every few moments. On the far hill each tree's pointed top stood out against the sky, then faded back into the horizon's dark line. Rain streamed off the edges of the roof, enclosed the house with its sound. Her mother rocked and she sat in that lap, her head leaned back into the curve of her mother's throat and chin, her mother's breath against her scalp, her mother's hands clasped around her as they counted. Five miles, four. Even if it had been pouring down buckets, she had said. The storm had climbed over the hills from Colebrook and Clarksville instead of following the river's bends. In the morning her father had come back from Baldwin's and said that on Ben Young Hill Hal Dobson's barn had burned. Until the rain had slowed to a slap and patter among leaves she had sat against her, their legs tangled. Soon you'll be too big for my lap. Her mother's hand stroked her hair. Back to sleep. For two years, the house had seemed unsafe at night. Even though Charlie Chase's wheeze sounded through the hall. Boards creaked, shifted; outside, the woods seemed too quiet. The summer he and Marshall Young, among the few who went that day the band played in Colebrook and the men, alike in their drab uniforms, marched along Main Street to Bridge Street where they boarded the train, the gathered people clutching flags and clapping, whistling—that summer had been damp and wood swelled against the nails and joints holding it in place. And some nights her mother slept at the lake. We need a cook as good as you, Mr Currier had said. We've all missed your pies this past year. You know these men have money to burn and the man who eats well will be happy to spend it here. Charlie can keep up the herd, that's all man's work anyway. And one of my boys can fetch you in the mornings and drive you back to the village most nights. I'm tired, she said. All I think about these days is sleep. Is supper ready? Charlie Chase pushed open the door from bringing in the cows, sat on the bench to unlace his boots: for two years he didn't move the other pair next to where he placed his own. He pulled out a chair. Aren't you going to wash, Charlie? On Wednesday mornings, after Charlie Chase had tended the herd, he went to Baldwin's for the paper, then after supper read it word by word, his hands inky when he folded it into a square and tipped it into the stove. There's another day, he always said. He stood over a shallow basin of water, sloshing his hands back and forth. As he creaked down the steep cellar stairs for cider, her mother asked What's the news from France?

One night. Martha was unsure if it was her mother's arm across her or if she had been already awake before her mother had slipped into her narrow bed. You're all I have, all I have left, her mother sobbed. Her mother's legs had felt hot against her own; she pressed close against her, tugging the covers loose. He'll never be back. Down the hall Charlie Chase did not wake. He may already be gone and his letters would still come for weeks before they stopped. How would we know? After supper, each night that there was a new letter, her mother would read it when the dishes had been washed and polished with a cloth to stack in the cupboard. Charlie Chase looked at the floor, or out the window, but Martha watched her mother's eyes move across the tissue-thin paper that rustled as she flipped it to read the other side. It may not even be him writing anymore, her mother said. In the morning her mother was gone to the lake already, and Charlie Chase was in the barn when she walked down the hill to school, and when, that night, Tom Currier drove her mother up in the wagon and she walked in to the table she had set, her mother said nothing but I'm tired.

There are dishes to be washed downstairs. I sent them all off before they took over my kitchen. For the little time it remains mine we'll do the washing-up ourselves. Her mother stood and walked to the door; Martha swung her feet over the edge of the bed; springs and slats creaked. Soon enough she would have dishes to wash. In the summers, and again in October and November, sports from away drove their Hudsons through town, one man leaning an arm out a window to ask the directions to the lakes. Under the stiff brims of their caps, their eyes seemed always to dart and flicker, touching everything they lighted upon. In a day or two the same cars would pass again, heading south, a bled buck strapped to the hood or the roof with loops of knotted rope. Which lake is that? Windy Williams would say, standing and scratching his stomach. I believe you're turned around somewhat. Light from the hallway slanted across the floor. Martha blinked her eyes. Stretched and pulled the bedspread's corners, smoothed a hand over rumpled sheets. Her mother stood aside as she passed through the door. The day after her father returned, he had held the door wide with one hand while she walked before him. Show me what's changed in the woods, he had said. They're the same woods, she answered. Across the pasture they had said nothing, his voice and the cast of his eyes unfamiliar. She had heard him breathing behind her as the land climbed in small folds and outcrops of granite showed through the grass. Your mother tells me you've been helping her up at Mr Currier's. A bit. Do you like the work? The tops of the spruce waved, cones dangling in clusters. It helps out. As they stepped into the trees he looked back and her eyes followed his to the cows standing on knobby legs, the house and barn amid silvery grass, the light already failing this day. He coughed and spat. Shadowed, she paused. He turned again, then looked up at her unmoving at the head of the trail. May branches still bare cast dark lace. Well, you won't have to do that anymore, he said. Sure we can find enough around here for you to do. That man would set the hills on fire if he thought he could charge people to come see the flames. The previous morning Charlie Chase had driven them to Colebrook; she and her mother stood in blue dark while he led the horses nodding in their blinders from the barn. Clarksville and Skunk Hollow passed before the sun rose above the trees and even then they kept the blankets spread over themselves. Charlie's face when he turned to talk was streaked from the corners of his narrowed eyes. Balmy, ain't it? he said, grinning. At Colebrook the train had pulled in slow, engine chanting to a stop. Its black haze blew across the river. She had missed her father at first, wondering who was the tall man in uniform walking toward them. Her mother said nothing as he and Hayes McFarland and another man from Kidderville clasped hands and parted. Charlie Chase shook his head. Only three. She watched the man from Kidderville kiss a pale woman. And then her father stood before them, stooping to her mother as if to whisper words into her hair. The train breathed hissing steam and an old man wheeled a cart across the platform. Martha's ears ached from the ride's wind. She curled her fingers around her thumbs. But now Charlie Chase laughed and punched her father's shoulder. His lips brushed the top of her head, her hair, and his arm around her waist pulled her toward him; he said words she didn't hear. Against his chest she couldn't lift her head. Hayes McFarland wore cloth wrapped around his arm and she watched his wife look from the cloth to his face and then the wall of the depot. The wife covered her eyes with one hand, her daughters a circle around her. We'd better get home, her father said. She watched the knot of women around Hayes McFarland as Charlie Chase led them to the wagon, one of her father's bags tilting him to the left. Her mother and her father looked at the platform as they walked. At the wagon Charlie Chase gave the reins to her father who gave them back to Charlie Chase. Some months later she saw Hayes McFarland again when he had driven upriver in the Model T he had bought secondhand after returning. Where the road met their pasture he stepped out, a can of gasoline in his hand, his other arm awkward at his chest. Her father had walked toward him already thin that first summer. Can't I get you some more, her mother was always asking, you've eaten just a bit. I met him only on the train ride home from Camp Devens, her father said. Didn't know we were both from up north until we'd talked a while. He is not a harmful man. Together her father and Hayes lifted the front seat cushion and she watched the back of her father's shirt ruffle as he stooped to help Hayes fill the tank. When they had replaced the cushion he slid onto the seat while Hayes cranked the motor. Charlie Chase had come beside her, one arm on the fence. Must be swapping old tales, he said, lots to remember I bet. The engine misfired; blue smoke dispersed on the breeze. But in a moment Hayes was pressing twin circles into the grass with the tires as he turned, her father waving at them as the car whined downhill in low gear. Looks like a '13 or '14, Charlie Chase said. Her father had returned on foot that evening as swallows snapped bugs and the last light left the sky. He walked straight to the barn where Charlie Chase pitched hay out of the loft; pulled a stool under himself and milked. Then helped Charlie Chase shovel out the gutters. Later, at the table, long after the dishes had been cleared and washed, he told her that he had forgotten the quiet. McFarland had asked me what it was like that last morning. He had been in the hospital then. We were driving in this car of his toward the lakes and he asked me to tell him what it was like. How absurd to shout my answer over the noise of his engine. A quiet we had never dreamed of hearing in that place, I told him. I remember leaning against the mud, waiting for the word to go over. A foot from my face, a beetle struggled up the damp wall. The artillery had ceased. The clouds were small scraps that day. No one moved, our hands tight on our rifles, all of us expecting the call at any moment. Instead we heard shouts of Fini le guerre, fini le guerre; we heard bugles. Some French soldiers threw their helmets into the air. The word came down the trench and men cast down their rifles to weep or pray and then shouting climbed out. Laughing, they shot the sky. Not long after eleven o'clock. My fingers stayed bloodless around my rifle, the bayonet I had fixed moments before. Beside me, a man staggered to his knees, weeping. Twenty yards away the Boches were packing their equipment; some of them drank beer. McFarland told me that since he's returned he has thought of little else. A week earlier and I would be in the same shape as you, he told me. I told him we were both lucky to be back, that we both have many years left to us. Every man writes the tale of his life, I told him, and holding his loose sleeve between us he said in that case he would have no tale to tell. Charlie Chase came in from the porch, setting his empty mug in the sink. Goodnight Charlie. We turned around at Happy Corner and he let me out at the bottom of the hill. And who knows what could have happened in that week, I told him. A gunner in our company was killed at nine that morning. He shook his head and did not look at me. In the hospital we had word long before you, he told me. We knew of the signing beforehand. I stepped from the car and watched it vanish around a bend though I heard the sound of his engine for a long time through the trees before the river washed it away. He is not a harmful man. He says that with his pension he'll hire someone to work his fields. Next time, he says, he'll let me drive. Her father's hand rested motionless on the table, each curled finger's shadow waving over the cloth as the wick burned down. For long minutes they sat silent. The lamp flickered out and he made no move to fill it. Across the table from her his body was a blur of shadow. His voice spoke on a long breath. And all I have to tell of myself is eighteen months apart from everything I've known. Who will remember that? His chair scraped back across the floor and his dark form rose against the lighter wall; the trace he left in the air, scented of the barn's weedy hay, leather, warm skin, swept him from the room and his feet took the stairs in twos.

The water in the sink had stood two days. Cool, it coated Martha's hands and wrists like oil as she slipped the plates under, circling their faces with a cloth. These are clean enough to be wiped, her mother said behind her, stacking saucers dusted with cakecrumbs. His boots had kept the creases years of wear had worn into them, the wrinkles and folds where, stooping in snow gone slushy, he had unhinged a trap and lifted a limp fox into a sack. Where, following the loops his own feet had worn through the woods, branches had carved welts in the leather. One morning she had taken the bootstraps in her fingers and moved them a bit. When Charlie Chase came in from the evening milking, sighing as he bent forward to untie his laces and then slowly kicking his own boots off, she watched him, but neither he nor her mother seemed to notice; nor when a few days later she arranged them in their original position. Her mother had offered to Charlie Chase his shirts, but he had taken only one with him to Putney, draping its sleeves along his arms, the cuffs loose over his wrists. He had been a tall man. You don't want a man you must always look in the eye, her mother had once said in the kitchen at the lodge. Dough spread wide under her hands which heeled it back into a ball. Flour ringed the board. Her mother swiped her cheek with the knob of a bent wrist. Would you pull this back, her mother asked, puffing air up from cornered lips, and Martha reached to replace the loose hair behind her mother's ear. Saturdays and some nights it was stories, two years of stories while Charlie Chase whittled and swept curled scraps into the stove, pretending not to listen. I had never considered anyone else, her mother said. After him, how could I have? My mother would have sold me to the Indians if I'd let him get away. And when father heard he was a ten cord man. But he was shy. His clumsy hands raw and needled from the woods holding out a doily for me, his first gift. I imagine his mother or one of his sisters made it. He was not like the other men who worked the camps to escape women or lawmen or both, who spent their week's pay on Saturday night and passed Sunday bedded in shacks like sick animals. He told me it was the quiet of the woodlot he loved. Only axes and wind high in the spruce, a man shouting and each tree's ripping fall. The horses snorting as they twitched the logs to the yard. But even then he knew he would take over the farm. If I keep working this it will get so stiff we'll need his old saw to cut it. Her mother balled and patted the dough between two palms, spun it in the bowl's oil, and draped a cloth over it. Martha lifted a dripping plate to the drainboard. Under the water her hands found another. At the lodge she had stood before a sink of heated water, her mother and the other girl bringing to her so many plates she believed it must be more than a dozen men around the dining tables. You won't have to do that anymore, he said. Do they breed all the girls so pretty here? Come away with me and you won't have to do that anymore. We need another plate, Mrs Currier said at the doorway, have you fallen asleep back here? And her mother pressed beside her as she woke, her hands like mice on her skin. He is dead I know it. The sink was empty; searching, her fingers gathered up only water that ran down her wrists to her elbows. Behind her, her mother said There may be some sandwiches left if you're hungry. I'm going to bed. Be sure to clean these here too. When she turned her head, her mother was already gone. At the lodge, the young man had skulked by the kitchen door all morning as if he wanted to cadge a bite. Washing, Martha could see him among the trees, scuffing toes at the ground. On the step she swung dirty dishwater in a vanishing arc, trying to hit the nearest tree, and from where he stood some yards away he appeared not to notice her. Water slapped packed dirt. Saturdays in hunting season, her mother had said, just to do the washing up he'll pay fifty cents and you can take your dinner after they've all eaten. Her mother and Mrs Currier had gone down cellar to count jars. And when she shouldered open the door, another tub of water in both hands, the young man now leaned against the wall and under his hat his eyes skimmed quickly over her and into the kitchen behind before returning to the tops of his boots. His hands clutched something dark and shapeless, and thrust it toward her. Here. His voice unexpected, a fish jump- ing and all she saw were ripples. She poured the water out slow; drops spotted the hem of her dress. In one hand she held the tub and with the other took the pelt from him, a tiny shriveled paw and his finger brushing hers. Have your mother make you some mittens with it, he said. And as if they had been hiding behind trees four men appeared, shotguns broken over their crooked arms. Look here, one said. Ready for another hand of cards, or are you otherwise engaged? Martha stuffed the furry strip into the apron's pocket and let the door swing shut. Behind it, laughter. With a clean cloth she wiped the breakfast dishes dry. These men can't be trusted, her mother had said, if anyone gives you trouble let me know and I'll give him holy-old hell. On the steep stairs to the cellar she heard her mother's voice and Mrs Currier's, rising; their feet scuffing the rough planks. And she had not seen him since. The pelt, wrapped in a piece of calico and hidden in a drawer, she had shown no one.

She let the water on her hands and wrists dry in the air, waving them to cool her skin; plucked at the neck of her dress where the fabric was stuck to her. She did not drain the sink. Upstairs there was no sound. She carried the lamp from the drainboard to the table and, wide awake now, pulled out her chair. Only nine months ago she had risen one night for water, and coming down the stairs had heard her father's voice, and Charlie Chase's, the low rhythm of murmur and pause: they sat here in pushed-back chairs, Charlie Chase rocking his on its two back legs, his hands clasped behind his head, and her father slouched forward holding a mug of cider with both hands. A pitcher stood in the middle of the table beside a sheet of paper covered with numbers and crossed-out numbers in her father's cramped hand. Hello dear, Charlie Chase had said as she turned the corner; her father looked up at her and then back down at the tabletop. He rubbed his eyes with his fingertips. Can't you sleep? I wanted some water. Charlie Chase leaned forward and the chair legs tapped the floor. While she drew a glass and drank it neither man spoke a word. Only as her feet made the risers creak had she heard their voices resume, indistinct. In the morning, Martha knew, Mr Currier's sons would bring the wagon for another load, her mother watching as they tipped up the sideboard and lifted it through the doorway. They would hoist this table sideways, gripping the legs and turning it to fit it around corners. And they would refuse the water her mother offered them while she refused their refusals and all the while the glasses she had filled as they worked caught the sunlight. Peeling potatoes one Saturday morning for the men's dinner, Martha heard footsteps in the hall and they came into the long kitchen where pots and pans hung in rows and a dozen knives stuck out of a block of dark wood. A pail filled with moist skins at her feet and, on the table, an enamel pot of yellow potatoes, holes where she had carved out eyes. Your father's a brave man, Tom Currier said. She dropped a curled peel into the pail. I suppose so. Wish I was older, he said. But my father says it won't last the winter. Frank Currier leaned his elbows on the counter and lifted his feet from the floor, scraping his boots against the cupboard doors; she would have to clean the scuffs before Mrs Currier returned. She turned the potato in her hand. The blade rasped over the skin. What are you doing with them potatoes, Frank Currier said. I'm getting hungry. When they knocked at the side door tomorrow she would let them in, their heads bowed, their feet banging against each other's or the table legs. Hello. Their eyes would not meet and a silence would befall them. Her mother would set on the table a plate of leftover cookies someone else had baked and they would take only one each. And she would sit here watching as they cradled boxes and backed through the door, a cat flicking its tail in the shade beneath the wagon they carried them to. In the circle of wavering light she unfolded one of the sheets of paper she had for weeks now carried with her. Marvoisin, Belleau,

Givry. Columbia, Colebrook, Beecher Falls, Bungy, Clarksville, Pittsburg; the woods, the river, the lakes. Her mother said that at night, at the lake, there was no sound but the loons and the wind through the trees. Some cloudy summer nights, she said, men would row out into the lake and from the shore you could watch the tips of their cigarettes shrink into all that dark until they faded completely and the only sign of them would be the splash of an oar, a rusty oarlock creaking, a man's curt oath—these sounds drifting back so that it was impossible to tell if the men were twenty or two hundred yards away. And why do you think he's so pleased to be up there, on Second Lake? Where there's no one else but the timber company? her father said one night. They all sat around the table, then: her father in his place to her left, her mother across from her, Charlie Chase to her right. The food, centered between them, steamed. Charlie Chase did not look up from the roast and the boiled carrots and turnips he cut with the edge of his fork; Martha let the meat's strands soften in her mouth while she glanced from Charlie Chase to the smears of gravy on her plate, tiny beads of fat shining. It's the nicest spot on the lake, her mother said. Her father set down his tea. Yes, the nicest spot. And the closest to Canada, and the most secluded. How do you think he can afford to pay her fifty cents to wash a morning's dishes when men working dawn to dusk in the woods bring home thirty-five dollars a month? He coughed then, a husky chant. Charlie Chase lopped the lump of butter with his knife and smoothed it over his vegetables. I'm glad to see someone has an appetite, her mother said. Martha chewed again and swallowed; a thread of meat caught between two teeth and she worked it with her tongue. There was no one else to take me on, do you understand? Without you we needed the money. And then for weeks she had carried his dinner to him on a tray, sat by the bed while he lifted the fork to his mouth, and carried it back downstairs to the kitchen where her mother, wiping the counter with a rag, would say Is that all? At the table, she and her mother and Charlie Chase sat in their habitual places and in silence broken only by the scrape of cutlery on the plates listened to his coughs, until her mother pushed back her chair, went into the pantry and then up the stairs with a glass of water. Charlie Chase would look up at her. This pork chop sure tastes good but I can't wait for some of that pie. Upstairs a door opened and closed. Me too. The woods, the river, the lakes. The farm. The lodge. But you never let me finish my story. Which story? Not knowing what else to do, the farmer paddled his log toward where the village had been before the flood had drowned the houses. For seven days and seven nights he circled above the chimney-tops that stuck only inches above the muddy water. On the eighth morning the earth began to swallow the waters, and here and there the roof of a tall house poked above the surface. The farmer lashed his log to a chimney and climbed onto a peak; by noon he sat at the edge of the roof, dipping his feet in, and when, the next morning, he woke, stiff from sleeping curled against the chimney, he saw that the waters were gone. He climbed down the side of the house, where the tree he had cut now hung, and walked through the town. He knocked at every door, but there was never an answer, and finally pushing one door open he hunted from room to room of an empty house, where now there was only mud and green weeds like tangled hair. In what was once a bedroom, he kneeled beside a ruined frame and a mattress leaking water and began to pray that his wife and children were safe. He thought that he spoke only in his head, but then realized that he was crying, saying the words aloud, and that they echoed in the abandoned rooms of the strange house. And the echoes were the only answer. Then feet creaked on the stairs. He turned and rose from the bed, thinking that somehow his prayers had been heard, that he would find his wife and children climbing the stairs toward him. What are you saying? Her mother stood on the bottom step behind her, squinting slightly in the lamp's dim light. Who are you talking to? Martha turned toward her. Oh, her mother said. Here. Her mother came across the floor and put her arms around her, warmth rising from the neck of her nightgown as she bent forward; against her mother's loose hair her face felt wet. Shhh. Here, now. Come to bed.

Mr Ephraim Currier, of Lowell, Massachusetts, raised the frame of the lodge he named Idlewild on a gentle slope overlooking the Second Connecticut Lake in three months. That summer, 1893, ignoring the beginnings of his home city's severe economic crisis, he hired any boy he could distract from farming the fields around Pittsburg village or milking his father's Guernseys and Holsteins to saw planks and carry stones and mix mortar while the Italian and Portuguese and French-Canadian carpenters and masons he had brought with him from Lowell nailed joists and laid the foundation and men from the village rode up from the valley before dark to watch each day's progress. Currier and his workmen and their caravan of wagons had arrived unannounced one afternoon as May faded into June, the leaves and pastures as green as they would be that year, and, as boys ran from farmhouse to barn to Baldwin's general store telling that wagons were coming along the River Road from West Stewartstown, by the time they drove through the center of town men had long been assembled on Baldwin's porch, or leaned against fenceposts and on shovels; women watched from doorways and windows, and children and dogs galloped in the wagons' dusty wake. The workmen, sitting on bundles of tools, bouncing and swaying as the wheels caught ruts, waved as they passed the villagers, but the wagons did not stop until they had reached Second Lake, as one farmer who followed them on horse later reported. By nightfall every household from Clarksville to Beecher Falls to Back Lake had heard of the men in the wagons, though no one knew their intentions.

Every foot of Second Lake's shore, and much of the undeveloped country for miles around it—north to the border with Québec and east into Maine's Oxford county—had been, almost since the days when the territory was claimed by both the United

States and Canada, the property of the St. Alban Paper Company, but with the earnings of his textile mills on the Merrimack River Currier had persuaded the Company to sell him twenty acres, six of them waterfront, along with the promise that no other land on the lake would be sold to any interest but timber. In addition to the undisclosed purchase price, Currier agreed to blaze an access road from the highway, then little more than a cart track at its northern terminus, to the shore of Second Lake, and every board foot he cleared after his lodge was standing he had guaranteed to St. Alban's logging teams. It was only in the early years of the next century that anyone in Pittsburg learned that Mr Jacob Wainscott, who married the heiress of St. Alban and later became its president, had been a classmate of Currier's at Harvard, and that neither he nor his wife had ever set foot on this tract of their company's land. Until the early 1920s, when the Wainscotts sold the St. Alban Paper Company and all its assets and holdings to The Everett Company—a group of private investors and land speculators from Boston, who in turn sold the land around Second Lake in parcels to several smaller timber companies prior to the Depression—little of the timber on St. Alban's lands was ever cut, most of the logging in Pittsburg at that time centering around First Lake and Perry Stream, on lands owned by the Connecticut River Lumber Company.

All summer, the workmen fought the blackflies hovering around their faces and crawling behind their ears and under collars, the horseflies that would leave a welt the size of a quarter, the mosquitoes that found the backs of their necks, their ankles, their wrists. Early mornings, when the men stepped barefoot out of their tents onto damp grass, mist floated over the lake, lifting in shreds and scraps to reveal the dark water. Hidden loons wailed and laughed, and later, when the sun had burnt through the haze, the men would see them near the middle of the lake, only their dark heads and necks visible from shore before they dove, disappearing for minutes at a time and surfacing far from where they had vanished. Currier stood in the shade with his foreman and, over a stump still bleeding pitch, spread the plans a Boston architect had drawn. Occasionally he shared in some of the work—spending an afternoon helping to dig the foundation or to carry wall studs and end girts, since, despite his strength, he was clumsy with most tools—and at these times the men felt some of his urgency, and hammer blows echoed across the lake. By August's end, when the grass shone with frost some mornings and the swamp maples had begun to turn crimson, the glaziers had installed every one of the four-hundred and forty-eight panes in the lodge's fifty-six windows; the painters had whitewashed the new clapboards and limned every sash and porch rail and the soffit and fascia boards the dark red Currier had chosen to recall his home city's brick; the roofers had nailed down the shingles; and smoke lifted from the three chimneys at night. At the edges of torn earth stunted fir thrust spiky branches toward the sky that had been opened above them. Wind blowing through the maples' curling leaves sounded, to the workmen dreaming of home, like rain.

The interior was still rude, with only rough flooring in place and no finishwork, but by the end of the next year oak paneling had been installed in the sitting room, stoves and furniture shipped to West Stewartstown station before being hauled overland, glass-front cabinets put in the kitchen and pantry, and every room plastered and painted. Currier hung, on the wall above the head of the dining room table, an oil portrait of himself—a commission by a minor artist then briefly popular for his paintings of Massachusetts society—outfitted in breeches and hunting jacket and posed lifting a limp pheasant in a dusky woodland. For three-quarters of an hour, two servants nudged and repositioned its corners until Currier, several paces across the room, was satisfied that the heavy gilt frame was perfectly level.

Despite its remote location and hurried construction, Idlewild, with its clapboard siding, steeply pitched roof, and great central chimney and smaller chimneys at either end, was a fine example of the New England Colonial style, and though the lodge was a rustic cabin compared to Currier's home in the Belvidere district of Lowell, still it was far grander than most farmhouses north of Littleton. Its dining room could accommodate quite comfortably some thirty people; upstairs, a narrow hall gave onto a master bedroom suite and seven other bedrooms; a separate stair from the kitchen led to a servants' quarters. From Idlewild's front porch one looked across a sloping lawn to the lake's unbroken blue, the far shore a tangle of spruce and fern and laurel from which Camel's Hump rose to the northeast, at the boundary with Maine.

For several years Currier came to the lake at the end of April, when ice still floated in the water and before the last snow had melted from the north-facing hillsides and sheltered hollows in the woods, to open the lodge for the season and repair whatever damage winter storms had caused, and each time he brought with him servants and cooks, handymen and drivers, and apparently so many supplies and provisions that his servants would appear in Baldwin's store but once every week or two, their suits damp and wrinkled, their cuffs and shoes dusty. Throughout the summer months he returned for weeks at a time and it was during these visits that the people of Pittsburg village observed that he was not the bachelor they had at first believed but a husband and a father, though few of them saw his decidedly younger wife nor his children save the local men he occasionally hired to guide him into the deep woods toward Mount Magalloway—not to hunt, for he usually carried no gun, but simply to learn, he told them, the deer trails and old Indian paths that crossed the brooks and bogs and ridges. The pale and silent son Currier had fathered in his forty-second year accompanied his father on these excursions at Currier's request, though as they forded streams still nearly snow-cold and slapped the blackflies drawn to their sweat it was clear to the guides that the son would rather have stayed at the lodge with his mother and sisters, or, perhaps, remained in Lowell for the summer.

Sometime during October's smoky beginning Currier rode in on the stage from West Stewartstown, accompanied by a half dozen other men—managers at his mills, newspapermen, municipal officials—outfitted in wool jackets and trousers, peering at this new and unknown countryside while he pointed out its landmarks. Currier again hired guides, though now he and the men he had brought with him carried shotguns and rifles, some of them never before fired. But Currier proved to be a better marksman than his guides would have guessed, and each fall grew more skilled at stalking and tracking his quarry. When he and his companions retreated south for the winter, closing shutters over Idlewild's windows, locking its doors and carrying with them anything perishable, the men who had steered them through the woods would return to their homes after two weeks with less money than Currier had offered them; with tales of his shrewdness at cards, of the whisky they said Currier drank with every meal; with the furs of the bear, moose, marten, and lynx Currier and his associates had killed and left for carrion once they had hacked off the heads, telling each other that they would properly decorate the walls of Idlewild's sitting room, though their attempts at taxidermy mainly failed and one of the guides, walking past the lodge months later, would see a whitened jaw or a skull still bearing a few scraps of flesh that the snow cover had preserved.

The reason why Currier chose such a remote location for his summer retreat, a place neither fashionable nor accessible, was the subject of a great amount of discussion not only in Pittsburg but also in Lowell, where the other successful families were more likely to build summer cottages in Newport or along Massachusetts's rocky north shore. But by the end of the nineteenth century, the once prosperous textile mills in Lowell and Lawrence were already beginning their slow decline that would last decades and eventually see the industry depart for the south, where the workers were less organized, and where cotton fields surrounded the mills. Already, competition from the huge Amoskeag mill upstream on the Merrimack, in Manchester, and from mills in places such as Fall River and New Bedford—located, more conveniently than Lowell, on shipping routes—had diminished Lowell's importance as a textile city. After the departure of the skilled labor during the Civil War years, during which the mills closed their doors, and the arrival of the immigrant workers who worked longer hours for less pay, a series of strikes and lockouts hampered manufacture. From 1867 to 1884 there were at least four major strikes, and by 1893 the economic depression had caused all the mills to drop production to half-time; now, formerly contentious employees were satisfied to have any wage at all, though mill owners' profits suffered as well. Currier, despite the immense expenses he incurred in building Idlewild, was still largely immune to hardship during these years.

Indeed, the villagers often saw mysterious crates and parcels being driven on the stage toward Second Lake, and occasionally Currier himself appeared at the post office, whistling happily off-key, to receive such parcels—their unknown contents the subject of that afternoon's talk in the village—from the counter clerk. Nevertheless, perceptive to changes in the business, Currier may have planned to shift his assets into the timber industry, which had yet to reach its peak, and perhaps saw Idlewild not as a summer home but as one that would become permanent as the focus of his endeavors moved northward.

As the turn of the century neared, Currier's autumn visits to Idlewild, without the company of his family, became longer, and each year he brought with him more and more men. His local guides, when their employer had left for winter, often departing in a sledge rather than a wagon, now told stories about the two- or three-week long hunts into the wild country toward Parmachenee and Kennebago lakes, past Hellgate Falls to the Dead Diamond River, crossing and recrossing the border with Maine, or up into the highlands north of Idlewild, the ridge of hills that separates the basins of the St. Lawrence and Connecticut rivers, into Québec and back depending on where Currier's urges led him. Hip-deep in a cedar and tamarack bog, Currier and his companions all turned and fired at a bull moose startled by the noise of their passing, the meat so full of lead that two nights later men spat shot into the campfire as they ate it. Currier was said to have challenged his companions to wrestling matches, both men stripped naked on the dry earth under a stand of fir, needles and dirt clinging to their skin as they rolled and grappled, and when it became clear to the other men that Currier could rarely be beaten and then usually only when he had just wrestled and was still slick and cut, welts from roots and rocks across his shoulders and back and chest, he began to offer wagers to them—twenty dollars if a man could bring him to both knees, fifty if he could pin him—and while Currier would sometimes lose money this way, the gambles made him fight with even less regard for his person, so that he and his opponent both finished the match bleeding and bruised, panting heavily as they cursed and bent to pull on their trousers. One October one of Currier's friends brought with him several dogs, not pointers or hounds for hunting with but muscled terriers bred for fighting, and Currier hung fresh flanks of venison or moose from a tree to watch the dogs leap and tear at it, clutching the bone in jaws Currier's friend claimed could snap a man's leg in half. Nights in the camp as embers wafted above shifting logs, or around a table in Idlewild's sitting room, Currier hosted card games, and it was said that whether he was using his own deck or one he had neither seen nor touched he was so skilled not only at playing but at cheating that in a round of five card draw he ended up with eight or nine cards in his hand though no one else noticed, and knew at least two of the cards everyone else at the table held. The stakes increased from one night to the next and one of Currier's floor managers, gone bust double or quits, ended up working at half salary for one year to repay an evening's debt. Soon few of the villagers agreed to serve as guides, telling Currier that even at his wages they could not afford to spend a month or six weeks in the woods, that they had too much work at their farms—though soon Currier needed no guides, knowing the land nearly as well as some men who had lived on it all their lives.

In 1897, Currier wintered at Idlewild, and though his wife and children stayed in Lowell, the villagers began to realize that the Currier family would add its name to the local registers. Most of Pittsburg's inhabitants were men and women originally from northern New Hampshire and Vermont, or from various points in Maine, and everything from Currier's speech to his manner to his dress made them suspicious of him, as did his wealth, which they felt was unearned given that they never saw him work. The stories that began to circulate during this time only heightened the villagers' sense of his difference, and even though he likely knew what the general opinion of him was in the Connecticut Lakes region, he did little to ease the villagers' doubts—rather, he seemed content to let various stories drift downriver from the plot he had carved into the woods on Second Lake, and though while his family was with him he made brief public appearances in the village, at the Methodist church or Baldwin's store, the times he passed in Idlewild without them he made no effort at such mannerly gestures and played host to any number of rabid and extravagant events. Though even in Lowell he had been known as a reckless and rather untamed man who had bought his way into textiles with an unknown source of capital and whose volatile and unconventional business practices— refusing to lock out his mill's weavers and creeler-boys during the 1884 strike while at the same time resisting the unions' demands for the ten-hour day—had caused among the older, more conservative owners of other mills such as Boott and Hamilton and Middlesex as well as among his own shareholders some degree of concern, still he was regarded as a member of society and had been on intimate terms with mayor Pickman and many other notables.

The following spring, Currier's wife and children joined him in Pittsburg, and the family retired to the lodge and was seen only infrequently during the months of May and June. During this period of Currier's life, he had very few dealings with the men and women of Pittsburg, and was visited by few who later offered recollections of this time, so it was only when his son returned north in 1906 that the villagers learned that in 1899 Currier had sold his mills for little more than he had paid for them nearly twenty-five years earlier. As the century ended, the villagers simply knew that the Curriers returned to Lowell only for brief intervals; that, even in the presence of his family, Currier still went into the woods for several weeks with those men who had made it a habit to travel to Idlewild each fall. Hunters and trappers from Pittsburg or Clarksville or Errol encountered Currier and his retinue, unwashed and wild, butchering a moose they had killed in the Magalloway valley or scouting along the Diamond Range or ringing a bonfire while one man dealt cards upon an overturned rock. The single incident of those years that most villagers were able to recall later occurred during the spring of 1900, when Currier's wife came to Pittsburg village, her two daughters and son riding in the wagon one of Currier's servants drove, to ask for help in locating her missing husband, who had, she said, departed four days ago for the afternoon and not returned since. A dozen men from town—taking pity on her frantic dishevelment—rode out to the lodge in wagons and on horses and set off into the woods where Mrs Currier told them her husband had gone. In twelve hours they had found him sitting alone by Smith Brook under a lean-to of branches and heaped leaves and spruce boughs. His shirt, ripped into rags, was scattered across the ground, and his bare arms and shoulders were scratched and muddied. As they approached, he stood up and asked them if they had brought any whisky, and then agreed to return to Idlewild with them when they told him of his wife's worries, though those who observed him said that he did not appear drunk or disoriented or confused.

Ephraim Currier died on August 17, 1901, aged fifty-seven years, apparently the victim of a sudden stroke that felled him as he mounted the stairs, and once again the villagers would have had no news of it but for the wagon passing by their farms the next morning, Mrs Currier wearing a black veil no one knew how she had obtained, her face behind it nearly invisible, the children sullen and unmoving but for the jostling of the wagon as they looked out over the rising fields and pastures and fir trees, and the body housed already in a temporary rough coffin one of Currier's handymen had fashioned overnight. By the week's end Currier's servants had closed the lodge and departed themselves. For five years, Idlewild lay vacant, disturbed only by hunters, who, finding themselves caught in an early storm, climbed in through a ground-floor window a branch had broken to shelter in the still-furnished rooms while snow buried the dead grass, or even to build a fire in the woodstove and spread wet clothes on the hearth and, perhaps, given the stories of Currier's amazing wealth, to search through the mahogany desk or the master bedroom closet for a stash of money. Instead of coins or bills they found only folded maps and notes and letters still sealed with wax and crates of leatherbound books. Young men from town climbed onto the porch roof where they forced open a window and on their bellies slid over the sill into the bedroom of Currier's eldest daughter to steal the strange and lacy garments secreted in a chest of drawers as gifts for their own sweethearts. Bears clawed the front door, carving deep white gouges in the wood. Winds worked shutters loose and slammed them against the clapboards, and the sound carried across the lake. Ice dams along the edges of the roof at winter's end forced water through the shingles and into the ceilings of the second-floor rooms, where it seeped through sagging plaster in brown blotches. Summers, swallows nested under the eaves and in the three chimneys. Paint ten years old buckled, blistered, chipped, peeled. Grass grew tall, competing with the maple and spruce seedlings that had taken root, and which, in 1906, when Currier's son returned to Idlewild, stood waist-high between the porch and the shore. As the weather turned colder, lazy farmers drove a wagon to Currier's woodpile and carted as much of it as they could back to the village until, after two or three years, only a scattering of half-rotted logs overgrown with grass remained.

That Currier's son—Phillip Currier, though at first none of them remembered his name from the summers he had spent at the lake, and, when they had learned it again, even when he had lived among them nearly as long as his father had, still would not speak it except in his presence, referring to him instead as Mr Currier's boy or Currier's son, himself not earning the right to be called Mr Currier until the days when he achieved his own degree of prosperity and so surpassed that of his father—returned to Idlewild, not only to re-establish ownership of belongings and land which the villagers had considered abandoned and therefore free for the taking, not only to gaze once more upon the site of his father's last turbulent years and perhaps to reconsider his own recollections of the place and the man, but to bring his own wife, and to restore and inhabit the lodge which in its brief five years of untenancy had suffered a decrepitude far swifter and more extensive than many of the village's elderly, surprised and confounded those villagers who remembered him, anemic, close-mouthed, scratched by burrs and branches on the rambles for which his father drafted him during their first years at the lake. That he, admittedly a tall man now, with shoulders and arms sturdier than those they would have imagined the boy would grow into, but still to them forever a boy on the cusp of an unattainable manhood, stamped with the sooty mark of the city he had been born into and raised in, dressed in clothes they could never have afforded and would very likely not have worn had they been able to afford them, had returned with a wife to the edge of the woods was another thing entirely, and, following his arrival, as had happened with his father, speculation began from supper table to fencepost to the woodstove at Baldwin's store, rumors that his father's wealth had been gambled away during his father's last years, the decades-long run of luck inevitably souring, or that the neglected lodge was all the son had inherited from the father, or that Currier had discovered that this son so unlike him in temperament was actually not his son and had disowned him. In any of these rumors may have existed some measure of truth save the last, for soon after his return the villagers began to realize that Phillip Currier was indeed the equal of his father, if not in strength and stature then in shrewdness and force of will.

What he told them was simply that he had had enough of the city life and that among his childhood memories those fondest to him were of the times he had spent at Idlewild, and if the villagers doubted him they said little, nodding and looking anywhere but his eyes as he spoke. Impossibly, he brought with him no workmen as his father had, no tools or supplies, nothing but his wife and the half-dozen bags and chests which the stage had carried from West Stewartstown, and it was in Baldwin's store—while he selected nails and a claw hammer, a hacksaw and an axe, bundles of shingles—that he announced his intention to restore the lodge himself. He might hire a helper, a handyman, he added, someone to assist with those jobs a single man, no matter how proficient, could not do alone, and though ultimately several men from Pittsburg village did receive contracts for certain jobs at Idlewild, Currier completed most of the work himself, pitching a tent on the lawn he had cleared of saplings and weeds his first days back, and, much like the Portuguese and French-Canadians who had built the lodge some thirteen years before, working as long as the sun gave light for his labor. His wife stayed in the village, renting a room at Young's hotel where by October's end Currier joined her, riding the horse he bought from a farmer out to the lake to work each day the weather held. Among themselves, the circle of loiterers at Baldwin's store gave Currier until the first hard snow to retreat south, but he surprised them by staying through the winter, attending the Methodist services with his wife and by all appearances resolved to stay whether the village would have him or no. Before the ground had thawed he was riding back to Second Lake each morning, building fires to keep warm and working inside, replacing floorboards where snow had drifted through a broken window, re-plastering buckled walls and ceilings, and though no one could guess how, in his brief absence from the village, he who had certainly never had need to learn or practice them had acquired such skills, the work was deemed of a fine quality by those who inspected it later that summer, rowing close to shore or gathering blackberries within sight of the lodge, while Currier climbed a ladder propped against the clapboards to scrape and paint the walls.

Nearly fourteen years to the day that his father had first opened Idlewild, and nearly six years to the day of his father's death, Currier's renovations seemed nearly complete, the great house restored to a near duplicate of its former appearance to those who had seen it through trees or from the lake, smoke lifting from its three chimneys, its clapboards the clean white they remembered, every window reflecting the sky. Maples along the shore had been red a week under pewter clouds that had blown in from the north and seemed to hang unmoving. Currier hired a farmer to drive him and his wife and their few belongings from Young's to the lake, and on his return the farmer predicted to any who would listen that the couple, young and childless, citybred and inexperienced, would not last the winter in the lodge's isolation, that they would either make it to the village at some point, having burned all their wood or eaten all their pantry, or that they would be found somewhere along the road come spring. And again Currier, whether he was ignorant of them or determined to prove them wrong, defied all of the villagers' predictions by sledging to town occasionally, buying more lumber or nails or plaster or attending services with his wife, and then vanishing into the snow for another month before he would be seen, bundled in an overcoat and scarf, a cap pulled low over his reddening face, driving the sledge back. By spring, the second since Currier's return to the north, the villagers were accustomed to the irregular appearances of Currier and his wife as they had become accustomed to those of Currier's father, though now it was apparent from Mrs Currier's appearance that the couple would be childless only a short time longer. During that following summer, when Currier's wife bore him the first of two sons, wagons again passed through the village on their way to Second Lake, some of them containing boxes and crates, and others furniture, all of which the villagers believed was most likely the couple's belongings from the city being sent north, and which they took to mean that the couple—or family, now, they corrected themselves—was perhaps settling on Second Lake indefinitely. What no one expected were the groups of strange men, flatlanders by their look and dress, who passed through the village that fall, north, on the stage or on horse and once, memorably, in a Model T Ford, the first automobile many of the villagers had ever seen and perhaps the only car, with its high clearance and light weight, that could have managed the rutted road to the lakes and the corduroys of logs that covered its low spots. In their appearance and manner and their speech as well these men recalled those whom Ephraim Currier had brought north with him from Lowell a decade earlier, the municipal officials and bureaucrats and businessmen, though if the villagers had known how to distinguish between an upper-class city man and a middle-class one, they would have realized that these men passing by Baldwin's store and the town hall and the schoolhouse and the pastures and Young's hotel were less prosperous than the associates of Currier's father. But to them, all of the men who had followed either of the Curriers to their village, as well as the Curriers themselves, were one and the same: more foreign than the men and women and children who lived a day's ride north and spoke a language they did not understand. Currier hired several villagers, still dubious and hesitant after the memories of his father, as guides, and the woods around Second Lake again echoed with gunfire. But it was soon apparent that these city men were not known to Currier any more than they were to the villagers, and it was about that time that the villagers learned that during the winter he spent at the lodge with his wife as well as the following spring and summer, that even as his wife lay—attended by a midwife and Dr Rowell from Colebrook and several female relatives from Massachusetts—in the same double bed where Ephraim had been laid to await the construction of the temporary coffin which would carry him from the north for the last time, Currier had engaged in further renovations to the lodge's

interior, putting up walls, adding doors, so that now Idlewild's upstairs hall gave onto the remodeled master bedroom suite as well
as ten small rooms, each with a pair of narrow beds or bunks and
a washstand between, the windows overlooking either the lake's
wrinkled surface or dark spruce woods—the waters abounding
with lake and rainbow trout, the woods home to black bear, moose,
deer, and innumerable smaller animals and game birds, and the
altitude and healthful climate such that hay fever was unknown
here, according to the two-column-inch advertisement Currier
took out in the *Lowell Sun*, the advertisement running twice a
week from May to September, 1908, by which time the lodge was
nearly booked through hunting season. David Young and two of
his brothers, all of them part owners of Young's hotel, rode out to
the lodge one afternoon to speak with Currier, but as soon as it
was obvious to them that he intended no competition with their
business, that his own would be largely seasonal, that his guests
would all be coming from out of state, and that he would happily
recommend their establishment to any of his guests seeking lodgings closer to the village or when his own rooms were filled, they
departed. Currier offered to purchase the baked goods of various
women his wife knew through the church, and made a contract for
milk and butter with Bill Coombs, and hired several men to serve
as guides to the city men who'd as likely fired a gun as not before
they arrived at his lodge, and paid Windy Williams to deliver his
mail from the post office, and during the busy weeks would bring in
girls from the village to cook and clean under his wife's eye, so that
soon the money the city men brought with them was circulating
throughout Pittsburg village, and despite their complaints about
the foreigners' rudeness when they stopped at Baldwin's store to
ask directions or buy a Coca-Cola or a Mission Orange tonic, or
their worries about the habits and beliefs these outsiders would
bring with them, the villagers began to accept his presence, as well
as that of his restored and converted lodge, though he would never
be anything but an outsider himself.

Within two years, two men from the village had built competing lodges, The Glen and Camp Otter, on First Lake—both
of them on the lake's north shore, both of them only half as far

to town as Idlewild. Following Currier's lead, these men bought advertisements in various newspapers from Hartford to Springfield to Boston to Portland, and so almost overnight an area which had been something of a secret as a resort for sportsmen—most of them instead preferring the grander hotels at Vermont's Lake Memphremagog, or further south in the more impressive setting of the White Mountains—began to draw travelers from southern New England and even the lower Hudson valley. By the time President Wilson asked congress to declare war on Germany in 1917, and so put a brief, temporary halt to further construction in the Connecticut Lakes region, several smaller lodges had been erected on Back Lake, and the villagers had become inured to the annual autumnal procession of Fords and Nashes and Hudsons passing north along Main Street, and the extra stage that had to be hired to bring men in from the train station.

Given the terms of the agreement his father had arranged with St. Alban for the deed to the twenty acres upon which Idlewild stood, Currier's business did not suffer much since on First Lake and Back Lake the cabins and lodges were beginning to crowd one another and he could advertise his lodge as the village's first and still its most pristine remnant of the Abenakis' old hunting grounds. But in the years immediately following the war and after the passage of the Volstead Act, rumors began in the village that Currier was using his secluded location for various additional and covert business ventures, renting his barn and cellar to the men crossing into Québec and importing unmarked crates from Sherbrooke. Though few in the village would have opposed such actions, if substantiated, for their morality or legality, some of them resented the fact that once again an outsider had shown more foresight than they had in developing a network of enterprise in their own country, while others resented the attention such rumors would inevitably attract to their own affairs and the increased scrutiny they too would have to endure, and still others resented the presence of the Packards and Hudsons driving through the village, sometimes at sixty miles an hour where the road flattened out along the river, either for their noise and nuisance or the flaunting of wealth in a place where most people still drove wagons. Whatever the actual reasons, Currier was successful enough in the 1920s that he was able to raise Idlewild's rates to a level significantly above those at The Glen or Camp Otter or any of the smaller lodges, and began to attract a different clientele than he had previously, the middle-class hunters who saved all year to come north for a week in November now staying on First Lake while at Idlewild the guests were much younger, dressed in the raccoon coats which had not yet made it, and with this exception never did make it, to Pittsburg, showing less interest in hunting or fishing than in rowing their fussy girl-friends three hundred yards into Second Lake where they would let the boat drift, or in sitting all day on the front porch with their feet on the rail, smoking one cigarette after another, complaining about the weather and the boredom and wondering aloud to the guides and serving girls how anyone could choose to live here. At night the lodge was said to be host to card games no less heated than those Currier's father held in his sitting room, which was now part of the great dining room where Currier had recently hung a crystal chandelier, and on certain weekends Currier hired bands to play and pushed the tables against the walls for dances, and young men from the village hid in the bushes beyond the circle of light cast by the lamps inside to listen to the music and watch the men and women who stood on the porch for a breath of that clear and wholesome air Currier advertised and a nip from a silver hip flask before they returned inside. Currier's sons, Thomas and Francis, now young men themselves, purchased a Ford roadster in 1925, and many assumed that they were assisting in the business the village believed their father was engaged in, since the car was often seen passing the customs house at Beecher Falls and even as far south as St. Johnsbury or Littleton, if not racing along the River Road between West Stewartstown and Second Lake, overtaking wagons loaded with hay or causing cattle crossing the road to scatter while, wreathed in dust, an angry farmer hurled rocks at the roadster. Though the villagers predicted that the Currier boys would kill either themselves or whoever was unlucky enough to be caught in their path when they rounded a curve or crested a hill, Thomas was instead shot to death in the woods north of First Lake the follow-ing year, allegedly by a man whose name had once been scrawled in Idlewild's guest register, and who was later jailed in New York for smuggling, the dispute claimed by some to have arisen from a dozen crates of Canadian whisky which disappeared from Currier's barn and which, others said, had actually been impounded by patrolmen from Colebrook and destroyed in that town's dump before a gathering of interested citizenry. Idlewild was closed for the remainder of the season, and, save for the burial, Currier and his wife and son did not appear in the village all winter. When the lodge reopened the following spring, the rates had been lowered and the hunters from Lowell and Lawrence and Lynn stood on the lawn each morning, stuffing new shells into their pockets before vanishing into the predawn darkness with guns broken over their arms.

Currier closed Idlewild after the 1929 season and did not reopen the following spring as he had no reservations. While he had not lost much money, if any, in the actual crash, he had no income the villagers could see while his lodge stood vacant. Some of the villagers he had previously employed brought small gifts of milk or corn or flour, since he had no land to raise any food of his own, but they all imagined that during this time whatever fortune he had accumulated began to erode rapidly. It was, therefore, no surprise to them when, in the fall of 1930, he announced that he would be closing Idlewild indefinitely, until the economy recovered, but that as soon as times were better he would return at once. He and his wife—his remaining son, Francis, had enlisted in the Navy the year after his brother's death, when he turned eighteen—drove away in their five-year-old Auburn after shipping many boxes south on the train and leaving Idlewild's key with one of the former guides, who was to inspect the property each spring, perform whatever small repairs he judged necessary, and notify Currier in the case of extensive damage. The caretaker fixed loose shutters and replaced broken panes of glass, and in summer maintained the grounds, and twice yearly a check arrived at the village post office bearing a return address in Lowell, though there was no letter. When the 1938 hurricane devastated much of New England, particularly along the Connecticut River valley, Idlewild, in addition to losing many shingles and windowpanes, sustained severe injury when a fir breached the roof and the heavy rains poured into the upstairs rooms and streamed down through the walls and floor. The caretaker wrote to the address in Lowell from which his checks had been sent, describing the wreckage and asking Currier what he wanted done or if he would prefer to come examine the property himself before deciding, and waited several months for a response though none arrived, after which time some in the village suggested that Currier had written off the property as a complete loss. That winter, snow drifted inside the lodge, through the hole in which the uprooted fir still rested, and much of the interior was further spoiled during the spring thaw. In the ensuing years, hunters or loggers—for the woods around Second Lake had been logged since the early 1930s, when the various small firms which had bought parcels of land from the Everett Company began operations—who stumbled upon Idlewild now saw only a sagging ruins, the clapboards rotted and loose, the glass nearly entirely gone from all fifty-six windows, the roof collapsed, the central chimney a jagged turret from which smoke had not risen in a decade, the grounds a fury of weeds and saplings, a few half-skeletal rowboats and canoes growing moss and swamp maple or cedar seedlings from their overturned bottoms along the lake's edge. If he ventured a walk across the decaying porch to peer through one of the missing panes of glass, the man could see wallpaper buckled and waterstained or peeled away from crumbled plaster in strips, warped floorboards, chairs and tables dusty though still usable, and the chandelier, now tarnished, cobwebbed, and missing some of its prisms. But soon even the locals stopped noticing Idlewild, stopped expecting to see Currier, perhaps looking older, his hair gray now, drive up to Baldwin's store with his wife to herald his return, stopped even discussing the lodge or its former owners—for now it seemed to belong to no one or nothing but the weather—stopped mentioning its progress toward complete disintegration. It was only the lodge's burning, early in September of 1947, under circumstances mysterious to this day, that again caused the villagers to mention it, to recall their memories and stories about the Curriers, who even now did not appear. How the fire was started was never answered to anyone's satisfaction, some saying that it began in smoldering brush, others saying that it was deliberate though purposeless arson by local boys or out-of-town fishermen, or that it was quite intentional arson set by Currier himself or his son or even his son's son—though no one had any proof that such a person even existed—to claim insurance money, though why such a claim was not made after the hurricane was never explained either, others saying that it had been some sort of freak lightning strike even though later the skies over Pittsburg the afternoon of the burning were recalled to be clear, one man insisting that the only logical explanation was that rotting flour in the pantry or some similar substance had spontaneously combusted, and most of the village's wives saying that their husbands had done it simply for something to talk about during afternoons of loafing now that the war was over and even the war stories of the village's several veterans had been told and retold and compared against those of the veterans of the earlier war and exhausted. What had survived of the lodge to that day was now smoke dispersed above the lake and a heap of ash and sooty rubble and charred timbers. The foundation still stood, but the heat had been such that even what had been in the cellar had burned. Those who lived on First Lake or in that part of town called Happy Corner or north of the new lake—Lake Francis, the one created after the hurricane by damming the river and flooding the valley—could see the black smoke rising from the trees to the northeast, and many of them, dropping whatever they were doing to head that way, witnessed some of the burning, and sent word to the village that something was ablaze near Second Lake, so that most of the villagers had assembled by the shore, their cars parked at skewed angles to one another, some of them with doors still flung open, to watch the last bits of wood frame burn in the approaching dusk—some working to see that the fire did not spread and some merely watching the violent flow of flames, their voices displaced by the heat and orange light, by the swaying shadows as it grew darker.

Though the woods surrounding Second Lake remain in the possession of several small logging companies, and though nearly all of the old-growth timber that once surrounded the lake has been cut, the corridor of woods along the Daniel Webster Highway, which runs parallel to the lake's western shore and on to the

Canadian border, has been designated state forest land. Since the only access to the far side of the lake is through this protected forest or along logging roads little more than washed-out dirt tracks barely wide enough for the logging trucks, it seems unlikely that Second Lake will suffer the development of First Lake or Back Lake, where cabins and summer cottages and lodges crowd the available shorelines. A boat ramp has been built on its western shore, not far from the site where Idlewild once stood, and a faint path leads from the ramp through blueberry bushes and birch trees to a scoop of earth, green with weeds and tangles of blackberry, ringed by a rectangle of tumbled and overgrown rock, where, standing below tall spruce and fir, one can see Camel's Hump rising from the trees to the northeast, or Mount Magalloway in the deep woods to the south.

THREE

1925

Tom Currier's face, in the last light of this September day, glowed. The sun burned atop a stand of fir just south of the lodge, their edges blurred against its light. He pulled the oars dripping from the water and rested them on the gunwales. Trailed one hand in the water and flicked his fingers at Martha. The boat swayed as she shifted, its sides spreading ripples. Drops darkened her sleeve. Around them the light shaped patterns on the water. They drifted until the sun was behind him and she in his shadow. Orange light haloed the hair she knew he had wet before parting it on the top of his head, mussing it and combing it straight again while he looked at the mirror. She squinted into the sun, watching one of his hands move toward her ankle, then instead reach to pick at a flake of paint until it came off. She would not speak but twined her hair around one finger. Let him. Let him ask again. He had come to the kitchen door that afternoon while she chopped onions and potatoes on a board crosshatched with brown lines, wiping her eyes with a bent wrist. The hat he had begun wearing after the men from Boston and Hartford first came he held in his hands, turning it as he talked, and she watched his fingers circle and circle the brim while his words merged with one another, water pouring into a cup. It isn't what he's doing, her father had once told her mother, it's the men he'll attract by doing it. And the sedans drove through the woods, along the highway to the lodge or else on to the road's new end by the fishing shack at Third Lake. The men from Chartierville or La Patrie or wherever they'd come from this time sat on the bank, holding poles they paid no attention to, most likely not even baited, tackle boxes and backpacks strewn on the mossy ground beside them. From the bottom of Prospect Hill, in P.Q., it was a mile and a half walk uphill through thick woods, and the men were tired, but for the extra fee they could ask for that mile and a half and for crossing the line of blazed and girdled trees themselves they did not mind. And soon, people said, the two roads would connect. A man standing on Third Lake's northern shore could near throw a stone into Canada, and there was no customs house between Beecher Falls and Jackman, Maine. Slouched caps shaded the men's faces and the wind made a sound in the trees. A sedan stopped by the roadside and from it a man stepped into the weeds and whistled. One of the men waiting threw his rod on the bank and stood up, shouting across the still water. Ostie de tabarnac! Où t'étais? Dépêche-toi! The boat circled, washing slowly toward the center of the lake. The sun had fallen behind the trees and slanted through the trunks, bleeding into a point smaller and smaller as she watched it wink out; the waters darkened. Behind them, at the lodge, a light burst from a single window and spilled onto the grass, onto the abandoned camp chairs and the overturned canoes lying side by side along the shore. Inside, the men would be gathered before the needless fire, swirling whisky and melting ice around the sides of their glasses as they waited for the food to be brought to the table. Her mother, throwing a last measure of salt from her cupped palm into the stew, watching to see the dumplings did not overcook while Ellen replaced the forks she had dropped on the floor with clean ones. Mr Currier in his study, his arms behind his head or folded beneath it on the paper-strewn desk as she, walking past the open door with an armful of linens, had once seen him, or flipping the pages of the immense leatherbound dictionary her father had told her was among the few things Mr Currier brought with him when he came from Massachusetts, teaching himself new words or pressing the tip of his pocketknife against the pages to cut out, her father had once said, whatever words he didn't want to know the meanings of, or else wanted to forget. Somewhere in the shadow collecting among the far shore's trees she heard an owl's sonorous call. Asking a question, she had always thought of that sound. What would she answer? Tom ran his thumb across his fingertips, frowned at the white paint under one nail, and lifted his face to hers. Martha, he said. He paused. Yes, she said, isn't it cold now the sun's gone down. She cupped her elbows with her hands and leaned forward, bringing her shoulders almost to her knees. Will you row us back? She half-turned on the seat to look back east across the lake, the trees a dark smudge, their pointed tops indistinct against the sky, and only heard him drop the oars into the water, felt the jerk as he pulled on them and the rowboat moved forward. Curling ripples his strokes left reeled past her; the oarlocks creaked; drops hissed into the water. The lake's weedy smell: this moment still almost summer. Already she could hear voices from the lodge. Next year I'll be gone, she had told her mother, staring at the slope of white ceiling they both woke to, though then it had been dark and that dark was what allowed her to speak. Martha only heard her, the rustle of the blankets as she turned four feet away from her, and though she did not look, she knew her mother was up on one elbow, or sitting, the covers thrown back. Next year we'll have enough and I'll finish sch—. Next year you'll do no such thing, her mother said. She laughed. Where will this money come to support you? Who will hire you? For a moment neither spoke. You wouldn't even last. A month and you'd be back here begging the Curriers to take you back on while in the meantime they'd have had their pick from all the village. Anyone can cook and clean, and there are other pretty girls. Do you think they'll wait for you? Her mother sniffed, and rearranged her covers. And the cirrate wake of the boat she heard rather than saw, the water too dark to reflect her face as more than a pale blur, only the scraps of clouds above the lodge she would not look at showing any trace of this day. Tom had stopped rowing; was using the oars to slow the boat as the weeds and rocks of the bottom came to greet it. Then he was out, pulling the boat half out of the water by its painter so she could step onto the clipped grass from which crickets now called. Shadowed, men stood on the porch, arms on the rail, the light from his father's new chandelier glowing behind them. Full dark now. Thank you for the ride, she said, but he kneeled beside the boat, tying a knot, and did not lift his head. The smell of cigarette and cigar smoke as she walked across the grass and up the porch steps, and she wondered when it had become so late. Nice evening for a paddle, one of the men said, and she nodded, head bent. His feet on the steps behind her. Had he run across the lawn? There he is, another man said as he breathed out smoke through his teeth. There's our man. She closed the door and walked through the empty unswept dining room and into the kitchen where Ellen leaned over a stack of plates, circling them with a dishrag. Your mother, Ellen said. I know, she said, already rising the stairs as Ellen spoke. But her mother was not in their upstairs room, one wall slanting up to the ceiling so that getting out of bed Martha had first to reach an arm up, the room that smelled always of the meals that had been cooked or were cooking in the kitchen below it. Through the single window she looked at the yard, the moon not yet waxed enough to give much light so each tree and clump of bushes and the spaces between them were irresolvable into their singular elements, appearing as they did one stretch of differently-shaded dark which the quiet breeze stirred into shifting patches. These fall days evening gathered the trees and hills and the lake's still surface into itself so quickly, drawing with it the scent of approaching cold, winds that rattled the handful of curled leaves still clinging to the swamp maples. A lantern's light turned from the road and at the pace of someone walking moved toward the lodge, winking through the branches it passed beneath; footsteps on the gravel. As it neared the house, her mother's voice said Tom, you're back; the murmur of men's voices from the porch stalled in its fickle rhythm. Is she in the kitchen? Martha turned from the window and sat on the edge of the bed she had made in that morning's blue light, waiting for Ellen's voice below her and then for her mother's feet to climb the narrow stairs. The door opened. Why are you sitting here in the dark? I've been out trying to find you. I was looking for you too. Well certainly you saw I wasn't here, her mother said. Why aren't you helping Ellen? Do you think that missing the supper you were supposed to help serve excuses you from cleaning up after it? No, I—. I already told Ellen that you'll take care of tomorrow's breakfast yourself. But for now there's enough still to be done downstairs and you'd better go and help her. Martha rose. As she passed through the doorway her mother said Please shut it, and she pulled the door to behind her, tugging it into the jamb to latch, the wood here and on the steep steps she descended crooked. Nothing fit. I'm sorry, Ellen said, and she said Never mind. It's not your fault. She soaked a dishrag in the tub, squeezing water through her fist, and began on the mugs tipped over and piled in the sink, their sides streaked with coffee or dark tea-rings at their bottoms. Did he ask you again? Ellen asked when they had established with their hands and the dishes and water a faltering cadence, not lifting her eyes from the plate she scrubbed her cloth across. The stack before Ellen seemed no shorter than when Martha had walked through ten minutes earlier; the front of Ellen's dress was dark with water, the floor puddled. No, she said, and if he had you know what I would have said anyway. The men had moved from the porch into the dining room and she heard them from down the hall, their voices rising one above the other, their chairs creaking as they tipped them back on two legs or thumped forward, their combined laughter defeating any other sound. His voice was among them tonight as it had been most nights since midsummer though she heard it say little, only the occasional tone of his laugh as one man concluded a story or a joke. It was Pete Morrison, that big lump from downstate. He's stayed here before, some of you must know him. He'd been up here one night last March and loaded up his new Cadillac and was driving back south the next morning. Just down to Lancaster. Said he'd found a bunch of people he could sell to, and even if he wouldn't get as much as he could down in Boston or even in Manchester he thought it was worth it for the short trip and as he said the low risk. Told us he'd be back in a day or two, after he rounded up everybody'd given him an order. He left here with another fellow who agreed to drive pilot in his Essex in exchange for a few dollars. So this fellow leads Pete all the way down past Groveton, till they can just about spot the smoke from the chimneys in Lancaster. Pete says he comes over a rise not far from the fairgrounds when he sees a farmer bringing all his cows across the road and that Essex nowhere in sight. He swerves but clips the first cow. It crumples up his hood and breaks the windshield and he can't see anything until he spins into an old elm and the car stops. First thing he hears is the farmer shouting, and he pushes open the door and takes off running, down into a swamp, and somehow gets away from the farmer who he thinks must be having enough trouble with the rest of the herd. Pete says he estimates it's about ten o'clock by then and he sits in a thicket in that swamp trying to figure how much the cow he got was worth and how much above that he'll have to pay the farmer to keep him quiet and how much he has on him. And besides all this figuring he thinks he'd better wait until the farmer cools down enough so that he can talk to him. You know how some of these old guys are about their animals. So he guesses it's about six or seven when he makes his way back to the road, past dark and turning cold enough he doesn't want to wait much longer because he's pretty bruised and rattled, not to mention stiff and damned hungry as well. Says he finally gets to the road and finds that the farmer has run a logging chain through the car's frame and padlocked it to the tree. All the whisky is gone, of course. But worst of all it looks like the farmer has taken an axe or a maul to the car because even where it didn't hit the cow or the tree it's all banged up, the metal all torn and the running boards and bumpers knocked off and the windows all smashed and the tires cut up and the dashboard and the steering wheel wrecked, knobs pulled loose everywhere and even the upholstery torn to pieces. Said before he saw it he thought he might have been able to salvage it or at least sell it cheap to some dirt farmer in the hills who wouldn't notice the dents and the twisted frame or at least wouldn't care. But Pete decided he'd best just head out of there. He showed up here a few weeks later telling how he bought a pistol and hijacked a car he heard would be coming through St. Johnsbury one night. Said it runs smoother than his Cadillac did, and has a smoker installed too. Said at least next time he hits a cow he can lay a screen to be extra sure the farmer doesn't catch him. A few of the men chuckled. She overturned another mug on the tea towel she had spread on the counter. Tom had told her he and his brother would buy a Ford from a man they knew and then the money they earned would be ten times as much. And suppose you wreck it or it gets captured? she asked. We'll just go down and buy it back at the auction, he said. Do you think they'll come help you if something happens? she asked. How many do you think they can find to take your place? Listen, he said. We're not going to do it for someone else, just ourselves. There's a spot on that old dirt road running along Hall's Stream, out past the Wheeler school-house, where the water curves west and the road follows it. Right at this bow the stream's far bank is the road that leads from Beecher

Falls up through customs and into P.Q. and at that one point the
distance between the two roads is less than a quarter mile. Frank
can wait on the American side while I drive up into P.Q. and load
up and then carry it all down that bank and wade across the stream
and put it right into the wagon. Then Frank just has to drive back
to the lodge and hide it until we're ready to take it south. I can drive
back through customs clean. Tell them I have a sick aunt in Coati-
cook if they ask why I'm always passing through. I'll even offer to
let them search it. And no one from outside the village will bother
with that dirt road since it just follows the stream a ways and then
dead ends at an old farm out back of Tabor Notch. A car can only
get a mile down it anyway before it's too washed out and overgrown
to keep on. She held the last mug dripping over the tub. Watched
as beside her Ellen's hand traced slowing swathes across a plate, the
loose knot of her hair slipping to her neck. His voice silent and the
voice of the other one she had listened for those nights she stood
here washing, the wood before the sink worn pale by her own feet.
She too always waiting to speak. Men's voices, smoke, drifted.
Ripples spread across the surface of the tub's gray water, rings inside rings. She remembered how a lazy rain finally began to fall
after a gray morning, the air so humid the cats did not jump from
the steps she walked down. The rain increased; water dripped from
the eaves. While everyone else had rushed out, let the rain soak
them through their clothes, she walked back inside. It will rain
again someday, he had said. Her father had called her from the
kitchen to walk the woods: half-hearted drops in leaf veins, beading bent grass blades; spiderwebs silver water constellations. Or
had it been someone else calling her? Someone has to know the
trails when I'm gone, she had heard him once tell Charlie Chase,
and you're too lazy to walk with me. True enough, Charlie Chase
had said. The lines around his eyes like the creased leather of his
boots, untouched for two years by any hand but hers, the back of
his hand on the blanket banded with clumped veins, his skin dry
and cool. No—earlier, a time before that time. His feet leaving
hollows in the new powder, those same boots scooping troughs
leading deeper among the trees. She could not step from one of his
prints to the next and between them her ankles sank into the drifts.

The wind had given her skin this flush she felt tight across her cheeks, had wet the corners of her eyes where her lashes froze together. Snow hid the shapes of the spruce limbs which bowed toward them on either side; as he walked his shoulders brushed the snow loose, but the branches stayed bent after it cascaded down. His back retreating before her, his scarf draped over one shoulder, the snow unbroken but for the tracks they had made, wind, the woods, the throb and itch of her fingers fisted inside her mittens. And as she let him increase the distance between them, she thought of the trail of crumbs, each spilled wish. Wait, she called, wait. Why had they never drawn a map? You're the one who'll have to tell my tale, he had said. Once upon a time, in those days when wishing still did some good, a king lived alone with only his one daughter in a dreary country of dark woods and crooked hills. For the queen had died as the child was born and the king's heart had been heavy since. As the years passed, the daughter grew into a lovely young woman, but, instead of rejoicing, the king's heart grieved that his beloved queen could not witness this fair change with him. He no longer took pleasure in his minstrels' songs, nor his falcons and hounds, nor the court dances, nor his grounds and gardens which a hundred men tended each day. And one morning he sent his messengers far and wide throughout his land to find a new queen who would break his spell of unhappiness. After seven days and nights the messengers began to return to the castle, but none of them had found a queen. All of the women in the kingdom are already married, sire, or else too young or too old, they told him, and as the king stood by his window watching the day end beyond the hills, it felt to him that as the sun set so too did his hopes fail. But even as he watched, two figures approached the castle's dusky gates. The last messenger had returned with a beautiful woman from the farthest reaches of the king's country. The next day the king was married to his new queen, and he took her to meet his daughter, who curtsied politely and offered her stepmother gifts of an embroidered gown and a silver brooch. But the new queen refused them, saying, My child, a moth-eaten dress and a scrap of tin? Such gifts do not become your new queen. Secretly the new queen was jealous, for she thought the king's daughter more beautiful than she, and her pride would not allow her to accept signs of affection, no matter how splendid, from the king's daughter. And after brooding for a week she summoned one of the castle's huntsmen to her chambers. Take the king's daughter into the forest, she told him, and there you must kill her and bring me her heart as a token. The huntsman obeyed the queen, for even though he loved the king's daughter as all the kingdom did, he was sworn to loyalty to the new queen as soon as she married the king. He led the king's daughter deep into the woods, where the trees grew tangled and thick and no light fell; where there was no path leading away. As he drew his knife the king's daughter began to weep, and pleaded for her life. If you spare me, I will stay in the woods and never return home, she told him. Only once that she remembered had her father come back from the woods with a buck, lashing its hind legs to a stout stick he tied to the barn's beam with rope he uncoiled from his arm. Seven points brushed the crushed hay and the white tail curled down over the back. He was so pretty it was a shame to shoot him, he said. But that year two of the cows had not freshened, and by November they had eaten boiled potatoes with a meager gravy three nights in a row; the next morning he was gone after tending the herd, and returned an hour past dark dragging the trussed carcass on a litter of birch poles. But we've got to eat, he said. Keep Jerseys for butterfat and Holsteins for bulk and you will never want. And she would stay for this? This snowed-over or washed-out road among black trees and bracken leading to a drafty lodge by a frozen lake? These greasy knives and forks dropping which, Ellen once told her, meant company would arrive. A fork is a man and a spoon is a woman and a knife is anyone's guess. So that is why he hired you, she said, I wondered. No. And already years had passed since the morning Mrs Currier had shown her into the kitchen, opened the cupboards wide to mason jars of vegetables, shown her the barrels of flour and salt pork, the sack of coffee, the stacks of china in the glass-fronted cabinet. When a girl comes to work for me, she learns that a room has four corners and a dish has two sides, Mrs Currier said. Later, Martha would remind her mother of these things—the apron-string at her neck, the ache at her back the bowed mattress only troubled, the skewed wall, the ones who put a hand still sticky with pine pitch to her when they asked for more coffee. When, in later years, gathered about the table or on the porch, they read her letters home they would at last concede. They would say. After all. Yes, she knew. Let me tell you a story, she would write to them. The story I will tell is not the one I heard. Every man tells the tale of his life, he had said, and she answered And every woman must listen. But who will tell mine? She swashed the water back and forth, dried her hands on the tea towel. Beside her Ellen slouched above the drainboard, drying the last plates. But what's wrong with him? Ellen asked, looking up. Martha paused, the damp cloth still bunched in her fists. He's from here. But he must want to leave too, Ellen said. I don't know. It doesn't matter, I would just be bringing it with me. Martha twisted her arms behind her and worked the knot free; hung the apron on the back of the door. Here. A village of white-washed clapboards and brick chimneys loosing smoke into low skies. Every time she passed it she tried not to look, the wagon bouncing her along the road to where it briefly smoothed out in the center of the village and then the hill rising away from her. One afternoon this past spring Mr Currier had driven her and her mother and Tom and Frank in the new Auburn 120 he had bought, folding down the top, she sitting in the back between Tom and Frank and hoping they did not notice while, as they drove by, she watched the dirt road leading uphill, which disappeared from view before she could see even the peak of the roof, a single window. And whose face would peer through it now? Vern Amey, delivering some of his wife's mincemeat to the lodge one forenoon, had told her mother that even the new folks persisted in calling it the Hennessy farm as everyone else in the village still did. But someday she would be free even of that name and those who knew it. Instead of climbing the steep stairs, she walked into the hall, the cigar smoke thick, blue at the doorway to the dining room, where the men had broken into smaller groups, some standing beside the fireplace, resting their drinks on the mantel or holding them in one hand while they gazed at the hearth and another man spoke. Some sitting at the tables in groups of four or five, knocking ash on the floor, a shrinking accordion of cards in one's hands which he flicked face-down before his friends. Kerosene flames burned behind glass; through the open door the shapes of several figures darkened the porch. Tom Currier stood, one hand in a pocket, the other holding a nearly empty glass, with another man she did not recognize. His trousers were a bit muddy at the cuffs but of a cut and fabric similar to those the man he spoke to wore. Sure, sure. Of course, he said, nodding. Whichever you prefer. He looked at his watch, bending his wrist from his sleeve as effortlessly as any Boston man. And what if the ones your father rents storage to find out you're keeping some of your own here? she had asked him. That won't matter, he said. Not until someone takes yours, she said. Not until you try to get it back. She watched the man touch his hand to Tom's shoulder, steering him toward the door, and they walked outside, disappearing into the darkness beyond the steps. None of the men seemed even to notice her, as they faced each other around tables they plinked coins, cast creased and rumpled bills into piles on, the air barred in strata of smoke. She walked back down the hall and into the kitchen; Ellen gone to her own crooked bed now, saucepans and skillets hanging from hooks in the dark and the aimless light behind her filling the iron sinks and cupboards with shadow. One night. She could not say what had woken her, saw only the cloudy glimpse of her own feet against the stairs, the wood cold on her soles. Downstairs the fire was long dead. In the dark the objects seemed disarrayed. And in one chair a figure sat, legs draped in an afghan, thinning hair rising from the skull in wisps and tufts. Her father restored to her after these years. At his feet a book had fallen on its spine, its pages fanned wide. She stooped over him; his eyes blinked open. Is it so late already? he asked. And what a shame, the new queen said, that you did not have a son. For of what use is a daughter? She sits and sews and is pleasing to look at; but a son could be riding across your country at this moment to fight your enemies, or clearing your dark forests for farmland. Why did your old queen give you a daughter and not a son? I could give you a strong son, she said. And when the new queen said these words the king hushed her; but she insisted, telling him every day what wondrous tasks his son could perform while his daughter fashioned flowers into wreaths and practiced music. For months and months the king bade his new queen be silent, but at last she poisoned his heart so much that one night, as she repeated her tales, he asked her what they must do. You must take her into the forest, the new queen told him, and there you must leave her. They walked into the woods. The clouds suggested snow. Dirt, dirt worn smooth, the twigs ironlike, the spruce bark and frozen pitch, the pattern of fallen needles, orange. All cold. Still. Lake a swept field of snowy ice. Drifted. In two years' time, he said. And he. Kneeling beside her. I won't be gone long. I'll write as often as I can. A letter describing the river and the round orange moon. I am sure she has it still tucked in a drawer. We walked those woods. Come with me, he said. I am certain of you. Four years I've waited. Martha turned the knob and stepped from the kitchen into the dooryard. Yellowed grass. A wind had come up from the lake and among the spruce and fir it said hush. A loon's mad laughter from the dark. They were once men, he had told her. Enchanted? she asked. No, just wild. Think of the money to be made, he had said. Even the customs house at Beecher Falls has mirrors and lights to see underneath every car driving through, so the border guards won't have to dirty their knees. It won't last. But any man can make a small fortune right now. Think of that. You can't work here your whole life. Come with me and you won't have to work at all. Well I wish you luck, she said. I'm sure you'll do well, but I'll take care of myself. Through the darkness she heard a horse's hooves on the gravel and a wagon's turning wheels, the horse at an easy trot, whoever drove the wagon whistling as now she heard the faint snap of reins, not ungentle but close. The horse slowed and the wagon turned off the road toward the barn and as it did she heard a voice. With the man he had been talking to in the lodge, Tom walked toward the wagon as his brother jumped down from the seat. He won't last, her father had once said. When it becomes too ordinary here for his city friends, or when Washington regains its senses and overturns Volstead and the money leaves, he'll follow it somewhere else. How far is it to Boston? she had asked him the night they stood beside the dark lake's worried waters. I didn't come straight, he said, my feet haven't measured that road but it is far enough for you I'd say and large enough to swallow you in and no one would know. His breath in her hair. Their three figures a single dark form by the wagon. One separated itself from the others and walked toward her, past her, up the steps to the porch and into the dining room where the light seemed lower, now, the man clutching to his tailored shirt a bottle. And as the door swung to behind him she walked to the wagon, them turning around as she stepped on a leaf, and Frank saying It's just Martha. How are you? he said to her now. Evening, Tom said. Sorry about before, I didn't know I'd made you late. It doesn't matter, she said. If you really want to do me a favor, she had told him once, drive me to Boston when you buy your car. Sure, he had said. We could go to some of the clubs when we get there. We will go and look at that ocean at least once, he had said. It is nothing like our lakes. There are gaslamps on every street, he had said, they light the city until they blink out at dawn like lying in the woods under the trees' ragged roof watching stars disappear. If you spare me, I will stay in the woods and never return home. And the huntsman took pity on her and put down his knife. Flee, he said, and watched her disappear among the trees. Returning to the castle, he killed a deer and cut out its heart to bring as proof to the new queen. This is no girl's heart, the queen screamed when she lifted the lid of the box where the deer's heart still wept blood. Take him to the dungeon and there chain him for fifty years that he may learn the price of treachery. The huntsman was locked far beneath the castle in a dark cave dripping water. Often before he could eat such food as he was brought rats chewed it, and spiders knit webs around him, and bats flapped their charcoal wings about his head. He dreamed always of the forest, the dark trees and endless trails which the rest of the kingdom found gloomy and fearful but which he prized even above the king's marvelous gardens. Yet each time he woke to unyielding stone, to iron cuffs about his wrists. At last the fifty years had passed and the guards came to unlock the door and usher the huntsman, now a very old man, from the dungeon. He blinked at the light when he was led to the castle gate and told not to return. For days he wandered through the kingdom, eating berries and roots whose names he could not recall and drinking from the clear streams he had all but forgotten. Slowly his strength began to return. One day, in the midst of the forest, he heard a voice singing, and followed its sound to a small hut of sticks and leaves, where a woman sat before a smoking fire. Though she was not much younger than himself, she was still so fair that at once he recognized her as the king's daughter whom he had brought into the woods fifty years ago. Forgive me, he pleaded with her, and when she assured him that she was much happier here than she had ever been in her father's castle, he said Show me what's changed in the woods. They're the same woods, she answered. Boston is no different than here, her mother had once told her. You bring yourself with you wherever you go. But you'll see that only when you've been. How would you know? Martha said. You've never been there. No, but I've been enough different places to know. The sky above you will be the same blue. Some afternoons, he had said, if I forgot myself for a moment, if I let the sound of guns fade and looked out on a landscape yet unmarred by men I could imagine myself here. The yellow grass of our first fall reminding me of harvest and the snow I knew would soon come. Come winter, when all of the out-of-towners can't drive their cars on our snowy roads, we'll hitch up the pung and go through the woods. Until April we'll be the only ones in the village who'll be able to get it. Take it down to Lancaster or St. Johnsbury. Anyone would rather have some good Scotch whisky than cider during the cold spells. In the spring Charlie Chase would bottle the applejack he'd made during the winter by letting the cider freeze in an old tub and tapping it before it thawed—the water freezes, but the alcohol in it won't, Charlie Chase had once told her, pointing to the slushy tub. Waste of good cider, her father always said, though he'd join Charlie Chase for a drink some nights. Oh, it's a durable drink, Charlie Chase would say. A chunk of wood snapping in the stove; her mother behind her, brushing her hair. It doesn't matter, Martha said to Tom. Even if I'd been back in time for supper she would have found something else. Well, Tom said. Frank lifted a box from the wagon. Help me get this down cellar, he said. Here the grass was long, uncut since summer, and as they walked to the kitchen door it bent and whispered before them. Spruces swayed. Tom lifted the latch, held the door wide against tangled grass, while Frank disappeared into the dark space beyond. She had walked beneath that stretched arm into the woods one night, him stepping past her after he'd shut the door and saying Follow me, and then his shape before her, the back of his shirt pale in the dark. Through the woods a path twisted along the shore, so close to the lake that at times it seemed to lap their feet, blueberry bushes screening the moon's smear on the water until he parted them where a smooth rock lifted from water as dark as the sky. Here, Tom said. We can just sit a while. Her skirts spread over the rock, she sat on her heels against the rock's slope. He reached a hand into the water, drew it back through his hair. A nice night, he said. Yes, she answered, but did not turn her eyes from the rippled light on the lake. Beside her he coughed and cleared his throat. I'm like you, he said. I don't want to stay here either. In fact I'll be gone as soon as I can. My father doesn't need me here. Where will you go? she asked. Boston probably. But that's where I'm going, she said. It's big enough I think. I won't get in your way. You're not in my—it's just. Just what? he said. I want to look for someone there. He stroked his hand through the water again, lifting it in a cupped palm to run down his arm or pour back into the lake. The moon behind a cloud now, his face was only shadow. She inched down the rock. Maybe I could help. I don't know. I don't think so. Who is it? he said. Tell me who it is. You know, ever since your mother started cooking here. Ever since, he said, and trailed off. I know, she said. I know, but I'm sorry. Just tell me who, he said. I've known you long enough you can trust me. It doesn't matter who. Then just tell me. I'm sorry. It's not that old hobo, he was saying, but already she had jumped from the rock and turned back down the trail, hearing him coming behind her. Sorry, he was saying, I'm sorry, Martha, wait. The bushes clutched. Invisible spiderwebs broke across her mouth, her forehead. Just wait. But his voice was farther now; he had stopped somewhere behind her and alone she'd emerged from the woods, the lodge dark before her, the moon lighting only the edges of the obscuring clouds. In a moment Frank climbed the cellar stairs and shut the door. How much did you pay for it? Tom asked. Did you hear about Lavoie? one of the men had said to another one night as she cleared their plates onto a tray, forks balanced over bones, gravy skinned over, potatoes gray and cold. No, what? Fool broke into a barn over in Newport. Place some farmer had rented out to some boys from Manhattan. So you know what price it was supposed to get. The men leaned to one side as she reached to retrieve crumpled and stained napkins, a knife, the breadbasket. Can I bring you more coffee? Sure sweetheart. They took him out to the woods when they heard he'd sold it already. No one's even found the spot. She backed down the hall and into the kitchen. Set the tray on the counter and took the carafe of coffee by its cloth-wrapped handle. Sure, Tom told her later, a lot of fellows disappear up here but they always have haven't they. It's just miles of nothing. And no one will notice if he's not even from around here. No. The trees sifted afternoon light; she knelt at his feet as he drew his knife. Please, she said, if you spare me I will tell you a wonderful story. What wonders can a child tell? the huntsman asked. Listen. Once upon a time a king lived alone with only his one daughter in a dreary country of dark woods and crooked hills. For the queen had died as the child was born and the king's heart had been heavy since. As the years passed, the daughter grew into a lovely young woman, and one day she told her father that she wanted to leave his kingdom to travel into the wide world and seek her fortune. Oh my daughter! the king said, I would grant you any wish but this one, for having lost already one so dear to me I could not bear to lose another. As you will, so it shall be, the king's daughter answered, though from that day forth she would spend hours gazing through her window, where the hills of her father's land met the sky in a blurry line. At dusk she watched the day end beyond the hills, and it felt to her that each time the sun set so too did her hopes fail. Three more times, when she felt her heart could stand being in her father's castle no longer, she asked his permission to leave; and each time he refused. At last, after a year and yet another year had passed and she felt that she would surely go mad if she did not leave, she exchanged her clothes with those of her maid, and in the guise of a peasant fled the castle gates for the city she imagined lay somewhere beyond the hills and forests of her father's lands. But the king quickly discovered the ruse, and sent his swiftest huntsmen into the forest to pursue his daughter. Deep in the woods they overtook her at last, and as she stumbled to the ground exhausted from the pursuit, one huntsman drew his knife. Please, she begged him, if you spare me I will tell you a wonderful story. And when she left? Would they follow? His Ford, finally purchased, rumbling along the road behind her? I didn't come straight, my feet haven't measured that road. Crooked then, a dreary country. A trail of crumbs to find the way back. Why had they never drawn a map? I want you to keep these, he said. The few pages, creased from countless foldings and unfoldings, the pencil marks smudged, the strange names, spread in the lamp's circle of light night after night on the kitchen table. When I'm gone someone must remember. Show me what's changed in the woods. In two years' worth of dreams, I walked here, but now you'll have to remind me of the paths. Fifty years of dreams, sleeping on stone. Every man writes the tale of his life. You're the one who'll have to tell my tale, he had said. Tell it to whom? To yourself. To your children. There will be someone who wants to hear you tell it. Not much, Frank said. Four dollars a bottle. We can get sixteen for it easy. And if we could get it to Boston, probably twenty-five, Tom said. The breeze shifted, breathed the scent of woodsmoke. Did you know this is the deepest of the lakes? Tom had said once, rowing her toward its center. Ninety feet down right here. Below her, silt hung where the sun could reach; above, the sky opened at last from the trees. And what could she explain to him, what answer could she give? Her heart was no bleeding jewel; it was proof of nothing. Martha remembered the simple possibilities of a morning in Lancaster, a store full of coiled rope and tinware, horse blankets, harnesses, peaveys and spades stacked in a corner, snowshoes and boots hanging from the ceiling, a glass case of patent medicines; her father spoke to a man across a tall counter, both of them leaning on elbows, their eyes flicking from the counter where their fingers traced circles to each other's faces to the faded posters and broadsides tacked to the walls. Outside, the purple and gray sky. Clouds so low the hills were lost in them. Rain. Twenty, she heard her father say. Through the smeared glass she watched a boy and girl little older than she step into the muddy street, arms linked, both bareheaded so that their hair fell dripping against their foreheads. They walked through puddles, the hem of the girl's dress dark and heavy, the boy's boots dull, and passed just before the window she watched them through, though neither noticed her there, the glass between them cloudy from her breath. Water poured from a drain spout, slapping the earth outside the door. Mud splashed up. An instant she felt she understood, though that understanding exceeded telling it. Those months he lay in the bed before her it was a story she wanted to return to, to ask him if he too remembered, had noticed this boy and girl, could recall this shared morning, yet she could not speak it: it was no story, only one moment among countless others—this she knew. But still a moment she recalled more than most stories; a moment that turned into a story as the nameless boy and girl disappeared, leaving her in want of what she had seen: their errant ease, their shared solitude. One night. Mr Currier had a word with me tonight, her mother said. The lamp on the single table between their beds giving a last light to the day, the windowpanes rattling against the sash. Martha pulled the brush down, feeling her scalp pull with it. Her mother already under the covers, shapeless beneath them. He said that you and Tom have been walking into the woods at night, her mother said. Is that true? The ends of her hair waved, following the brush as she lifted it again. Yes. He told me he's afraid that you'll both get into trouble if you haven't already. He said he would speak to Tom and asked me to speak to you. Do you know what we would do if we couldn't stay here? Do you think there is any other place we could go? Only her mother's head and neck showed on the white pillow. Will you hurry and come to bed? she said. And think about what I'm telling you. How is he watching us? she had asked Tom the next night. I don't know. Don't worry what either one of them says, we can always just leave. No, she said. Then I'll tell them what I've asked you, he said. I'll ask your mother if she'll allow it. No. Well just forget it, then, he said, heaving himself up and walking away while she watched the water. Just forget it. Someday you'll find a place you want to go, Charlie Chase had told her, bending to lift his two suitcases into the stage. And when you do, be sure your way takes you through Putney. I'll expect you. That old, my old hobo, she would say, when the trees gave way to brick and tall buildings, polished glass, streets leading one to the next in a pattern she would not know, when she would see him leaning against a pole, sitting by a window, walking toward her and finally looking up. I'm going inside, Frank said, see what they're up to. Will you be in soon? Soon, Tom said. They watched him walk away, blending into the dark until he mounted the porch stairs and opened the door; then she felt Tom turn toward her, but kept facing the house, the windows throwing stretched squares of light onto patches of grass, the leafless lilac, the sweep of gravel leading away through spruce. Silhouettes passed before the windows or paused there to look out at what she knew could not be seen, only a faint reflection on glass. The trees spoke among themselves. What, he said. What is it. What? she asked. You're quiet. I guess I don't have much to say. Do you want to take a walk? No, I'm feeling sleepy tonight. Well why did you follow me out here? I didn't follow you. I was in the kitchen and I just wanted to get some air. I saw you. You were watching me talking to that fellow and then you watched us wait for Frank to come back. Well you're pretty choice of yourself tonight, she said. He turned toward the trees and was still. She heard him swallow. I don't know why I ever asked you, he said. Why I ever thought you would. From a half-open window came a sudden burst of laughter, and in a minute three or four men stepped onto the porch: the tiny flame of a match winked among them and went out. You already knew what my answer would be, she said. I guess I did. Well. I think I'll go back in. All right, she said. She saw him turn back toward her and for a moment he hesitated, glancing from the ground to her face though with the light behind him and only the curved sliver of moon she couldn't see his features. Neither spoke. I, he said, and paused. She waited. She could hear the voices of the men on the porch but not what words they said. Fine, her mother had said. Go if you want to. But don't come back to me later. You've always had foolish ideas, and I hoped you were going to grow up and forget them but it seems not. I don't imagine you even know how you'll get there? Just tie up your things in a cloth and start walking? You'll be tired before you even reach Happy Corner. I think I'll go back in, Tom said at last. All right, she said. Already his feet made a sound in the grass and then he was on the porch too and across it and inside. From all the woods around her there was no sound but the wind and the sounds it made in and among the trees, the branches rubbing together or creaking and the needles trying to catch it, unable. And then. Once upon a time in a dreary country of dark woods and crooked hills. And then. When a year and yet another year had passed and she felt that she would surely go mad if she did not leave. And then. She tucked her maps into a fold of her dress and imagined the country ahead. And then. She turned to discover that the birds had eaten every last crumb she had dropped along the path. And then? the huntsman asked her. What happened next? And then she told her pursuers the most wonderful story they could imagine, there among the bent trees and green ferns and pathless woods, a story both beautiful and sad, a story of lost dreams and places now vanished, a story of a time when even their grandparents were children, and as they listened to her speak they forgot why they had come. Quietly, then, she slipped through the woods and escaped. That's all there is to it? the huntsman asked her, rising to his feet again and loosing his knife from its sheath; thinking of the long miles back to the castle. Please, she said, please. You never let me finish my story.

FARMHOUSE IN A FOLD OF FIELDS

CONNECTICUT VALLEY, PITTSBURG, N. H. 167K.

Now that they are gone and
To be dreamed of
. . .
What might have been written down is seen
To have been said, and heard, and silence
Has flowed around the place again and covered it.

—John Ashbery, "Litany"

As the sun rose the morning of the day when the walls and floors

The blacktop has buckled. The car jolts. Roots from these tall trees

and roof of her house were to be sawed into pieces, broken apart

have stretched beneath the road; water has seeped through the bed of

by crowbars, raised on jacks, lifted onto flatbed trucks and driven

gravel and sand, and frozen during the winters; spring thaws have

six and a half miles southwest through Pittsburg Village to Indian

weakened the road's edges. She notices several potholes. So even this

Stream, Miss Linnie Abbott packed the last items in her

surface is now old enough that the summer months when shirtless men

pantry—a tin of tea, a single cup and saucer, and the sugar

leveled and graded earth, smoothed hot asphalt with a steamroller,

bowl—in a straw-filled box she then nailed shut. She closed every

marked curves with stakes and twine, and dynamited boulders—even

window, walked through the rooms that had been emptied of

that summer, whichever summer it was among all the summers she has

everything save a single suitcase, several crates and boxes, a

been gone, was some years back, and this stretch of road—despite its

kitchen chair, the woodstove, and her bed, which she had un-

cracks and heaves, still far more level than the dirt and gravel bumps,

made as soon as she'd risen from it. The floors creaked as she moved

the muddy holes and ruts she remembers—has become as familiar to

across them, and though she'd swept every corner, mopped the
those who live here as the dusty track it replaced was to her. She looks

pine planks, and scrubbed the baseboards, she'd been unable to do
out through the windshield, smudged with flies from her drive through

anything about the discolored rectangles on the walls where the
the mountains, at the roadside grass, the spruce, the flashes of moving

china cabinet and the lowboy had stood, undisturbed, since her
water between them. She has driven hours and there is more beyond

father had put them there as soon as the wallpaper he'd hung be-
this strip of asphalt vanishing into the trees which seems to her

hind them had dried. She walked through the hall and sat on her
unexpected if not entirely false. She cannot tell how much she has

step to await the men who would move her house from the valley.
forgotten, how much has been altered; what she only thinks she recalls.

Her skirt, which she had sewn herself from a heavy cotton weave
Woods have sprung up or been cleared; new gravel drives emerge from

she had ordered from a dressmaker's shop in Manchester, draped
dark stands of fir to meet the highway, and unrusted mailboxes stand

her to her shoes, and she wore a fine shirt, with lace embroidery
on posts to mark them—the names painted on their sides are none she

tipping its collar; about her shoulders she had drawn a white
recognizes. Each mile north, for the past two days, she has imagined

cardigan sweater trimmed with grosgrain. From her neck, a silver
she's seen something familiar, whether the shape of a hillside, the faded

pendant, which her father had given to her mother on the twenty-
lettering in a storefront window, the sunlight through the warped boards

fifth anniversary of their marriage, hung on a delicate chain. Miss
of a particular gray barn, the narrow view from a crossroads. And

Abbott had never married; never borne a child; and had made her
though she spent last night in a small hotel just south of the mountains,

home here some sixty-odd years to those in the village who troub-
not only so that she would pass through the notch in daylight but also

led to figure the dates—twenty years, at least, she had lived here
to draw out the trip, the countryside beyond them has felt less wide

alone, since the death of her mother, who had outlived her husband
than she would have said it was two mornings ago, leaving the city. On

by some dozen winters. Tabor Notch is a pretty place, Mrs Cook
either hand trees crowd the road's curve; the road itself follows the

and Mrs Parker had told her at tea last week, their last together
swells and folds of the land, and the muddy pastures edging each

here before she finished packing; for years now it had been the
small village appear before she expects them. Even the drive along the

custom of Mr Cook and Mr Parker to drive—once, in horsedrawn
river from Colebrook has seemed shorter, the route to a place she has

wagons; now, in secondhand automobiles—their wives from their
never been. She has seen a pair of red gasoline pumps tended by an old

homes in the village to Miss Abbott's house at the valley's far end
man wearing loose and somehow immaculately clean coveralls at West

for Saturday afternoon visits, since Miss Abbott herself left her
Stewartstown, though the train station windows were cobwebbed, and

house only when she could find someone to drive her. And she
the booth and platform empty. Has seen the house, crooked and

supposed it was pretty, the narrow hollow leading back into the
somehow skewed, that now stands by the road at Indian Stream. The

hills from which Indian Stream flowed—curling, there, through
new restaurant beside Baldwin's store; the few new homes—cramped

one of the village's few tracts of interval land other than this one,
and close, each looking to her as if it had been both erected and

which they would soon drown beneath a hundred feet of water—
inhabited within two weeks, and had remained in a perpetual state of

to meet the Connecticut little bigger than itself. A dirt road ran
unfulfilled progress ever since—between the town hall and Baldwin's.

back from the highway to the old Tabor farm, now Seb Cowan's
It could be, she thinks, any one of the small villages she has passed

farm, a mile past the site she had selected for her house. She would
through on this side of the mountains: a scattering of shabby homes, an

dig up her mother's peonies to replant by her doorstep, and in the

auto garage and a general store and a post office, a saw mill or

rich soil near the spot where the two waters met she would tend her

lumberyard perhaps, a hollow used as a dump where last year's

bean garden, though the sound of the two streams might drive her

leavings are picked through by the bears and crows, all of it circled by a

mad, she thought, that water's endless tale. All through the brief

screen of dark trees and guarded by close gray skies. But now she is

spring and summer the noise of trucks and machinery had dis-

already here, the gravel popping under her tires and knocking the wheel

rupted the valley's quiet, the days of cows scratching their necks

wells of her car. She parks beside long-unused hitching posts, takes her

along fence rails and flies tapping window-glass inside the kitchen,

purse from the seat; observes her face in the rearview mirror and

dusty afternoons when she would walk to the River Road bridge,

adjusts her hat. Her watch reads just past noon, the dinner hour; the

where boys cast lines into the slow water and hurried home with

street is nearly deserted. She does not recognize the faces looking back

brook trout hanging by the gills from a forked stick—hoping to

at her from the store's porch, though they are not unlike those she

eat supper in time to catch the movie Mr Baldwin would show on

would—tanned and deeply lined, dark eyes narrowed to a near squint

his new projector and one of his wife's freshly-ironed white sheets
though the day is not bright. The wooden steps she remembers are now

at the town hall. But this summer the boys had watched the trac-
cement, and as she climbs them past the men watching her—this

tors and dump carts and men downriver, at the end of the valley
unaccompanied city woman of middle age, about to enter the store—

nearest to the village, where the workmen the state had brought in
she wonders if the transformation is complete or if a single spoken word

scraped and piled earth to build the dam the governor had named
will undo the spell. But none of the men speaks and she does not have

after himself. And spent their wages in Baldwin's store and the
to answer. She pushes the door open to a room that seems unchanged

restaurant Baldwin's nephew had opened next door; some weeks,
since she last saw it, stopping here to buy some picture postcards of

Mrs Cook told her, Baldwin would run a film twice to keep the
the lakes and a bottle of tonic to drink while she waited with her bags

workers occupied in their off hours, or because they were bored
for the ride to the station and only one of the men on the porch that

enough here in the woods to pay him again to see the same story.
day, Windy Williams, had looked up from beneath his hat brim to

Everyone in the village who put up one or two of the workmen in
wish her goodbye. The same axes and snowshoes and fishing poles and

his spare room was earning money and Miss Abbott's neighbors
various other tools hang in the near-dark—have, most likely, hung

had all been paid far more than the actual values for their short-
nearly undisturbed during her absence; so too the jars of penny candy,

season crop farms, the slowly collapsing barns, the dairy herds
the wooden counter nicked and bumped and stained with overlapping

they had sold, but she had refused to accept the state agent's offer
rings where Mr Baldwin had set down his bottle of root beer to tally a

when he had knocked on her door last year; then, when the state's
customer's purchases on the pad he kept in his shirt pocket. But now a

lawyers told her she must leave the valley—eminent domain, their
younger man stands behind the counter, a newspaper unfolded before

papers said—she vowed to bring her house with her, and took only
him, his white shirt his most visible feature until her eyes adjust to the

as much of the state's money as she would need to hire men to move
low light. Beside him is a flimsy rack of comic books and magazines,

it. I was born in that bedroom upstairs, she told the state agent.
their corners drooping and creased, which she does not remember. Can

My father raised these walls. I saw both my parents through right
I help you find something, ma'am? the clerk asks, while she stands

here. This view down the valley is all I know. But already the valley
in the doorway. No—no thank you, I remember where everything is,

was deserted and the view changed, the empty farms and un-
she says, realizing even as she says it that now he will only take her

tended corn somehow more desolate to her than even an overcast
for someone who has vacationed here before and hopes to prove to him

January morning with snowdrifts up to windows too frosty to see
her intimacy with this place which he has never traveled fifty miles

through. Across the road, Mrs Blood's curtains stirred, the breeze
beyond. Well I'll be right here if you need anything, he says, and returns

slowly filling them with air and then letting them fall back; she had
his attention to his newspaper. She walks the worn and creaking

not even bothered to shut her windows. Forgotten cats still hunted
floorboards between aisles of insect repellent and lead sinkers, sacks

among the green rows of cornstalks and in the mornings clawed at
of flour and sugar and coffee, bins of screws and nails, bottles of ink

the barn doors where no cows were now kept, where at dusk she
and pen nibs. Some of the shelves are covered with finger-marked dust.

saw boys sneak inside to scavenge any rusted odds and ends or
Behind her the clerk slowly turns a page and smoothes it. She selects a

broken tool handles that had been left, or to carve their names into
spool of thread she has no need for and carries it to the counter. Though

the beams and timbers that would soon be submerged. Even she'd
there is no one else in the store, the clerk waits until she is almost upon

half-fancied chiseling her name into a flat stone to mark the spot

him before he looks up from the newspaper, half-smiles at her, and in

where her house had stood, once it was moved, but in her more

one quick motion sweeps the glasses from his nose and folds them into

sober moments had persuaded herself that such gestures were use-

his hand. From his blue eyes and freckles she takes him for a Young,

less, for once the valley was flooded it would not be drained in the

though she cannot guess who his mother or father must be. As he ac-

lifetimes of those who remembered her or her family's name. And

cepts her coin and picks through his drawer for change, she asks him,

each evening, as the day the dam was shut and the river allowed to

Do you expect Mr Baldwin back in this afternoon? Again the clerk's

overflow its banks drew nearer, men from Skunk Hollow and

lips pull back from his teeth in a gesture which she cannot decipher. No

Clarksville and occasionally as far as Columbia drove up in bat-

telling, really, he says, dropping the change into her palm. He's in some

tered and muddied sedans or junk-filled wagons to dump whatever

days and not in others, though I think he said he'd be down to Colebrook

scraps and rubbish and broken machinery they could not burn in

this morning. I can leave him a message if you like. Or Jack next door

the barrels beside their shanties. When one unkempt young man

the restaurant might know. From under the counter he produces a tiny

and his wife had attempted to unload a rusted separator and a
paper bag, shakes it open, and slides the spool of thread into it. He

trunkload of garbage not far from her house, Miss Abbott had
folds the top and hands it to her. No thank you, she says. I'll stop

flung open her door and aimed at them the shotgun Mr Cook had
back later. As the door swings shut behind her, the men on the porch

loaned her when all of her nearest neighbors had left. Take it back
again fail at their effort to conceal the immediate breach in their con-

where it came from, she shouted at the couple. People still live here.
versation; do not bother to look at her from the corners of their eyes

The wife, dressed in a man's patched jacket, her hair done up in a
only, but instead turn their heads as she steps down to her car, opens

dirty scarf, tugged her husband's sleeve, and together they looked
the door, and gets in—even as she sits before the steering wheel she can

at her in silence for a moment before heaving the separator back
still hear the pause in their talk and knows they will not resume it

into their car and driving slowly away. The next morning, walking
until she has driven away. Certainly, she thinks, she should not have

along the road between shaggy rows of corn, she had seen the
come alone, though neither can she imagine having brought anyone—

separator lying in a tangle of broken stalks a half mile past her
someone to point out barns and streams to, and say This is the place

house. Mr Blood had loaded Miss Abbott's furniture into his truck

I told you about: no place itself could ever match her telling of it; the

to store in Seb Cowan's barn until her house was moved, the day

pebbled lakeshores, the miles of evergreens and rugged hills would only

before loading the few things of his own he believed worth hauling

disappoint. But even if these men could recognize her face, could fasten

down to Orford, where he'd purchased a twelve acre hill farm with

a name to it, how would she be remembered here now? And who would

the proceeds from the sale of this one. What else would we do? he

now remember her? As if this place were less a home than a delay in

asked her when he returned from Tabor Notch for the tea she had

some unknown course, nearly all of those with whom she lived here

waiting. There's no land worth buying here unless you're one of the

have now been gone almost as long as she has, she thinks. Once upon a

timber companies, and they already own most of it anyway. She

time, there was a girl who thought she was special among everyone else

watched from her window as later, after supper, he and his son

in the village. Her father loved her very much, and she him, but after

lifted boxes into his truck as the sun slipped behind the hills and

a journey he fell ill and died, and from that day on she lived with her

the fireflies winked among the closed-up daylilies beside their

mother at a guest house on a lake—but even her mother had left, in

house. They said that the valley was wide and long enough that the
search of work, once Mr Currier had closed his lodge nearly twenty

lake's surface would be two thousand acres, though no one knew
years back and none of the other camps had had need of a cook, how-

how much time it would take for the river to fill it, for the tallest
ever renowned her cooking and baking, since the hunters and fishermen

trees and the barn roofs to vanish. How long, she wondered, would
themselves had disappeared, gone to stand in lines to receive food rather

the swallows continue to nest under those eaves? Bing Davison
than spending large amounts of money for the privilege of trying to

had been the first in the valley to sell, and even before the next
catch it from woods or water, and then, a few years later, marshaled

person had sold he had mortgaged an old tarpaper hunting cabin
and shipped overseas—And where does a woman with no husband

up on the ridge above the valley, and to anyone who listened while
and no home go? her mother wrote to her that year, in the letter which

he bought new shingles or stovepipe joints or tenpenny nails at
told of her remarriage. When Mr Currier returned to Massachusetts

Baldwin's store, he told how he planned to clear away the trees
I had no choices left me until I met Victor. I would have asked you

below his cabin to give him a generous view so he could watch the
to the ceremony if I'd thought you'd come, her mother had written,

water rise above his old front door from his new one. But that's
but you are welcome to visit us any time. Vic is very eager to meet you

just fool's talk, Mrs Cook had said when she told the story over
after hearing so much about you from me. Nights here we walk down

tea. Why he's got more to do than a man on the town, in Baldwin's
to the beach, sit and watch the sea unrolling itself toward us. I had

buying supplies every day. He just likes to stir manure to see what'll
never imagined how big it was, even after your father had described it

happen, Mrs Parker said, tapping a spoon of sugar against the side
to me. Now I can't remember a time when I hadn't yet seen it, hadn't

of the bowl before spilling it into her tea. Let him wait a year and
heard the wash of waves on the rocks every day. As we sit there he

see what he says then, up there in the woods. Maybe so, Miss
often asks about you, or the farm, or Idlewild, which he visited only

Abbott thought, though she was not certain that was what Bing
once. I think our lives there seem strange to him, though now they some-

Davison was up to. She could imagine herself the need to watch as
times seem that way to me as well. And I am very eager to meet Daniel.

long as she could the valley as it was, now, and even as each farm-
As I've said, our door is open to you. She had, at first, read these letters

house became an island. For weeks she had sat by her window,
as they arrived, one appearing every week or two in the box she rented,

gazing out on the fields, the hills framing this low ground the river
bearing the postmark of some Maine village she had never heard of,

twisted through, the setting sun filling the valley with light these
and which she spelled out carefully on the few occasions she had re-

summer evenings. Then she would shut her eyes. And when she
sponded to one of the letters. Later, she would sometimes wait several

looked again, something had already changed—the shadows
weeks to go to the post office, not wanting to see the thin envelope

a bit longer, a blackbird perched on the clothesline. To herself she
marked with its familiar script, though when she did finally open the

had sworn never to come back; never, once she was settled in
box there was still only the one envelope angled there, never two, as if

Tabor Notch, to pass north or east of the village except by taking
her mother knew. When she felt she could no longer read them she

Back Lake Road to Happy Corner; never again to cast her eyes
placed them unopened in a desk drawer, though after a time she

over this stretch of country. The Haynes family, who had been in
covered them with other papers and remembered they were there only

the valley as long as anyone in Pittsburg could remember, had dis-
when she had need of something in the same drawer. At last she let her

interred nine coffins from the family plot to be reburied in the hill
lease at the post office expire, and returned her key to the clerk rather

cemetery, and that day there were few in the village who had not

than pay the fee to renew the contract. Only once since then had she

gathered on the hillside's cropped grass as each one of their people

allowed herself, during her business of mailing notices or bills or

was given the proper services again. A new monument, carved

Christmas cards, to look through the tiny glass window of the box that

simply HAYNES, and far grander than the hand-cut stones that had

had been hers: it was empty. Eventually she found she could not

stood in the valley, now marked one corner of the cemetery, but

remember the name of the village, and though she knew it was im-

even that marble paid for with the governor's money seemed to

pressed in ink on the envelopes still sealed in her drawer, she did not

her to speak for no one but those who had also quit town, leaving

allow herself this either. For years now the allowances have been few.

only this trace of their years here and the dust settling on the road

The car her one extravagance, she thinks, as she slowly turns onto the

behind them. And everyone who abandoned the valley offered the

blacktop and heads north, though until now she has not driven it much

same apology. Been losing money on this place long as I owned it,

beyond those streets on which she received her lessons—could imagine

Jack Haynes said. Would have been tied to it forever, otherwise.

nowhere to aim it, since every road connects to countless others and

To this she could say nothing, and only at night as the river mouthed

she cannot bear the thought of circling, of doubling back. And those

the same words it had always said did she wonder how he would

streets, in the city where she has lived now more than twenty years, are

free himself from it when he stood in his new house and called it

lined with buildings whose many-paned windows reflect each other's

home, when he slept beneath a roof another man's hands had raised

light and that of the sun, and whose walls cast early shadows; it often

from materials still another man's money had purchased. She, at

seems to her that from none of those streets can she ever see far enough

least, would not betray the mother and father who slept among the

to imagine or remember what lies beyond them. But still this road

stones on the hillside by disowning this country for another of

continues, spanning Back Lake Brook, then rising gently to the lip of

which she knew nothing. Three months ago, when the last ice had

what she does not expect to see quite yet, quite so close to the village: the

broken on the lakes, Seb Cowan had walked with her over his

grassy dam at the end of a dark stretch of water, longer and even wider

lands, along the edges of fields still unturned. She had not seen or

than she has imagined. There is a gravel pull-off, and she parks there,

spoken to him since he was one of the barefoot boys fishing from

then walks along the dam's wide top, gazing the length of this new lake.

the River Road bridge and she was younger herself, driving the

She sees the low silhouette of a loon far out. From here, her back to the

hay rake through her father's fields during second haying, or riding

village and her face to the forested east, the lake, even at midday, seems

north to First Lake where, in hunting season, she swept rooms and

more wild to her than any of the others ever did—there are no camps

made beds at Camp Otter. But in the weeks and months after the

along its shoreline, no fishermen nosing their canoes through its shallows

storm, when the state's surveyors and engineers had determined a

or paddling across it. Only dark trees ring the mute waters. When the

need for a dam to control the headwaters of the Connecticut, and

dam was finished, she read in the newspaper that, at the ribbon-cutting,

when the talk of Miss Abbott's defiance had spread through the

the governor's speech—before a gathering of villagers, two hydroelectric

town, he had stopped her after services at the Methodist church

plant owners from the lower Connecticut, and newspapermen— was

one Sunday. Beneath the brim of the crushed felt hat he had pulled

interrupted by applause only when he acknowledged the desire of many

on once outside, his eyes met hers only briefly before turning to-

of those assembled to reverse the order of the words Murphy Dam.

ward the ground; in his bearded face she could still see signs of the

The grainy photograph that accompanied that story showed only the

boy she remembered. Come out to my farm around sugaring time,
front of the dam, a thin trickle of water down its face, and not the

he told her, and though she had not spoken to him again during
deserted valley beyond. Now, looking over the lake's unbroken surface,

the winter, she'd asked Mr Blood to drive her there three months
she cannot believe that the waters have risen so swiftly, that a decade's

back. When she knocked on Seb Cowan's door and he saw her, he
time could swallow this valley. Water laps the roots of firs on the far

simply said, You come on inside while I get my boots on. In a mo-
shore. When she looks back across the lake, the loon has dived. Behind

ment they were outside again and he was pointing to different plots.
her, a logging truck downshifts as it approaches the village; its exhaust

You want to make sure you're not too far from the road, he said.
hangs blue in the air. In the newspaper, she'd also read that—because

What about right here? No, she said, no, I don't think this will do.
of pressure from Concord to complete the project quickly—when the

My dooryard would be too close to your cowpath. He held his arm
last of the valley's residents had moved, their abandoned houses were

for her but she took it only when they came to a fence she wanted
not dismantled; and among the stands of tamarack and birch, the elms

to cross. The gate's up this way, he said. I can climb over if you'll
marking property lines, the swamp maples rooted along the curved

just give me your hand, she answered, lifting her skirt and placing
banks of the slow river, and the spruce and fir on the valley's southern

her foot on the stile. There, by that stand of birch, she told him
slope, where the land climbs toward Clarksville, only some of the taller

half an hour later. That's it. Just before the highway bridged it, the
trees had been felled in a mad rush of men sent to clear timber after

stream shaped an oxbow, then swirled into the Connecticut on the
the dam was shut and already the river had begun to flood. Most of

road's far side. An acre here would do nicely, she said. Across the
these men, the article had claimed, were not skilled lumbermen, but

river the hill rose, dark with trees, away into Clarksville; to the
rather the same laborers who had built the dam; they cut trees for only

southwest the river and the road that followed it blurred in the
two days, beginning at the river and finishing a half-mile to either side

pale light of afternoon. Other than Cowan's farm, the nearest
of it, where the engineers and surveyors had estimated the water would

houses were a mile upriver, at the edge of the village. For a long
cease rising, once the dam was reopened. And now she recalls what her

time she stood, watching the vanishing waters, and feeling Cowan's
father once told her, some morning they walked a loop of trail and came

eyes on her. At last he said, Let's go inside and draw up the papers.
across an old timber lot, where amid seedlings and ferns some stumps

She had not disclosed the terms of his lease to her even to Mrs
still stood, one with a rusting axe notched into its pattern of rings—

Cook or Mrs Parker, though they'd told her that some in the village
that no true woodsman would ever have done such a thing, that to leave

had speculated that she'd taken all of the governor's money after
an axe in a tree or stump overnight was to bring down the worst sort

all, for why else would Seb Cowan give up an acre of good interval
of luck upon oneself. He stood shaking his head at the foolishness of

land to let her move her house there. And besides, Mrs Cook said,
those who had left the axe there long enough for the rust to stain the

you may as well get the cream as the milk. Miss Abbott only smiled
stump's white wood, then gripped the handle and levered the blade out.

and raised the cup of tea to her mouth. A dollar a year, he had
He did not clean and sharpen the head, as she would have expected,

written on the paper they both signed, for every year that she lived
but buried it; the weathered handle he burned. She can imagine the

on his land. When she died the ownership of the house would be
murky chaos of rotting limbs rising from the lake's silty bottom, clusters

transferred to his name, or to those of his heirs should he prede-
of cones still hanging from them, then wonders, if she waits at this shore

cease her. As long as I know it won't be underwater with the rest of
until the shadows of the hills have fallen across the water though there is

that mess, she told him. You can do whatever you like with it once
still light left in the sky, will she be able to see down to the peaks of roofs,

I'm gone. She had hired a crew from Colebrook to dig the cellar
the tops of chimneys—and if she can, will she recognize any of those

hole with a steam shovel and then build a foundation after the
homes she once saw every night, a window's yellow light pale beside the

ground had thawed. Once or twice she had come in Mr Blood's
silver bands of the river, from the bedroom window of her own. She

truck or in the car with the Cooks after church to gaze at the
stoops and through loose fingers sifts a flat stone from those at her feet,

squared hole in the muddy earth. Clumps of yellow grass and root
then skips it out as she had afternoons at Mr Currier's when the dinner

ends showed amid the tracks of the shovel's tread. You'll have a
dishes were dried and stacked for supper, she and Tom and Frank

nice view of the hills, Mr Cook said. And you'll see everyone com-
vying to throw a stone the farthest, or to see whose stone hit the lake the

ing along the road to the village, and everyone heading down to
most times. It skims the water and bounces, shedding drops; spreads

Beecher Falls and Colebrook. Oh, you'll know all the news there
overlapping ripples as it sinks. At the other end of the lake, she knows,

is to know, sitting here by your window, Mrs Cook said. Right now
what was once the old River Road leads down to the shore and then

it looks just like the governor's dam site, Miss Abbott said, and
into the water, disappearing from sight only twenty feet from the edge.

she turned, silent, to look at the river until Mr Cook spun the
But she does not wait for dusk, nor for the loon to reappear. She

steering wheel in his hands and drove them back toward the village.
returns to her car and for a moment sits, watching the lake's shifting

Another time, after the gray-green Connecticut had carried away
surface while she eats an apple from the sack she bought at a grocer's in

the last of the snow and ice the earth had held all winter, she asked
Cambridge. She slowly works down to the spindle of seeds, and wraps

to let her off at the site on his way to West Stewartstown, and to
the core in the bag with the spool of thread. Then starts the car and

meet her there on his return. As he drove away, she scanned Seb
backs out over the gravel to the main road. Winter afternoons, Mr

Cowan's land to see if he or one of his sons or his hired man was
Currier sent Tom in the sleigh to bring her home from the village

in the nearby field, breaking ground for planting; none was. She
schoolhouse, and his horse would take well over an hour to trot back to

walked to the cellar hole, and stood there studying the fitted
Second Lake, along the road now tracing the bottom of the lake. The

stones and the mortar smoothed atop them for some time before
runners scraped packed snow. From the chimney of every house they

she slowly sat down on the edge of the foundation, turned around,
passed, smoke rose toward low clouds it helped color. Wrapped in

and, positioning the toe of her shoe in a space between two stones,
bearskins, a cap pulled over her forehead, she watched Tom's back.

 climbed down to the packed earth floor. The sky shrunk to a patch
Sometimes, when she emerged from the schoolhouse door, he had a

of pale blue streaked with white, and though she could hear the
peppermint stick for her, or a box of raisins he had swiped from the

wind among the fir across the river, she could not see the grove of
kitchen, and because he gave these things to her almost without speak-

birch. She brushed dried mud from several of the fieldstones. Here
ing, and because he was older than she and the son of her mother's

she would put shelves for her jars of relish and beans. Here she
employer, she did not speak to him either, did not thank him, but

would tell the men to build the stairs to the kitchen, the risers
simply took them in her gloved hands, only looking at these gifts after

short so she wouldn't break her neck. Here would stand a post to
he had turned away. She did not eat what he gave her but carried

to support the new central beam which, the head carpenter had
it home and placed it in the drawer of her nightstand; once, her mother

explained to her, he would need to reinforce the house's weakened
found among the old examination books, bobby pins, hairbrushes,

frame. In this corner of the house, in the living room, she would
folded papers, and forgotten dolls' clothes of that drawer two foil-

place her armchair by a window where she could look out and read
wrapped chocolate squares—which, during the ride to the lodge, had

the sky's changing weathers. But now she watched the breeze pull
half-melted from the heat of her pocketed hands and then hardened

the ends of Mrs Blood's curtains into the space between sash and
into odd shapes when the fire died that night—that Mrs Currier had

sill, then looked to her watch, where both silver hands pointed to
missed in the kitchen a few days earlier, and smacked her across the

either side of the six. The few clouds above the valley were still
mouth. Three years later, when she followed Tom into the woods

edged with pink. She patted her palms over her skirt and realigned
surrounding the lodge on summer nights, she imagined telling him this

her sweater. It would be a fine day, another day of gentle weather—
story, but never did. The chocolate disappeared from the drawer, and

as all these recent months had been, as if to taunt her for the weather
she never knew whether her mother had eaten it, returned it in its

of a single day and night. For she had heard too how Bing Davison
ruined state to Mrs Currier, thrown it into the lake, or done something

and some of the others who gathered on the front porch at Baldwin's
else to it. After that day she dropped Tom's gifts into the wake of the

store said they were praying for another storm like the one that
sleigh while he looked ahead at the darkening road, night coming gray

had followed the Connecticut from mouth to source and contin-
from the hills and smelling of snow that would fall. Why she

ued into the Canadian hills last September. Never seen one like it
remembers these things now she cannot guess, though save the few

and never will again, some of the men said, and throughout the
words she has shared with the store clerk, the hotel keeper, and the men

country few would forget either the winds and rains or the cash
who have filled her gasoline tank, she has been silent this trip too. In a

that had followed them. Mr Blood had told her this summer how
moment she passes one end of Back Lake, another sight she cannot

in certain places the woods were still a tangle of broken trees, not
match to her memory of it—now, tiny cabins crowd the shoreline and

just branches but entire trunks, and for weeks last fall, it seemed,
docks reach into the water; she sees at least a half-dozen boats as the

she had listened to Mrs Cook discuss the news she had tuned to
lake disappears behind her. Happy Corner is a few lonely houses in a

on her radio each day, reports of sandbags and flood crests in
meadow where the road crosses Perry Stream, which a half mile from

Springfield and Hartford; three hundred miles of ruined bridges,
here flows into the river. The road shapes an S and soon she has

overflowed banks, downed wires; towns and cities from Boston to

reached First Lake, then the unbroken woods beyond it, where Charlie

Sherbrooke without power; the National Guard flying anti-typhus

Chase once told her he had seen a wolf while hunting grouse, though

serums to parts of Vermont that had been entirely cut off by high

neither she nor anyone else he told had believed him. At Second Lake

water and washed-out roads. Even the State Liquor Commission

she thinks she has missed the turnoff, and circles back, but still cannot

at Concord had decreed that no beer nor liquor was to be sold

find it. Farther on is a new graded road, marked with a state forest sign

until further notice. In Pittsburg village the winds had stripped

and edged in gravel, and she turns here toward the lake. The road ends

shingles off roofs, broken countless panes of glass, knocked down

at a boat launch and thick blueberry bushes; two picnic tables stand

at least two old barns, blown over dozens of trees, and brought

in the shade beneath trees. Already the summer seems closer to its end

down a dying elm which missed the roof of the town hall but not

than it had at home; even in her sweater she was cold this morning,

the town clerk's new Ford. At Back Lake and First Lake, trees had

leaving the hotel, and the growth along the road stayed damp and dewy

damaged many of the camps and lodges, canoes and rowboats were

until ten o'clock. Now, the wind has increased and as she steps from

sunk, and a dock was torn from its pilings; at Second Lake, the
the car here it ruffles the water, rouses the heavy limbs of the spruce,

roof of Currier's old eyesore was stove in by the trunk of an enor-
presses her clothes against her. The clouds that have succeeded one

mous fir, and some said he would arrange to have it finally torn
another across the sky all morning begin to collect there, edges white as

down. And we should count ourselves lucky, Mrs Cook said. The
they pass before the sun. The access road has brought her near the

great hurricane of '38. They say the wind blew a hundred miles an
exact place she sought, and though the view of the far shore seems the

hour through the streets of Boston. Miss Abbott shook her head
same as that she recalls, she cannot find her bearings on this one. The

to think of the coming weeks she would spend with Mr and Mrs
laurel and ferns and blueberry have grown up around the spruce

Cook at their farm in the village, weeks of listening to the radio
trunks, where she thinks should be a lawn. She feels like a tourist,

broadcasts with Mrs Cook, weeks in the guest bed where the
searching among the trees for what she has been led to believe is here,

Cooks' daughters usually slept when they visited from downstate—
and though she cannot locate it, she walks back and forth over the

for it would be weeks, the head carpenter had told her when she
needled ground as the wind fills her skirt and flaps her sleeves.

hired him, while his men pulled off the roof sheathing, sawed
Spiderwebs stretched invisibly between bushes break across her face.

through beams and posts, broke the walls at the studs into pieces
Moss softens the shapes of stones. Above her she hears a woodpecker

small enough to load onto the trucks, numbered everything with
tapping a dead limb, and with a hand to shade her eyes she looks up

chalk, then drove every section and every scrap of reusable lumber
through the swaying lattice of branches but cannot see it. What could be

to Seb Cowan's acre and rebuilt it. You know it would be easier just
a path through the growth she follows; when she turns to look at her car

to build you a new house with whatever old lumber we can salvage
it seems, with the sky reflected in its windshield, tiny, abandoned. The

from this one, he told her. And a lot cheaper that way, since the
faint trace leads to a hollow filled with pearly everlasting, goldenrod,

material's mostly free and the work won't be as fussy. After we
queen-of-the-meadow, wild asters, the tall spikes of fireweed. Between

move it, it'll likely look a bit different anyway, he told her. No
it and the lake the trees have been mostly cleared, though countless

telling how the walls'll hold up, so we may need to replace some of
saplings—birch, swamp maple, spruce—compete with weeds still

the lath and plaster. At the least we'll need to plaster the seams
waist-high. As she approaches the hollow she sees that its sides are

when you get settled back in. And you'll need to rebuild the chim-
blackened fieldstone, and pauses there, trying to conjure the image of

ney, of course. She had looked up from the drawings he had spread
the house she had expected to see still standing, and though she can

over her table and stared at him as he spoke, his face flushing as he
remember details—the pans and skillets hanging from the scuffed

imagined the work. Just tell me you can do it, she said to him. Just
kitchen wall, the sound of feet walking across the porch, the dusty

say that it can be done. Oh sure, he said. Long as you're not too
corners of the dining room, the narrow stairs she climbed each night,

particular about the details. But the details were what she thought
the hard-packed dirt of the dooryard—the house itself is lost. In her

of whenever she thought of her house on this new patch of earth:
letters, her mother had only told her that the Curriers were returning to

the clay pots of geraniums she would place on her doorstep, the
Massachusetts, and she wonders how long ago this happened, how

morning light falling through her bedroom window, the brass
much of this news her mother has heard. The soot on the stones has

knobs and hinges she would buy in Littleton for her doors, the plate
told all it knows; amid this summer's fading greenery is no ash for her

of brownies she would carry out to Seb Cowan and his sons when
to sift, to scatter. She turns and walks to the shore. The dock has sunk,

they were in the adjacent field. She looked down the road toward
and its skeletal frame, foreshortened, stretches along the lake's rocky

the village, down the river's meander through the low valley, for the
bottom. Across the lake the balsams and spruce lift their branches in

men's trucks, but saw only swallows brushing the tops of the corn.
layers. Far beyond them rises that low double-backed mountain she

By eleven-thirty, Mr Cook had told her, he'd come by to take her to
remembers. In the wind she clutches her elbows with her hands, wishes

his house in time for dinner; he and Mrs Cook had suggested that
for her sweater left in the car. But she does not move for some time,

he bring her after he'd finished his early-morning chores, but she'd
simply watching the shifting patterns of light on the lake and breaking

insisted on staying at least until midday to watch the care the men
a twig into pieces. The water laps stones. Somewhere far below its

took with the house. You've seen how some of these fellows are, she
surface, she knows, a bracelet that slipped from her wrist one night

had told the Cooks. Seen them? I guess, Mrs Cook had said. It's
while she trailed her hand still shapes a delicate loop: she had not let

worse, being right in the village. It used to be you knew everyone
Tom try to dive for it. But whatever marks her own feet have left in

walking downstreet, and now I see men I don't know where they
this place have been buried by years of falling leaves, the settling of

came from. Between them and the sports, it's got so I don't know

dust, all the nights' soundless snowfalls; however long she has carried

who's coming and who's going. Or who's staying. Well, it'll all be

the place with her, it has forgotten her daily, and whatever lines she

gone soon, Miss Abbott had said. Just another lake for them to

once thought would contain it disappeared after they were drawn. The

float their canoes on and pull trout from, she thought now, watch-

slivers of sun move on the skin of water. She stands. Among the trees

ing the swallows. The only task left to her beyond waiting was to

the woodpecker still tests some dead limb. She walks back beneath it,

dig up her mother's peonies, which she had left this long only to be

toward the car, then leans on the metal roof and looks out over this

able to smell them through her windows, to see the rosy ruffled

lake another moment before opening the door. The hands of her watch

flowers each time she stood outside and looked at the house; she

have not yet marked two hours since she last looked at it. She twists the

knew that once she transplanted them a year or two would pass

key in the ignition. And though she knows this road no longer simply

before they bloomed again. She stood up and brushed her skirts,

ends in a clearing by Third Lake but now leads into Canada, she has

then walked to the barn for the spade and the burlap she'd placed

already turned back toward the village; there is another place she wants

there. Her mother had told her these peonies had grown from
to see. She wonders if she should take a room here for the night, and

plants she'd divided in her own mother's flowerbeds before she
passing First Lake again marks the VACANCY *signs hung out before*

departed the coastal Maine town she'd grown up in to come to the
the whitewashed cabins and lodges there, the empty camp chairs

Connecticut valley, where her husband had heard was cheap and
carefully arranged to face the lake and Magalloway beyond it rather

fertile land, despite the brief season. Her mother's father, a mer-
than the road; she planned to stay, has in the suitcase clothes for a week

chant sailor, had carried the original root—in a small wooden box,
of varied weather, but now she thinks she should drive as far south as

inlaid with silver and filled with a strange black soil he claimed he'd
she can tonight, take supper at whatever place she stops, hurry on to

scooped from the bank of the Yangtze—with him on a return voy-
Boston tomorrow. She can still recall her mother telling her she would

age from China as a gift for his young wife, and its flowers had
return before this place had disappeared among the hills behind her;

bloomed early every June for nearly a hundred years. Miss Abbott
has recalled these words each time she's imagined returning during the

had many times imagined her grandfather, a man she never knew,
past twenty-one years. And even though her mother left nearly as long

in the hold of the clipper ship her mother had told her he'd sailed
ago as she did, she has still felt that by returning she would only

on, moistening the soil from his water ration, or the first flower
be conceding her own failures, or else acknowledging the truth behind

he and his wife saw in their garden in Maine—or her mother her-
her mother's words. Now that she has returned, she cannot remember

self, twenty years old, leaving that foggy coast for a place which had
why for so long she has wanted to; nor, except to prove to her mother

been recognized as part of the United States for only thirty years,
how little she knew her own daughter, why she wanted to stay away.

and bringing with her trunks of clothes and dishes and quilts, along
What she has seen has shown her only how wrong she was to want to

with an uprooted plant to remind her of home. She pulled the barn
see it. She follows another logging truck into the village, then turns before

door wide enough for her to walk through; the spade leaned in the
she reaches the town hall and steers the car uphill, along a road still

shadowed corner just inside. By the time she had dug around the
unpaved, to an opening in the woods where, in rows, stones stand.

peonies, lifted the earth caught in the snarl of roots, and wrapped
Curled flowers gone brown and lacy lie before some of the stones;

the plants singly in burlap, the head carpenter and his men had
lichen has filled chiseled names. She walks between the even rows, man

driven up, parking their trucks on her lawn. She raised herself from
and wife laid together, the bones of entire families underfoot. The stone

her knees and waved a hand. You might at least wait till I'm gone,
she seeks is singular, and she flattens the grass beside it to sit: a cricket

she called. Those tires are ruining my grass. One man, his brown
struggles through the strands away from her. Below her, a valley now a

elbow bent through the truck's open window, shifted into reverse;
lake reflects light. The hole the sun burns in the sky has paled behind

clods of dirt clung to the tires. The head carpenter climbed down
the clouds, and she has brought the wind with her; it speaks through

from the other truck's cab and took his pipe from his mouth. It'll
branches. Lifts a clutch of leaves already yellow and scatters them; she

all be ruined soon, he said. Didn't think you'd want to wait around
watches their tangled flight as they reel and then fall back to the grass.

to watch us work. From the backs of the trucks men seized crow-
She has wrapped the sweater around her shoulders. The grass grows in

bars, claw hammers, and sledgehammers. I'll be here to keep an eye
tall tufts around the stone where whichever boy who cut it this summer

out for a while yet, Miss Abbott said, wiping the dirt from her
was unable to reach the spinning blades of his push mower. After such

hands. Can some of your boys help me move these flowers out of
an absence she is unsure how to begin; is not sure she remembers how

the way? Sure, he said. I'll do it. He knocked his pipe on the heel of
to tell at all. Not many years ago, it seems to her now, she held a boy

his boot and tucked it into his shirt pocket, then lifted the burlap
to her lap and recalled stories she had heard, stories she had read by

parcels. His men circled the house, shading their eyes with their
lamplight in a farmhouse on a hill; not many years before that she

hands as they looked up at the roofline; one opened her front door
curled her arms around a man's chest and shoulders at night, speaking

and disappeared inside; another held a pad on one arm and began
into his ear, his hair against her lips; and, even more years before that,

to sketch. They wore whipcords, puttees, suspenders, crumpled
sat in a chair beside a man's bed, her words occupants in a quieting

and battered hats, scuffed boots, and untucked shirttails. The head
house: and all of these stories may have been the same. Eyes closed. In

carpenter placed the peonies by the roadside. Well, he said to her.
her lap a boy's weight went limp; beside her, a man breathed quietly.

It won't look too good at first, but by the time we have you set up
Such things seem to her too terrible to tell now. With the boy, in those

down Tabor Notch everything'll look all right again. Little bit diff-
days, she could begin anywhere, and he would follow her. And this

erent, but it'll still feel like home. I hope so, she said. In the growing
man knows the beginning, but there have been countless beginnings

light her house shadowed them. Now I have a few things inside
since that one—and who can pick and choose among all of the days

I'll need you and your boys to carry out before you begin tearing
and nights to select one afternoon, an evening, to stand for all of the

everything down. Sure, he said. He went inside and in a moment
others? She does not know how to make simple what cannot be simply

emerged with the other man who'd entered the house. They placed
told. So she thinks she should begin with the boy, this boy whom the

her suitcase, chair, bed, and boxes next to the peonies, and then
man could never have imagined. Daniel, she says, was the name that I

several men went inside to disassemble the stovepipe and lift out
named him, since the naming was left to me. I had never known

the woodstove. Her feet in the grass, she sat back in her chair to
anyone with that name. The low lull of her voice fades; in the light, the

watch the men work. Two men lugged a ladder to the house and
grass, pressed to the slope by the wind, looks silvery. Then she asks, If

eased it against the roof; while one stood on the bottom rung, the
she failed me, and I have not let her forget it—not let myself forget it—

other, carrying a flat-bladed shovel, climbed it and began to rip off
how can I tell her that I have failed Daniel too? He has left

shingles the storm had been unable to loose nine months ago. They
home, saying that a boy raised with no father must become his own

fell in strips and clumps, raining debris on the grass. From the other
father, must find his own way in the world—but so must a girl, I

side of the house, Miss Abbott heard nails groaning as men pried
told him: that is why I came to this city. And that is why I must leave

away clapboards, and the sound of wood knocking wood as it was
it, he answered. I have not seen him since, though he has written me

flung into a pile. The man with the sketch pad licked a thumb to flip
from places I can't imagine. Chicago, once; the coast of California

a page, and in a moment he and the head carpenter went inside.
months later. She pauses. From a house downhill she hears a dog bark.

The shadow of the man on the roof, back bent as he swept shingles,
But for the apple, she has not eaten since breakfast, and though she

moved along the grass—and, as she watched it, Miss Abbott imag-
feels hungry she does not rise, only brushes back the hair the wind has

ined the first steps she would take, some weeks hence, from the
blown into her face and, addressing no one but herself, starts to speak.

door of her house onto the unfamiliar ground surrounding it.
She has just begun the story, and there is still so much to tell.

NOTES

MURPHY DAM, PITTSBURG, N.H.   1604

The italicized passage on page 5 is taken from *The History of New Hampshire, From Its Discovery, in 1614, to the Passage of the Toleration Act, in 1819,* by George Barstow (Concord, New Hampshire: I.S. Boyd, June 4, 1842).

The definitions on page 6 are taken from *Funk & Wagnall's Standard Dictionary of the English Language* (New York: Funk & Wagnall's, 1963).

The italicized passage on page 9 is taken from *Connecticut River,* by Marguerite Allis (New York: G.P. Putnam's Sons, 1939).

The italicized passage on page 14 is taken from *What They Say in New England and Other American Folklore,* collected by Clifton Johnson, Edited with an Introduction by Carl Withers (New York and London: Columbia University Press, 1963).

Vincent Bouchard's diary was suggested by, and uses certain lines from, *An Illinois Gold Hunter in the Black Hills: The Diary of Jerry Bryan, March 13 to August 20, 1876* (Springfield, Illinois: Illinois State Historical Society, 1960).

The italicized passage under "Prospect" (page 21) is taken from "Coos and the Magalloway," by Joseph C. Abbott, from *Harper's New Monthly Magazine,* February 1860, Vol. XX, No. CXVII.

The italicized passage on page 24 is taken from *More New Hampshire Folk Tales,* collected by Mrs. Moody P. Gore and Mrs. Guy E. Speare (Plymouth, New Hampshire: compiled and published by Mrs. Guy E. Speare, 1936).

The italicized passage on page 27 is taken from *Connecticut River.*

The passages under "Histories" (pages 29–32) are taken from, respectively, *Connecticut River; Collections of the New Hampshire Historical Society, Volume II* (Concord, New Hampshire: Jacob B. Moore, 1827); *Collections of the New Hampshire Historical Society, Volume Eleven,* edited by Otis Grant Hammond, M.A. (Concord, New Hampshire: New Hampshire Historical Society, 1915); *History of Coos County* (Somersworth, New Hampshire: New Hampshire Publishing Co., 1972; originally published in 1888 by W.A. Ferguson & Co., Boston); *The Struggle for the Indian Stream*

Territory, by Roger Hamilton Brown (Cleveland, Ohio: Western Reserve University Press, 1955); and *More New Hampshire Folk Tales*.

The italicized passage on page 37 is taken from, with slight alteration, "Wood-Notes," author unknown, from *Putnam's Monthly Magazine of American Literature, Science, and Art*, September 1854, Vol. IV, No. XXI.

The italicized passage on page 40 is taken from, with slight alteration, "Exploring the Magalloway," by Francis Parkman, from *Harper's New Monthly Magazine*, November 1864, Vol. XXIX, No. CLXXIV.

The passage under "Divination" (page 41) is taken from *More New Hampshire Folk Tales*.

The passage on page 53 ("Moose Hillock towers...") is taken from *A Treasury of New England Folklore*, edited by B.A. Botkin (New York: Crown Publishers, 1947).

The passage on pages 55–56 was suggested by a passage in *Indian Stream Republic: Settling a New England Frontier, 1785–1842*, by Daniel Doan (Hanover, New Hampshire: University Press of New England, 1997).

The italicized passage under "Topography" (page 58) is taken from *History of Coos County*.

The italicized passage on page 59 is taken from *Collections of the New Hampshire Historical Society, Volume Eleven*.

The passage under "Terminus" (page 61) is taken from "Coos and the Magalloway."

The italicized passage on page 63 was suggested by, and uses certain lines from, a passage in *More New Hampshire Folk Tales*.

The passage of Passamaquoddy on page 64 is taken from *Wapapi Akonutomakonol, The Wampum Records: Wabnaki Traditional Laws, as recounted by Lewis Mitchell and originally published in 1897*, edited by Robert M. Leavitt and David A. Francis (Fredericton, New Brunswick: Micmac-Maliseet Institute/University of New Brunswick, 1990). The following translation is that given by the editors: "When all had gathered together, they began to think about what they might do. It seemed as if all were tired of how they had lived wrongly. The great chiefs said to the others, 'Looking back from here the way we have come, we see that we have left bloody tracks. We see many wrongs. And as for these bloody hatchets, and bows, arrows, they must be buried forever.'"

The italicized passage on page 69 is taken from *Burt's Illustrated Guide of the Connecticut Valley*, by Henry M. Burt (Springfield, Massachusetts: New England Publishing Company, 1866).

The italicized passage on page 70 is taken from *History of Western Massachusetts, Vol. I*, by Josiah Gilbert Holland (Springfield, Massachusetts: Samuel Bowles and Company, 1855).

Vern Amey's story about Hap Jones (pages 72–73) was suggested by, and uses certain lines from, the story of Tom Brown in *The Last Yankees: Folkways in Eastern Vermont and the Border Country*, by Scott E. Hastings, Jr. (Hanover, New Hampshire: University Press of New England, 1990). This book was also helpful for its oral histories and descriptions of cider-making.

The italicized passage on page 76 is taken from *The History of New Hampshire, From Its Discovery, in 1614, to the Passage of the Toleration Act, in 1819*.

The passage under "The True Story of Jimmy Frye" (page 78) was suggested by, and uses certain lines from, "The True Story of Polly McFarland" in *More New Hampshire Folk Tales*.

"Toward the Interior" makes use of passages quoted or paraphrased, without attribution in the text, from the writings of Richard E. Byrd; specifically, from Byrd's books *Little America* (New York: G.P. Putnam's Sons, 1930) and *Alone* (New York: G.P. Putnam's Sons, 1938). My portrayal of Admiral Byrd is a fictional characterization and in no way pretends to be "true" information about him.

Certain passages of part one of "Quinnehtukqut" were suggested by *The Yankee Doughboy*, by Connell Albertine (Boston: Branden Press, 1968); *Leavenworth Papers, no. 10: Chemical Warfare in World War I: The American Experience, 1917-1918*, by MAJ(P) Charles E. Heller, USAR (Fort Leavenworth, Kansas: Combat Studies Institute, 1984); and *More New Hampshire Folktales.*

Certain passages of part two of "Quinnehtukqut" were suggested by passages from *Cotton Was King: A History of Lowell, Massachusetts,* edited by Arthur L. Eno, Jr. (Lowell: Lowell Historical Society, 1976); and *Surviving Hard Times: The Working People of Lowell,* edited by Mary H. Blewett (Lowell: Lowell Museum, 1982). My lodge Idlewild takes its name from an actual lodge of the same name, which also stood on the western shore of Second Connecticut Lake, though the history I have given it is in all other respects fictional. Camp Otter and The Glen are also the names of actual lodges on First Connecticut Lake, but are here used fictitiously.

Certain passages of part three of "Quinnehtukqut" were suggested by passages from *Goodbye Highland Yankee: Stories of a North Country Boyhood,* by Scott E. Hastings, Jr. (Chelsea, Vermont: Chelsea Green Publishing Company, 1988).

———————

Details about the hurricane of 1938 were found in unattributed articles in the September 22, 1938 edition of *The Boston Globe.*

Certain details about the construction and dedication of the Murphy Dam were found in *Dam It All*, by Isabel Tarrant (Manchester, New Hampshire [?]: self-published, 1973).

"Farmhouse in a Fold of Fields" modifies the structure of John Ashbery's poem "Litany," and, as in this poem, is intended to be read as separate but parallel narratives.

Although some of the names of people and places that appear in this book are based on historical figures and sites, this book is a work of fiction. In various instances I have changed dates and details to accommodate the truth of the fiction. And while many of its features seem to correspond to features in the actual Pittsburg, the Pittsburg of this book can be found only in these pages.

I would like to thank, for their readings and help with various aspects of this book, Heesok Chang, Paul Fenouillet, Natalie Friedman, Lamar Herrin, Molly Hite, Paul Maliszewski, Maureen McCoy, Jim Rutman, and especially Sarah Goldstein, its longtime champion.

COLOPHON

Quinnehtukqut was typeset in Jenson. The cover design was by Geoffrey Gatza. Proofreading was done by Christine Webb. The cover photograph is courtesy of the author. Other interior images are taken from postcards produced by Eastern Illustrating & Publishing Co., Belfast, Maine, and used with permission, or from the collection of the author. The maps in the frontispiece are used with the permission of the United States Geological Survey.

Printed by Marquis Book Printing, Inc., Cap-Saint-Ignace, Québec, Canada.

ABOUT THE AUTHOR

Joshua Harmon was born and raised in Massachusetts. He graduated with highest honors from Marlboro College, and received an M.F.A. from Cornell University. His work has been published in *Antioch Review, Iowa Review, New England Review, Southern Review, TriQuarterly, Verse,* and many other magazines, and he has received fellowships in fiction from the National Endowment for the Arts and the Rhode Island State Council on the Arts. He teaches at Vassar College and lives in Poughkeepsie, New York. For more information, please visit www.joshuaharmon.net.

Starcherone Books is a signatory to the Book Industry Treatise on Responsible Paper Use, the goal of which is to increase use of postconsumer recycled fiber from a 5% average at present to a 30% average by 2011. It is estimated that attainment of this goal would conserve 524 million pounds of greenhouse gases yearly, equivalent to keeping 45,818 cars off the road, as well as saving the equivalent of 4.9 million trees, 2.1 billion gallons of water, and 264 million pounds of solid waste each year.

The paper used for this book is Enviro 100, an alkaline, 100% de-inked, post-consumer, 100% processed chlorine-free stock, certified by both the Chlorine Free Products Association and the Forest Stewardship Council. We thank Marquis Book Printing, Inc., for making this option available.

Starcherone is a non-profit whose mission is to promote innovative fiction writers and encourage the growth of their audiences. We publish four books a year, including the winner of our annual, blind-judged competition. Information about the press and our authors, ordering books, contributing to our non-profit, and other initiatives in furtherance of our public-spirited mission may be seen at www.starcherone.com.